THE SERPENT AWAKENS

LUNA SAINT CLAIRE

Much Love

Luna St

A COMPELLED NOVEL

Published by Compelled Books
www.compelledbooks.com

The Serpent Awakens is a work of fiction. All characters appearing in this work are fictitious. Any resemblance to actual persons, living or dead, or events that took place, is entirely coincidental. Any names, characters, places, events and incidents are either the products of the author's imagination or used in a fictitious manner.

Library of Congress Control Number: 2022939809

ISBN 978-1-928816-74-4 (paperback)
ISBN 978-1-928816-75-1 (ebook)

Please follow @LunaSaintClaire
Instagram, Goodreads, BookBub, Facebook, Twitter & Tumblr

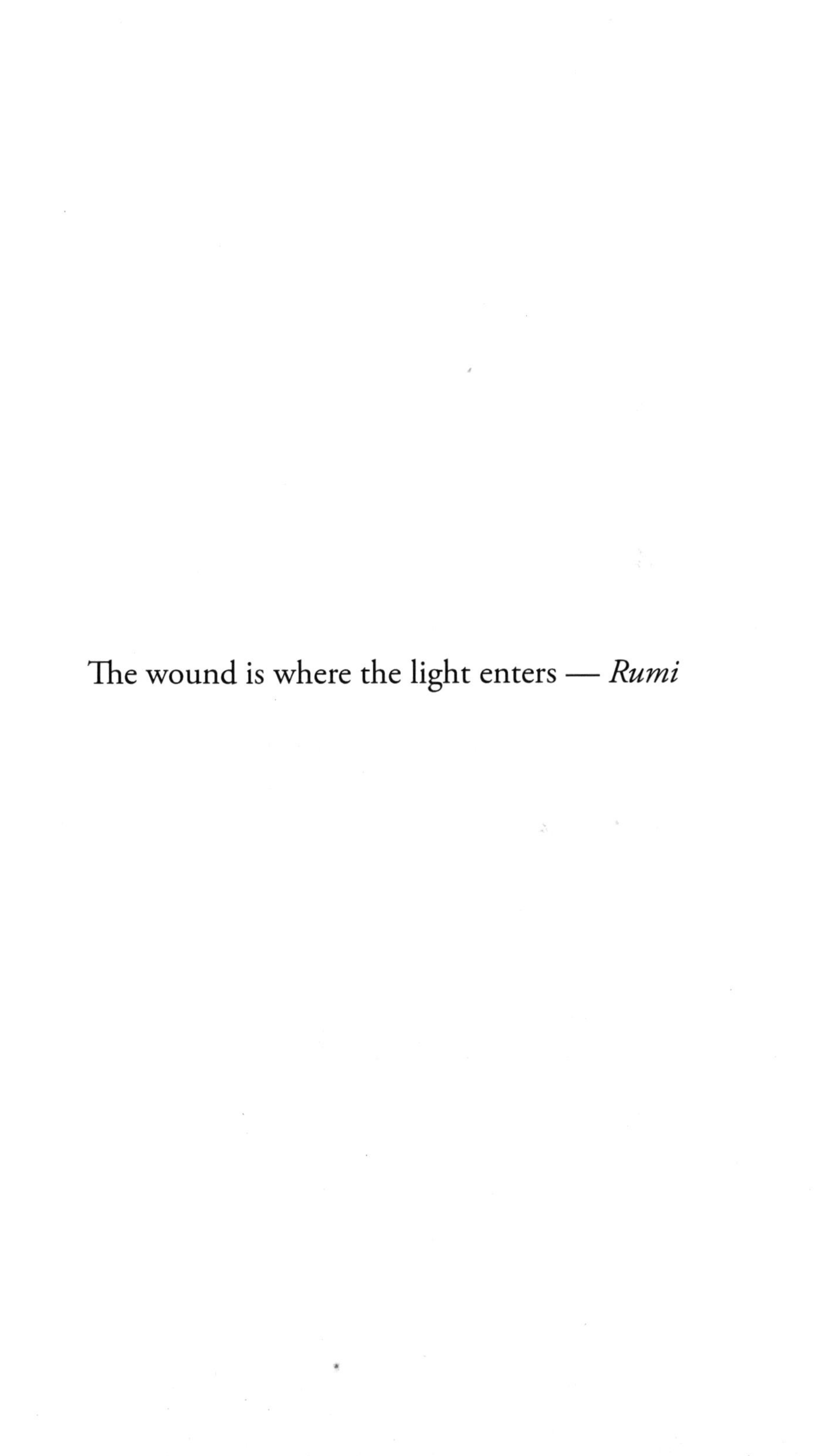

The wound is where the light enters — *Rumi*

1

The black lace treetops were silhouetted against the indigo sky as Nico made his way swiftly through the fog and shadows of the rainforest. His bare feet treaded surely even as they sank into the waterlogged moss. The gnarled roots and tenacious fingers of feathery wet ferns along the unfamiliar terrain snatched at his ankles like tentacles as he hastened toward his destination. He reached the riverbank just as the morning sunlight pierced the canopy.

A formidable baritone voice spoke his name before yellow eyes met his. The jaguar stepped forward out of the shadows, his gleaming tan coat decorated with rosettes resembling broken pieces of black pottery. "We must go," he said. "I will take you across on my back, Nicolás Romero."

Without hesitation Nico straddled the powerful creature, his legs dangling in the muddy water. Upon reaching the opposite shore he heard the mournful song of a wooden flute summoning him.

"That is no flute you hear. It is the call of the tinamou," the jaguar said.

"But I don't understand…"

"It is time. There is nothing for you here now."

Just then, a distinct metronomic signal invaded his senses. Determined to find its source he ran. His pulse beat loudly in his ears as he pushed through the thick vegetation covering the jungle floor. Lost and stumbling, his foot caught on a root, and he cried out as he tumbled forward in the mud, his arms splayed out in front of him. He woke with a jolt. His heart pounded fast and hard in his chest. The monitor next to his bed played an unnerving soundtrack of steady beeps.

° ° °

Maya was scrunched in a recliner by the window. She wore a rumpled oversized T-shirt dotted with visible food stains. Her dark hair hung loose below her shoulders and needed brushing. She had been sleeping in that chair for two weeks, ever since he'd been moved to a private room. Slowly she uncoiled her body and looked over at him. He was impervious to the television blaring an old episode of *Jeopardy!* It had been his habit to fall asleep with it on, the background noise a source of comfort to him.

"Were you having a bad dream again?" she asked.

It wasn't the first time she'd heard a muffled cry while he slept. Even awake, scenes of that night replayed for her as well. The visions play out, repeating the terrifying event—She is in the shower when she hears gunshots. She runs wet and naked from the bathroom to find Nico bleeding on the studio floor. She watches as they load him into the ambulance, not knowing if he is alive. At the hospital, she waits while they remove the bullet lodged near his heart. If she had not been there to call 911, he most certainly would have died.

She stood and stretched her arms over her head. Her hair was damp from sleep, and she gathered it into a high ponytail resembling an ink-brushed exclamation mark. She noticed the anxiety in his eyes.

"It was a stupid dream. I was running and fell." He kept his eyes on the television, managing to avoid looking at her.

"Was the jaguar there again?" she asked. He had been having disturbing dreams, but this one often recurred. The jaguar's ability to see into the dark parts of the human heart and their prescience frightened Nico.

"Yes. It was the same message."

She detected he was annoyed.

"I'm thirsty." He still hadn't looked at her.

She checked her phone. It was already six and his breakfast would arrive soon. The passage of time in the hospital was measured only by the delivery of meals. Taking the blue plastic pitcher from the tray table she went down the hall to the ice machine. The nurse at the desk looked up and smiled as she walked by. Maya smiled back and greeted her by name. She admired the courage of these nurses. As a stunt person she was trained to endure grueling days shooting a film. But she knew she couldn't withstand long days filled with sickness and the smell of death.

When she returned she saw he had fallen back asleep. She set the pitcher down and stood next to his bed. The mylar balloons sent by his adoring yoga students had become partially deflated and get-well cards decorated the bedside table. Even with the unfavorable aspect cast by the room's fluorescent lighting, she noticed the warmth of his olive complexion was slowly returning. His dark hair lay across the plain white pillowcase in curlicues resembling the mythological Medusa. His breathing was relaxed and measured. For now, he appeared peaceful. For as long as she'd known him, he'd had deeply etched lines scrawled across his brow, but now at forty-one they gave him a wearied look. It was hard to believe they were the same age, she thought.

She remembered when they met. It was more than nine years ago, she thought. She'd stood in the back row of his yoga class. After class she approached him. Her sleek body poised and alert like a cat. He'd invited her for tea in his living quarters in the back of the studio. She'd been reticent at first. But as they talked, she slowly unfolded like the petals of the Morning Glory at dawn. Eventually she revealed her reason for needing his help. There had been a fire on the set of her last film that left her traumatized, her doctor said it was post-traumatic stress disorder. Fear and hesitancy had impaired her performance. She'd read about kundalini and its power to clear obstacles. Nico promised he would help her overcome her fear.

Back then, his eyes gleamed with boyish mischief. He made promises of marriage and children, but as the years passed and his volatility and drug use escalated, she stopped asking when. Now he was fragile and broken, and his deep-seated agitation had intensified after his near-death experience. The nightmarish dreams he described were rife with obstacles and he was always searching. The jaguar had been explicit; it was time to leave. Maya reminded herself that dreams were messengers offering insight. She may not have lost him to death, but nevertheless she understood he would leave. The thought of losing him devastated her, but it had become ever more harrowing to be with him.

Her mouth was as dry as if she had eaten sand and the pit in her stomach reminded her she was hungry. She had to call her boss. He needed her to come back to work, but when she told Nico he had gotten angry. If she hurried she could get back before his breakfast arrived. She slipped quickly from the room to get herself something to eat from the cafeteria.

When she returned, Nico was sitting up in bed eating. The tray table was pulled over his lap and the volume on the television was louder than when she'd left. His eyes were fixated on a boxing match.

"Where were you?" he asked. Without averting his gaze from the screen, he shoveled a forkful of scrambled eggs into his mouth.

"I went to the cafeteria. I was only gone a few minutes," said

Maya defensively, noticing his scowl.

He didn't answer. His eyes were still fixed on the television, the ambient noise of it soothing his anxiety. Since the incident, he had to have it on.

When Nico asked her if she thought Élodie might have shot him, she was afraid to answer truthfully. She certainly thought it possible, even probable. He was obsessed with Élodie. He'd met her on a trip to the Arab Emirates. She was beautiful, French, and an international art dealer whose clients were some of the richest people in the world. Nico's plan was to open a posh yoga studio in Beverly Hills and Élodie had promised him the money. When the investment failed to materialize, he became desperate and his relationship with her turned volatile. He blamed her for deceiving him. In a murderous rage he kicked her until she yelped like a dog. She sobbed yet crawled into his arms and begged his forgiveness. As usual, they made violent love. He was ashamed of what he had done, but it bound her to him in a way he himself could not explain. They shared a deep intensity of emotion he never felt with Maya.

Maya detested Élodie. When the detective interrogated her, Maya told him she had smelled a fragrance she thought was Élodie's perfume. Her accusation enraged Nico. He made her tell the detective she'd been mistaken. What she smelled was the incense Nico burned in the yoga studio. As much as the police pressured him, he wouldn't name his attacker. He stuck with his story that they had appeared in the doorway as a silhouette backlit against blinding headlights that punctuated the darkness.

"Have you heard from Luna?" Nico asked abruptly.

"No, why?" she asked, concealing her alarm. She hadn't told Nico she'd called Luna the night he got shot. He ignored the question, and she buried her nose back in the phone.

The recollection of that night still haunted her. The rush of adrenaline as she spoke with the 911 operator and the panic while waiting for the ambulance to arrive. Even though Nico hadn't seen Luna in years, Maya felt certain she would come. Luna had been the only one she'd been able to confide in about Nico. And when Luna walked into the emergency room that night, Maya saw the unmistakable fear in her eyes.

Nico pressed on, revealing his uncanny ability for sensing what others were hiding. "Tell me the truth, Maya. There's something you aren't telling me. Was she here?" he prodded.

Maya hesitated before answering, knowing the consequence she would suffer for hiding anything from him. "Yes. I called her when you were in surgery."

"I can't believe you didn't tell me. And, neither did my father. Why not?"

"She told us not to tell you."

"Oh. I see…" He looked back at the television, appearing to be absorbed.

Maya glanced up at him. She thought he might be angry, but he wasn't.

"Do you think she would come now if I called her?" He flipped the channel and was now watching one of the Bourne movies he'd seen a dozen times.

"I don't know. Why don't you ask her?" Maya knew he missed Luna, even though he bad-mouthed her, saying she had betrayed him.

"Call her. Tell her to come," he said.

"She might come if you call her yourself." Not wishing to draw his ire, she tempered her statement with, "She never stopped caring about you."

Nico turned to face her full on. He appeared to be glaring at her, but there was something thoughtful behind his smoky-green eyes. The yellow flecks coruscated, and for a second Maya thought she had provoked him. Instead, he mumbled, "I'm not so sure…"

After he watched a few more minutes of Matt Damon leaping across rooftops, she saw him typing on his phone and suspected he was writing to Luna. No one could be more curious whether she would reply than Maya.

◦ ◦ ◦

Luna poured freshly brewed coffee into a mug and opened the book review section of the paper. She had the app on her phone, but there was something special about reading the physical paper. The smell of the ink and the sound of pages turning had a soothing effect on her senses. Hearing a ping from her phone, she smiled inwardly. Tyler usually texted her within minutes of leaving the house. Reaching for the phone, she thought to remind him to pick up milk on his way home. It took a second for her to register the text had come from Nico.

She already regretted having gone to the hospital, afraid he would find out and contact her. Cursing the flurry of butterflies in her stomach, she acknowledged it had been foolish to assume Maya would keep her visit a secret from him. Seeing the letters forming his name triggered her memory. His eyes when they flared with rage, his body curled in a fetal position suffering inconsolably from feelings of loss. The terror she felt when he had threatened her for coming between him and Élodie. Still, she could not dismiss the feeling there would always be a connection between them—one that transcended time.

She'd gone to the hospital that fateful night without considering how seeing Nico might affect her. The pull, like a bungee cord, had been too strong to ignore. They'd held vigil, sitting for hours in hard plastic chairs, drinking bitter coffee in the glaring light of the waiting room.

Nico's father and his wife Claudia had been there. Luna had met Roberto several times and found him charming. He had a big personality and loved life. After Nico's mother died, he married Claudia, who he'd met in New York. She was a long-time ranch owner from California. When Roberto sold his last restaurant, they moved to her ranch in the hills outside of Los Angeles. Claudia had a keen intelligence that showed on her face. However, Nico had a contentious relationship with her. He said she didn't like having him around. Luna suspected it was because Nico fought with his father which upset Claudia.

They'd been sitting in the waiting room for some time when Roberto said he'd predicted Nico's disposition would get him killed someday. At first, she was appalled. There was an awkward silence and then laughter. There was no denying it was true. Only Roberto, with his weird sense of humor, could make a joke of it. Luna noticed that even Maya cracked a smile.

Seeing him as he lay unconscious in the recovery room, tubes protruding from his body and his skin pale, she pitied him despite how badly he'd treated her. She left soon after and hoped he would never know she had been there.

Decades ago, when she was in college, Luna remembered studying the political philosopher Machiavelli, but never imagined she would one day know someone as unscrupulous, who employed such ruthless, self-serving cunning to get ahead. Nico manipulated her and she had been under his thrall for years. In hindsight, she should have recognized Nico's dread of being alone, the desperate need for stimulants, his cravings for women and sexual compulsions. Even his obsession with celebrity was rooted in his feeling of worthlessness.

Whether it was free will or fate, her encounter with him provoked a storm that shattered her sense of identity and self-worth. The storm hadn't blow in from the outside. She was the storm. Its turbulence forced her to confront the darkness, uncovering her secrets and her pain. When she finally severed the bond with him, it was as if a veil lifted from her eyes.

As she stood now in the dappled light of her kitchen, reading the cryptic text on the small screen of her phone, she tried to understand why, after all this time had passed, he wanted to see her. Had his near-death experience changed him? Would he apologize for the hurt he'd inflicted upon her? Maybe, as part of his recovery, he would make amends. Taking her phone with her into the bedroom, she sat in her reading chair next to the bed. Breathless, her heart galloped wildly, and her vision clouded. She read the text again hoping to decipher an esoteric meaning from the empty spaces between each word. *I'm getting out of the hospital tomorrow. I need to see you. It's important.*

Suspended in the moment of decision, she squeezed her eyes shut, struggling to quell the fear and irrational panic that stirred again. She had put him behind her, certain she had overpainted that canvas. But the past was still too near. Like a pentimento, she thought, where the vestiges of earlier forms were ominously plain. She had paid dearly for her freedom, yet there was something unfinished. As if they found independence, her fingers flew across the keys, *Where should I meet you?*

2

Luna headed west on Ventura Boulevard toward Amaru Yoga. The drive was both familiar and strange. She still avoided this route even when it was the most direct. There were times she had an impulse to drive by the studio, hoping to catch a glimpse of him, but chose to stifle that urge and not stir the past. Nico's training in Kundalini Yoga and his mystical ceremonies had restored her confidence and enthusiasm for life. When she won a prestigious design award, she attributed her success to him. She had relinquished her power and it had taken years for her to reclaim it.

In the present light it had become more transparent. She had worked hard to forgive herself. Why hadn't she seen beyond the fog? Every day she still judged herself, and with each thought she added clarity. Shame doesn't just disappear. It dissolves slowly, in layers, and always leaves a trace. She questioned why she had allowed herself to become entangled with Nico. She was a successful, smart, middle-aged married woman. Nico was charismatic, manipulative, and twenty years her junior. It was hard to accept she had been that vulnerable. Then, she remembered he'd made her feel young and desirable. He never tried to have a sexual relationship with her, he didn't have to.

She'd developed a cult-like devotion to Nico. It pained her to think how Tyler must have felt. Not a single day went by that she wasn't grateful for his love and patience. Anyone else would have given up on her. She wished he had been forceful and demanded she sever the bond she had with Nico. But Tyler said if he had, he would have been no different than Nico. Instead of control, it was his wisdom and devotion that had brought her to her senses.

She became less certain the closer she got to the studio. Her stomach somersaulted, rousing a firestorm of butterflies she thought she had extinguished. She hadn't spoken to Nico in more than three years. She remembered the moment clearly. Tyler was driving and they were on their way to her brother's house in Santa Monica. The wind, warm in the midday sun, blew her long hair about her face, and "Crazy Love" was playing on the radio. It was Tyler's song for her, and she was singing along when her phone rang. She had grown tired of Nico's drama and weeks had gone by without her speaking to him. She noticed her mind had become clearer than it had been in a long time. She must have let her guard down because for some reason she automatically answered, as if she'd been bewitched. She heard Nico, with an evil mocking tone in his voice. In the background Élodie was screaming. She concluded they must have been high on cocaine. Bolstered by Tyler's presence, she drew on her inner strength and ended the call. Within seconds, a text message appeared on the screen, Fuck you, don't ever speak to me again. We're done. He had written those words to her before, but this time, she knew it was true. Her heart suddenly felt heavy. Looking out at the road ahead, the sunlight seemed brighter, enough to shut her eyes. Tyler said nothing.

She regretted the time she had wasted and the futility of her efforts. Nico was like a vampire who compelled women to him. Élodie hadn't been the first girl to come to her with bruises. In her mind she thought she could save them. In retrospect, she realized she had been like the village busybody meddling in other people's lives.

Now, against her better judgment, she was going to see him. That little voice in her head told her that he must feel some remorse for the way he'd mistreated her. Surely, she thought, he would apologize. She laughed at herself and thought, he must have regrets. She reconsidered and said aloud, "Luna, you are such an idiot."

Pulling into a parking space behind the studio she turned off the engine and flipped open the mirror on the sun visor to check her makeup. With her finger she gently erased a smudge of mascara from beneath her eye. She left what remained of the natural tint on her lips. What might she say that wouldn't sound contrived? Almost laughing aloud at, how have you been? And his casual answer, I nearly died.

Her nerves tingled as she walked across the parking lot on unsteady legs. She knocked lightly on the heavy metal door. The yoga studio's red serpent logo had become faded over time. They hadn't found his attacker, and she thought how unsettling for him to return to the place where he'd been shot. When he didn't answer the door, she sighed with relief. As she turned to leave, she heard the latch click and Nico opened the door. Every hair on her body stood erect and she stifled the impulse to flee. He expected her, yet he stared as if she were a stranger. She remained awkwardly speechless waiting for him to invite her in. The fluttering in her solar plexus was a warning. There was a real danger he could reattach the psychic cord and regain control over her. But she resolved to hear what he had to say.

He wore slouchy black sweatpants low enough on his hip to reveal he wore no underwear. Other than appearing pale and a bit thinner then when she'd last seen him, he didn't look as though he had recently been at death's door. She spoke the first words that came to mind, "I'm glad you're alive." It came out strangled but sincere.

He laughed and smiled into her eyes, "So am I."

He stood to the side and gestured for her to come in. Stepping over the threshold, her eyes traveled down to the polished wood floor where he had lain bleeding. She followed him through the studio to the apartment in the back. His gait was slow and deliberate. Scanning the room, she became flooded with intimate memories of him playing guitar and serenading her with Spanish love songs. The kitchen looked the same as she remembered. As was her custom, she took a seat at the counter. The memory of watching him make empanadas was so strong she could smell them.

"How'd you get home?" she asked.

"Maya picked me up." He put the tea kettle up to boil. The grey T-shirt he wore hung loosely shrouding his damaged body.

She saw no sign of Maya. "How do you feel?" she asked delicately.

"Like shit… But I'm slowly getting my strength back." Leaving the kettle to heat he winced as he lowered himself into a chair.

She swiveled her chair to face him. "Are you sure it's okay to be out of bed?" She thought of the suffering he must have endured.

"Yeah. It's only bad when I move…and when I breathe." He winced and pulled his shirt up to show her the bandages that encircled him like a corset.

"Are you taking something…for the pain?" she asked reluctantly.

"No, I have to be clean, Luna…. You, of all people, should know. I want to feel everything." His tone was brusque, but he softened. "Do I need to explain…especially to you?"

"No, of course not…" She blurted. "Is Maya living here, so she can take care of you? I mean. . . It can't be easy. Showering and cooking…" She sputtered trying to regain her composure.

"For now." He pressed his lips together, a mannerism Luna had committed to memory. "She's loyal, Luna. You always said she would be… How did you say it? The last soldier standing." He regarded her quizzically. "You were right about a lot of things…" His voice trailed off and the tea kettle whistled, giving him a welcomed respite. "Can you make us the tea?" he asked, resting his hand gently on the left side of his torso close to his heart.

She moved quickly around the counter and turned off the gas. Everything was as she remembered. She took two mugs from the cabinet over the sink. The boxes of assorted teas were still on the lower shelf next to the spices.

"Which tea would you like?" she called out to him.

"The passionfruit tea. Maya kept buying it for me after you…" He dropped the last word intentionally. "And bring the guitar over here, will you?"

Luna carried the two mugs over, leaving the tea bag in his as he liked, then she fetched the elegant instrument, a gift from Maya. It was spruce and mahogany with inlaid mother-of-pearl, handmade in Spain. Maya had told her she saved up for months and gave the guitar to him when he returned from the Emirates. Unbeknownst to Maya, Nico had brought Élodie with him. Everything began to spiral out of control about that time.

Luna curled herself on the sofa. Again, that same familiarity and strangeness came over her. He seemed to be reconstructing scenes from their past. Her focus sharpened as she watched him. Was she being paranoid? He was being sweet and a bit needy. She became anxious contemplating what he wanted from her. He played tentatively at first. Perhaps he was in discomfort. The guitar rested gently against his torso as he maneuvered to find a comfortable position. It was as though he needed to play for her. He began to sing a ballad by Damien Rice. The lyrics were bitter and anguished. She knew he sang them for her. Listening to his voice, low and gravely, was a cautionary reminder of everything he had been—manipulative, controlling, abusive and at the same time, charming and flirtatious. He had been what she thought she needed. She clenched her jaw, repressing the urge to stop him mid-song and demand to know why he had called her to him. He remembered all the words, and when he sang he never meant to let her down, she looked away. When he stopped, she forced a smile against the words she couldn't utter.

"That was lovely Nico," she said, concealing what she'd been thinking, that he had deceived her and treated her badly. She was still recovering from the damage he'd wrought. But she also missed him, the way you miss the euphoric high from a drug you had once been addicted to. She got up from the sofa and poured herself another cup of tea.

"Will Maya be back soon?"

"No, she had to go back to work," he grumbled. After a considerable pause, he added proudly, "She's the head fight choreographer now. She has me to thank for that. I helped her overcome her fears, you know."

Luna held her tongue. She thought, of course he would take credit for her success.

"That's wonderful. I'm sure she must be thrilled," she said instead.

She never told Nico that Maya had confided in her. Nico had pressured Maya into doing drugs with him. She described it as a hell of all-night binges. At work, she began to lose her focus, putting her life and those of her co-workers at risk.

As if reading her mind, Nico continued, "She stayed with me in the hospital the entire time, you know?" The guitar lay across his lap, and he plucked the strings like words to a song. After a few beats, he added, "I trust her... she loves me. But there are other things I have to do now."

She wondered again what Nico wanted from her. Tyler questioned whether it was wise for her to see Nico, but she said she wanted closure. She sensed Nico was leading up to it. Feeling a shift in his voice, she waited for him to continue.

He hesitated, as if searching for the right words. "I have to recover…Not just from being shot. But from the drugs. I destroyed myself. I want to be who I was before the drugs…or I should say, the man I am supposed to be. I told you a long time ago that I didn't recognize myself anymore. I've become weak, Luna. You saw what happened with Élodie. I loved her and trusted her to keep her promise. She played me."

A pause opened in the room; it held a truth they shared. He saw the darkness in Luna's eyes as the knowledge passed between them.

"And Maya," he said contemptuously clear. "You think she is strong because she is a master of martial arts? She became addicted to coke…she did anything…everything I told her to do. See? Love makes people weak."

"Love makes people weak?" she said incredulously. "That's what you've learned through all this?" She made a sweeping gesture with her hand and stated in what she knew was her haughty voice, "You push people too hard, Nico. Élodie loved you. Maya still loves you. But to you people are just objects you use to get what you want."

"That's harsh," he huffed. "It's all done now… I don't want to talk about it anymore, Luna." He set the guitar down and shifted uncomfortably in the chair. Picking up his mug he drank the remaining tea. "Can you pour me another?" he asked impatiently, holding the mug aloft and adding, "Please."

She refilled the mug and handed it to him. "Tell me, why did you ask me here? We obviously disagree. I believe love makes people stronger. You need me to explain everything?"

"How can you say that? I tested them and they failed."

"If you love someone, you don't manipulate and control them. You have to trust them and accept them for who they are."

"Everyone has their own interests, Luna. Everyone left me. I'm alone."

"Nico, your arrogance is biblical. You are greedy, covetous of wealth and celebrity. Where has it gotten you? Your fear has made you selfish. You trampled over everyone."

"Fear? What do I have to fear? Besides whoever tried to kill me?" He cleared his throat nervously. "I'm a healer. I'm the best, and I've proven that."

He stood up slowly and walked haltingly to the kitchen. He opened the refrigerator and groaned as he bent to fetch a covered pot and put it on the stove. "Rice and beans?" he asked.

"You don't get it, do you?" She moved to stand next to him at the stove.

He took a wooden spoon from the ceramic utensil holder.

"Just stir," he said, leaning against the counter for support.

Automatically she took the spoon from him and stirred the pot.

"Look, I'm not talking about your success as a yoga teacher. You knew how to achieve all that. I mean your fear of loss. The fear everyone will leave you, that I would leave you. That fear turned into a weapon and drove us away."

"When I opened myself up and trusted them, loved them, they left me," he said bitterly. "They all had their own interests. Olivia and Sofia, too. They used me. Then left me. Even Nitya. She wouldn't leave that fucking bullshit village in India to be with me." He refilled the tea kettle and put it back on the stove.

Hearing those names reminded her of how long she had known

Nico. She had almost forgotten about those disastrous relationships.

"They loved you. Your dad loves you. Maya loves you..." She checked herself before saying, I love you.

"All my life, Luna... My dad left. My mom sent me away. And then Élodie... I trusted her...and she destroyed me. You see... everyone leaves me...even you." His eyes, dark wells, met hers. Not trusting the sadness in them, she looked away.

His hand went to his side in a poignant gesture that brought to her mind Caravaggio's painting of the apostle Thomas touching Christ's wound. Her breath caught. A sensation uncomfortably familiar and seductive crashed over her, like loud warning blasts of a train approaching a crossing. Masking her emotion, she took two bowls down from the shelf.

Nico took the wooden spoon from her and dished up the rice and beans. He watched her face as she began eating.

"Do you like it?" he said, fishing for a compliment.

Covering her mouth, she nodded and said, "Delicious, just as I remember." She swallowed and took a sharp breath. "Nico..." she began...but he was right...even she had left him. "Do you remember when we met...at La Forza?"

"Yeah, sure I do. Why?" Nico took his bowl to the sofa and slowly eased himself down.

"You were so full of yourself...acting all charming and seductive. I saw right through it. I saw something else. I saw a lonely, hurt little boy. Someone who needed a friend that he could trust."

"Oh yeah?" he smiled.

She saw the little twinkle in his eye. He winced when he tried to lift his feet onto the sofa. She jumped up and helped him, then backed away, embarrassed by the intimacy.

"You showed yourself to me and told me your whole life. You wanted me to understand you—to see the goodness in you. That's all everyone wants, Nico. To be understood."

"I let you down. I let everyone down," he said under his breath.

"You went home to heal your mom, but you couldn't save her. You were devastated. I said I'd be there for you."

"But you did leave me…" he scoffed.

"I had no choice, Nico. You treated me like shit. And besides, I knew you had Maya."

She remembered when Nico first told her about Maya. He was wearing a Cheshire Cat grin on his face. They were sitting in his apartment, just as they were now. He had taken out his iPhone and scrolled through the photos, stopping when he got to a photo of a dark-haired woman in mid-air doing a martial arts flying kick. When he swiped to the next photo of the same woman, she'd flushed uncomfortably. Maya's long black hair spilled like paint across a bed's white canvas. Her breasts overflowed a red lace push-up bra as she lay with her legs spread.

It wasn't until months later that Maya confessed to Luna, she was doing coke with him. When he left on a month-long trip to Abu Dhabi, she was able to straighten herself out, but when he returned, bringing Élodie onto the scene, he began using drugs to a greater extent. He frightened Maya with his tyrannizing demands for cocaine infused all-nighters.

Once Luna knew about the drugs her image of Nico shattered, but not her feelings. He had become part of her, like a tattoo. She cherished their friendship that contained within it a chaste intimacy. Setting fantasy and quixotic desire aside, had she been younger and single, she might have aspired for more. But she also knew he was possessed by demons that tormented him. When he fell into the darkness, he was unrelenting and abusive. Painful as it was, she finally severed all ties with him.

Nico's voice shook her from her reverie, "I'm leaving, Luna. I need to restore myself. I can't stay. There's nothing for me here. Besides, I am constantly looking over my shoulder." His voice was fading, and he'd closed his eyes.

She took the bowls and went to the sink to wash them. The kettle whistled and she poured more tea, though her instincts told her she should leave.

"I can't believe they haven't caught who did this…and you have no clue?" She called out to him, shaking her head in disbelief.

"I couldn't see…the lights were in my eyes…" He added under his breath, "It doesn't really matter, does it? I pissed off a lot of people…"

Luna moved closer to hear him. "Where will you go?" she asked.

"Home. Back to Buenos Aires." His voice cracked slightly.

She heard the hopelessness. Luna sighed. It occurred to her then, she would be relieved if he left L.A.

"Spending time with your grandmother will be comforting. It will raise your spirits. What did Maya say?"

"She doesn't know. I'm telling you first."

Luna wasn't surprised. He had always confided in her. There were still only a few people besides his family who knew his mother had died of AIDS.

"When will you leave?"

"In a couple of weeks. I should be strong enough by then," he said sleepily.

"I should be going, Nico. You're exhausted." He was at a low point, she told herself, but he hadn't changed, and he still hadn't apologized.

"Wait, Luna. Don't go. What do you think I should do?"

"What do you mean?"

"I was somebody here in L.A. What will I do now? I have

nothing left."

Luna paused a long while before answering.

"Have you thought about going back to the Q'ero tribe to complete your training?" she offered tentatively.

Nico's mouth curled up at the edges and he opened his eyes. "I have been thinking the same thing, Luna. You and Tyler always said not finishing would be my downfall."

"It would be a therapeutic place to recover," she said. She was supremely aware of being with him in this familiar place where her weakness had tugged at her desires.

Looking back, it was hard to fathom nearly thirteen years had passed since that night at La Forza. She recalled noticing him when he'd walked in; how his jeans fit, the way he'd carried his leather jacket over his shoulder. She remembered how charming he'd been during their dinner conversation, how everyone else at the table dissolved into the background. Beneath the façade of arrogance she'd seen his insecurity. He had just opened a yoga studio near her office and persuaded her to visit.

She'd arrived at his studio and had been let in by a young woman. He was late and already she was annoyed and thought him rude. She occupied the time looking at the collection of objects on the shelves. In a black metal frame was a photograph of a much younger Nico, a teenager. He was bare chested and bronze, standing on a beach that looked to be in India. On the wall of his office was a framed print of three indigenous women dancing, their long hair flying and their full skirts a blur as they twirled. It was askew on the wall, and she carefully straightened it. These must be the Quechua women in Peru, she remembered thinking. He had told her that he'd spent some time there. The image that most captivated her was of Nico with a Quechua man wearing a poncho and colorful knit hat with pompoms on the earflaps. Nico stared seriously at the camera, but the older man smiled broadly, his perfectly straight white teeth gleaming. As she studied the photograph, the light shining through an adjacent window glinted off the glass. She felt a bit like she was eavesdropping. These people, she remembered him telling her, lived in a most inaccessible region high up in the mountains of Peru. Behind their eyes and in the wide smiles on their faces she saw pure joy.

Only weeks after meeting Nico, he left for Argentina. His mother, she learned, was dying. Although she barely knew him, she had written him letters of consolation almost every day to ease his sorrow. When he returned to Los Angeles, a few months later, they took part in a San Pedro ceremony. He had called it by its native name, Huachuma. She could still remember the experience. It had left an indelible impression. Once the psychoactive substance took effect she'd been transported to an ancient forest. The visions had been clear and realistic. It was midsummer and the trees were thick with deep green leaves. She had a deep memory; perhaps this was the land of her Mohawk ancestors. Nico was there with her, his skin iridescent in the moonlight. The lustrous blue silk of night reached into the distance, into the sky filled with infinite brilliance as far as one could see. It made her dizzy. He took her hand and they climbed above a waterfall. The mist brushed over her body like a feather. He said something, but she couldn't hear him above the roar of the falls. A rainbow emanated outward from him and enveloped her. She became flooded with new knowledge and understanding. Past and future became one. Gazing into his eyes she fell into a dark pool. The distinction between self and other dissolved. He chanted her name, and they became one with the universe. It was then, with the magic, the intimacy of the plant's visionary power, that she'd bonded with him in forever time.

"Will your teacher take you back, Nico? Do you even know if

he is still there?"

"I'll do whatever it takes. I know, I left before I should have. I thought I had learned enough to heal my mother. I may have bought her more time."

"I'm sure you helped her. You're a gifted healer, Nico. You should complete your training. Remember when I told you about the myth of Chiron, The Wounded Healer?"

"Um, tell me again." He seemed to have perked up.

"The healer's own wound is the source of his power to heal others. It gives him empathy. However, unless he knows himself and is in tune with his unconscious, he's in danger of reopening his wounds, misusing his power."

"You think I don't know myself?"

"You never did the work, Nico. Until you do, you'll never control your demons."

"Maybe some demons can never be tamed..." His voice trailed off.

"There's a light in you. All that fear and anger...you can overcome that. Even when consumed by darkness the human spirit is capable of redemption."

"You inspired goodness in me, Luna. You were the only one who believed in me, and I fucked up."

"I still believe in you, Nico." She silently scolded herself for giving more of herself than she intended. Picking up her sweater, she tossed it into her handbag. "I really do need to get going, Nico."

"I failed, but I'll get myself back together. I'll regain your respect. I promise," he said with conviction.

She said nothing. She knew he'd say whatever was necessary.

He gingerly got off the sofa and walked with her to the door.

In the past, she would have hugged him, comforted him, and told him she would be there for him, whatever he needed. This time, they both knew that wasn't to be.

He didn't kiss her cheek. Neither did she reach for him. It would have made her uncomfortable. He unlatched the dead bolt. The buildings along Ventura were in silhouette against the fiery hues of blood orange and neon pink.

"How beautiful is this sunset?" she said.

They stood side by side with unwavering gazes as the colors intensified, and the rays of sunlight shone through breaks in high clouds like the long fingers of gods illuminating the lands over which they reigned.

"Do you remember the sunsets in Temecula?" he asked wistfully. "They were dusty lilac and rose. Never this orange."

"I remember how peaceful it was there..." She responded nostalgically. "This inferno is as if God were cleansing the earth. A way to say, it doesn't matter what today or yesterday held. Tomorrow we can begin again."

Luna looked at him, his face aglow with the last of the golden light.

"I don't know if I'll ever come back," he said. "I've lost everything..." His voice drifted.

She didn't say anything.

"You're a good friend, Luna." There was a deep sorrow in his eyes.

"We're not friends, Nico. I'm not sure we ever were." The words tumbled out instinctively. They sounded strangely unfamiliar. Once she realized what she'd said, she continued. "Look, I don't hate you for how you treated me. It's my fault for enabling you; all the emails and phone calls. I was always there to pull you off the ledge. But you are full of sadness and pain and can't feel anything else. You hurt people and manipulate them because that's the only way you know how to have a relationship."

He looked at her as if she'd struck him a fatal blow. It was her parting gift to him.

She took a gulp of air and sighed. "If I learned nothing else, it's that I'm not here to rescue people, I have to take care of myself."

Nico remained behind as she walked toward her car. She didn't look back, but as she pulled away, she saw him in the rearview mirror. He was standing in shadow, still staring at where the sunset had been and only the slate-hued twilight remained.

The time had come to leave again. Nico thought Los Angeles would have been different. He had earned a name for himself in celebrity circles, and the wealth he sought had shown every sign of materializing. And then, as usual, it all vanished. Maya helped him pack his bags. She said nothing when he secured his framed photos within the folded layers of clothing in his suitcase. Giving her his promise to return, he told her to find a new studio in Beverly Hills. Studio City wasn't exclusive enough for someone of his stature. She listened intently, nodding in agreement. If she suspected he wasn't coming back, she didn't let on. At his worst she never doubted him. She had been the only one who patiently waited for him to exhaust himself with the windmills of his obsessive desire.

The closets were empty, the shadows long on the blank walls. He tried with wounded voice to tell the truth, but the words moldered in his mouth, like rotten apples. They made love with mechanical movements and exchanged kisses anchored with questions. It was still dark when they drove to the airport. The halos encircling the headlights of the on-coming cars shimmered as they sped past. Their conversation was superficial and restrained in contrast with the nervous chatter that usually coincided with his fear of flying. The feathery fronds of the tall palms silhouetted against the distant hills waved, like hula dancers, a taunting farewell.

He pointed to the entrance ramp leading to the drop-off area.

She nearly missed the turn. He didn't want her at the gate. He felt the fear and sorrow that belongs to leaving, like a refugee heading into the terrifying unknown.

Maya pulled over at the curb. He brushed her cheek with his lips, as if he would be home for dinner.

"Be careful." She placed her hand on his chest.

"I'll call you later," he mumbled.

He hopped out of the car and hastily grabbed his luggage from the back seat. He turned briefly back and looked at her with melancholy eyes and then disappeared into the terminal.

Her eyes held pools of tears and her lip trembled, but she reminded herself, he always came back.

° ° °

He checked his luggage then passed through security. Shouldering his backpack, he boarded the plane and made his way down the aisle. An attractive woman in row C caught his eye and smiled. Had he held her gaze a moment longer it would have been a signal to hook up, but he looked away.

Nico climbed over the heavyset man on the aisle and took his assigned seat next to the window. Attempting to seal himself off from his surroundings, he put on his headphones and turned up the volume on a soothing playlist of acoustic guitar music. He opened the contacts on his phone and found solace in the inventory of his life. He began scrolling, his thumb briefly touching the names of people he struggled to recall and some he would surely forget. The announcement came to turn off all electronic devices and he quickly found Luna's name and texted the words wheels up and turned off the phone. He wasn't sure why he messaged her. It had been their habit years ago, a prayer of sorts. Closing his eyes, he thought about her visit. He made the sign of the cross. "Gloria al Padre, y al Hijo, y al Espíritu Santo," he murmured, as the plane lifted into the sky.

He dreamed of India, spearfishing in the Arabian Sea, the water pale as celadon porcelain. Ringed by lush hillsides, the pink sand glowed as the sun softened, inflaming the sky. Coconut trees undulated in the breeze for miles along a desolate and unspoiled beach. He came out from the sea proudly displaying his catch. Nitya was there dancing, and he heard her laugh with delight, like the tinkling of finger cymbals. He woke to the sound of the seat belt sign dinging, and it took him a moment to remember where he was.

He stepped from the jet bridge into the harsh light of the terminal. Lucia called out to him and waved wildly. He covered his face, embarrassed by her overt enthusiasm. Just two years apart in age, they had been inseparable as children. She was equal to him in height and had the same wavy hair the color of black coffee and penetrating green eyes. Everyone still asked if they were twins. Happy as he was to see her, he was annoyed she had brought her best friend, Gabriela. Too much had happened between him and Gaby, and he didn't have the energy to deal with her now.

Lucia threw her arms happily around Nico. As they walked to the luggage carousel, she began peppering him with questions about who shot him and why they had failed to arrest anyone. He assured her the detectives were working on it and not to worry. He said he was safe now that he was home.

Nico glanced over at Gaby and gave her a weak smile. He was ashamed to be returning home a failure. She looked good, he thought, the same shapely figure and sensuous mouth he remembered. The last time he'd seen her was at his mother's funeral. His entire family and all his childhood friends had been there. Life had been going well for him and everyone treated him as though he were a star. Gaby's voice shook him back to the present.

"I'm glad to see you, Nico," she said softly so that only he could hear her.

Her tenderness, the hesitancy of her voice overwhelmed him. He caught a glimpse of his reflection in the glass. He was vulnerable and weak. That everyone knew he'd been shot was humiliating. He didn't feel the need to respond. She looped her arm through his making it easier to keep in step with him. "I'm here for you…as your friend," she said.

He'd known Gaby his entire life and if nothing else he trusted her. He flexed his bicep, squeezing her arm. After weeks in the hospital and nights without sleep, he felt like the survivor of a shipwreck. He looked around the baggage claim area at all the people. He watched Lucia and Gaby as they dragged his suitcase off the conveyor belt. It was still not completely real to him that he was back home.

Nico looked out the window at the faded grandeur of the colonial era architecture as they drove down the narrow cobblestone streets. Lucia and Gaby kept up a brisk banter on the drive from the airport to San Telmo district. He didn't join in or listen to what they said, their voices were enough to quiet his anxiety. The cafés were still bustling, and the tango dancers in their ruffled dresses milled about the makeshift dance floor that had been erected earlier in the plaza. They dropped Gabriela at her house a few blocks away and parked in front of the iron gates to the pasaje, the interior passageway to the house. One of the grand historic homes in San Telmo, it had been built by Ita's maternal great-grandfather in the late 19th Century. He'd been one of the Lords of the Pampas, those of the landed aristocracy who raised cattle and exported beef throughout Europe when Argentina was among the richest economies in the world.

° ° °

When they entered the conservatory, the central patio of the house, Nico heard Astro barking as he bounded in to greet him, his paws sliding on the tile floor. Nico squatted down allowing the dog to lick his face. Astro was one of Stella's puppies and had the same black and white spots. Nico looked up and saw his grandmother in the kitchen. Even from a distance he saw her eyes glistening.

"Estoy bien," he assured her.

She shook her head. Relief was written on her face.

"Por fortuna, Nico." She walked over, wiping her hands on her apron.

He stood and hugged her to him. Melting into the comfort of her ample bosom, the grey-haired knot of her chignon tucked under his chin, and the scent of coffee and flour on her smooth olive skin brought a lump to his heart.

It's all too real, he thought, carrying his luggage up the narrow back stairs to his old room. Unzipping his suitcase, he took from between the neat stack of T-shirts a photograph of himself on the beach in Kerala. Studying it, he had trouble grasping the length of time that had passed. The places he'd lived came and went, as did the people. He was in the home where he'd lived as a child. His failure was embedded like a thorn, his life over in spite of his survival. He ran his palm over the worn surface of the mahogany dresser. Placing the photo on top, he went about filling the drawers. There was a gold key in the latch of the Louis XV armoire, but it wasn't locked. He opened the door and the ghosts of generations tumbled out. He hung his clothes contemplating the velvet dresses and waistcoats that had been there before him. The window in his room overlooked the patio and the aroma of sautéed meat and onions made his mouth water.

Downstairs, he paused in the doorway to take in the familiar surroundings. The water trickling in the stone fountain made it warm and slightly humid in the conservatory. As a child he'd caught frogs and put them in the fountain, only to have Ita return them to the pond. The palm trees in the courtyard had grown as high as the roof. He and Lucia would have tea at the garden table, like in Alice in Wonderland.

He watched Ita standing over an iron skillet making empanadas with her work-weathered hands. He knew exactly the number of blue and white tiles there were on the backsplash behind the porcelain sink. He'd learned his numbers by counting them as a child. This is real, he told himself. He'd expected to achieve the rewards of success in Los Angeles, but that was now lost. It wasn't the first time he had to start over. I'm home, he thought. Lucia was eagerly telling him all the gossip she thought he needed to know and Ita was making empanadas.

° ° °

Spills of sunlight came through the bedroom window bringing with it the aroma of coffee and caramelized onions. Nico lay under the quilt and surveyed the ledger of his life. His hair was damp from tormented dreams. The cloak of optimistic ambition that had driven him was in tatters. He'd thrown himself into countless passionate relationships thinking they were love, but none had turned out well. He'd chosen Élodie for her money and connections; it was a bonus that she was gorgeous.

It had been a disaster that nearly killed him.

There was always Maya. She was the most reliable. She would wait for him; except he didn't consider her his ideal mate. She lacked the money and connections he needed. He studied the photo of himself taken in India, his bronze skin, the lean muscles. It had been a past he belonged to, and it was now behind him. He contemplated his series of mistakes. For the first time he thought he could settle here with Gaby.

Pulling on his well-worn sweatpants and a loose white T-shirt he went down to the kitchen. He wasn't surprised to find a carafe of black coffee and a golden frittata on the stovetop. Lucia had left hours ago for the bank. His mother had worked there, and she'd gotten Lucia a job when she'd finished school. He was glad to be alone with Ita in the kitchen. Nico poured a mug of coffee and helped himself to a large wedge of the frittata, eating it from the skillet until Ita gently scolded him to get a plate. He sat down across from her at the kitchen table and watched her skillfully sew a button onto a sweater, her capable fingers effortlessly passing the thread back and forth. Returning home had aroused feelings that still haunted him.

That day, more than thirty years ago, had blanketed him with a sorrow that had permanently darkened his world. The memory of Ita holding his hand as they walked through the airport to the gate. Her sad, determined face was ingrained in his mind. He viewed his life as a parchment on which the writing has been erased and written over many times, like a palimpsest where all the possibilities still remained.

He remembered asking her questions that to him were enormous as elephants. "Why didn't Mami come?" His meek child voice projected over the boarding announcements in the bustling airline terminal.

She squeezed his hand gently. "You know she has to work, mijo," she said. Her voice was stern but didn't mask her love.

They waited by the gate. He remembered feeling sick to his stomach. He sensed there was something she wasn't telling him. He knew there were secrets, a time of whispers about the troubles in Argentina. There were thousands of people who had disappeared.

But he was too young to worry about that.

"Where is Lucia? Is she coming?"

"No, mi amor."

He was desperate to make sense of what was happening. "When can I come home?" he'd asked.

"There is nothing for you here, querido. It's time you went to live with your father."

Apart from owning several successful restaurants in Buenos Aires, Roberto had left his family behind. New York was where everything was happening, he said. Roberto was grand, vivacious, and generous. His restaurants were wildly successful, a gathering place for the rich and famous. He was a natural storyteller, and the joy and laughter of friends followed him. At Christmas Roberto arrived laden with splendid gifts from New York City. He took over the kitchen, and even though he was rambunctious, Ita couldn't deny he was a superb cook who made her laugh. In the summer they all went to the beach house in Pinamar. Nico was thrilled to be taken for rides on the back of his father's motorbike. When he closed his eyes to imagine it, he could still smell the sea air, taste the salt, and feel the wind in his hair. Nico didn't understand why he had left them. Underneath his love for him was anger and resentment.

Nico recalled the night before. He'd gone into his mother's bedroom. In the thin glow of moonlight from the window he watched her sleep, seemingly untroubled and without dreaming.

"I'm sorry Mami, please don't send me away," he whimpered. He felt ashamed of his earlier behavior.

She'd bought him a suitcase, the kind with wheels. You've grown up, she told him. But he didn't feel grown up. He had sat on his bed and sulked as she packed his favorite sweatshirts, sneakers, and baseball hats. She talked to him in a calm voice about how he would make new friends and go to a good school. She folded his clothes neatly and balled his socks into pairs. When she'd picked up the worn Snoopy from the bed and placed it into the suitcase, he pulled it from her and threw it to the floor.

"I'm not a baby," he howled and stormed from the room.

In the morning, while he and Ita waited for the car to collect them, he had unzipped the suitcase and looked inside. The Snoopy was there, on top. He wouldn't admit it but having Snoopy had lessened his anxiety.

When Ita handed him off to the flight attendant, he'd looked over his shoulder.

"For how long?" he pleaded, close to tears.

Not knowing when he would see them again was crushing. The acid burned the back of his throat and his legs, like rubber, had nearly collapsed from under him. At the time, he was certain it must have been something he'd done. He felt terribly alone as he boarded the flight, and when the plane lifted into the sky, a profound sadness took hold. He watched as Argentina and everything he'd known passed behind him as if he were leaving for the last time.

◦ ◦ ◦

Where had the time gone that he still felt the anguish of that day. He sat here in the same kitchen wondering if she remembered how he'd clung to her, his fingers gripping the neckline of her dress.

His father's Ducati had remained dormant under a tarp in the garage, and he wanted to get it running. He tossed back what remained of the cold coffee in his mug. He was about to get up from the table and took a hard look at Ita, her shoulders rounded over her still agile fingers. Her hair had turned grey, making her appear older than he remembered at the funeral, but that was twelve years ago. A scrap of courage took hold of him.

"Tell me why Mami sent me away?" he asked, swallowing the lump in his throat.

Ita looked up from her sewing. Her slightly clouded eyes, watery with age, were kind.

"Argentina had changed. This wasn't the place for you. Eventually, they would have brought you into the cartel. We didn't want you to get mixed up with them." Her words were choked with sadness.

"I was fine. They wouldn't have hurt me."

"Nico, they had you running errands. To you it was game, riding around on your bicycle, being helpful. You had no idea of the danger."

"I could have taken care of myself. I can't believe you sent me away…from you and Mami."

Allowing them both time to think, she fetched the coffee pot and refilled both their mugs. "It was inevitable. They were grooming you. Gloria Sanchez had been involved for years. Poor woman. Gracias a Dios, I got you out of here when I did."

At the memory, Nico shuddered. When he'd heard Mrs. Sanchez had been murdered he hid in his room for days and cried. A widow around his mother's age, she had been nice to him. Several times a week he rode his bicycle over to her house to deliver groceries. She made him lunch and gave him a can of Coca-Cola. He never told anyone that he knew drug money was inside the sack of groceries, and he didn't think anyone noticed he'd taken a few dollars from the bottom.

"And Mami? What happened?" He searched her eyes.

"Your father had gone to the New York to open the restaurant. He kept asking your mother to come and bring you and your sister. She should have gone. I think she was afraid to leave everything she knew. She had a good position at the bank. Here in Buenos Aires, our family was important, to some degree. But New York City… I think it was too big for her. The restaurant business, with its long hours… she would have been alone a lot.

Ita paused before answering the question he'd really asked. "She never stopped loving your father. They never divorced. When your father left, she started going out with friends from the bank. I imagine she was bored. She was still young, después de todo. There was one fellow, handsome, and he had a big job in the government." She paused and looked down at the sweater she was mending. "It was a troubled time in Argentina, and no surprise that he was corrupt. Drugs. Money laundering. I begged her to leave and take you with her, but she wouldn't. She didn't want to let you go, but I insisted on sending you away."

He frowned. It had been Ita's decision. He looked away.

"I missed you." He choked on his words. Unable to continue he got up from the table and paced the kitchen.

"Nico, look at me," she pleaded.

He turned to her. His eyes brimmed with tears. He saw the pain of regret on her face, and he fell to his knees and rested his head in her lap. She stroked his hair repeating, "Lo siento, mijo. I'm sorry."

He stood and raked his hair back. Embarrassed by his emotional display, he collected the dishes from the table and carried them to sink. The water from the faucet masked the silence. What was done could never be undone. They carried the relics of their past with them.

"Quieres locro para la cena?" Ita asked persuasively.

He nodded and smiled weakly. Offering to make him his favorite meal was her way of changing the subject.

His phone rang. Ita saw Gabriela's name on the screen.

"Watch out for that girl, Nico. I don't trust her."

"She's been friends with Lucia since primary school," he said.

He dried his wet hands on his pants and answered the call. "Gaby, I need to get the Ducati out of the garage. I'll pick you up and we'll go for a ride. Be ready. Chau bella." He longed for the wind on his face to sweep away the sorrow in his heart.

Ita shook her head but didn't say more about Gaby.

"Be careful on the motorcycle. You are supposed to be resting, no?"

He kissed her on the forehead. "Don't worry, Ita. I can take care of myself."

◦ ◦ ◦

It had taken him longer than he planned to get the bike working. Gaby was waiting for him in the foyer. He flipped up the visor on his helmet and watched her walk towards him. She wore tight white jeans and a pink shirt. The ringlets of her long curly hair cascading around her shoulders bounced as she walked. She fumbled with her hair clip. In his haste to buckle the helmet he accidentally pinched the skin on her neck. Climbing onto the bike, she wrapped her arms around his torso too tightly. The pressure on his wound caused him to flinch and he moved her hands to his waist. He revved the engine, and she patted his thigh signaling she was ready to depart.

They drove along the Plata, and he pulled over at a roadside stand. Gaby hopped off and bought sandwiches and beer. The routine seemed to echo the past. She clutched the paper sack while he drove the short distance to the service road and parked. Climbing over the low wall that divided the road from the riverbank, they sat on the soft silty ground with their backs against the sunbaked stone. She unwrapped one of the sandwiches and handed it to him.

Nico popped open a can of beer. They'd taken off their shoes and he felt the warm sand between his toes. There wasn't anything he wanted from her; he had no need to impress her. He meant it when he said, "I feel comfortable with you. It's as if no time has passed."

"We've shared a lot together, Nico. I'm so sorry about your mom…We didn't get a chance to talk…"

"Life's not fair," he said sadly. "That shouldn't have been her fate." Shielding his eyes from the sun, he looked down the river, its dark water moving slowly. A small fishing boat far off in the distance captured his attention. "It feels like such a long time ago…"

"What happened with that girl…the one who came to your mother's funeral?"

"Oh, Olivia? She left me," he pouted, feigning sadness.

"Why?" she pressed.

"She went to a fancy music school in San Francisco. That was more important to her than being with me," he said frowning.

"Ugh, Nico. You're such a faker." She laughed. "I'm not falling for your pity party."

Nico's eyes gleamed in the sun. He liked her spunk, and that she didn't play into his drama.

"Do you remember as kids, how you chased me in the school yard? You would grab my ponytail and demand my candy?"

Nico laughed and reached over giving her hair a playful tug. "I remember years later stealing something sweeter than your candy…"

"How can I forget? You were my first love," she said wistfully, and stared out across the river.

"You were the first girl I kissed," proclaimed Nico boastfully.

"Even then you were an over-sexed bully," she chided.

"What do mean over-sexed?" He laughed heartily. Reaching over, he cupped her breast. "Now, see? You are flirting with me."

Pushing his hand away she turned to him and asked seriously, "Why did you leave me, Nico? You came back from New York. I thought we had something...that you'd stay."

Nico exhaled sharply. "Gaby, I cared for you... a lot...but..."

"So, I wasn't good enough for you?"

"I was only seventeen. Just out of high school. You know the only reason I came back was because my mom was sick. There was much more I wanted to do with my life. I just didn't see myself getting married, having a family, being ordinary."

"Ah. You're far from ordinary."

He leaned his head against the wall and closed his eyes to the sun. The briny scent of the river brought back memories of his youth, riding his bike along the causeway. His wound began to ache. He reached over and finding her hand, pulled her closer. Curling up against him, she sighed and nuzzled her face in his neck. Being with her reminded him of younger, gentler years. He moved his hand into her hair and idly began coiling a tendril around his finger. Even with the heat of the afternoon sun on their bodies, she trembled under his touch. In response, he pressed his lips to hers in a soft, lingering kiss.

He became aware of his body relaxing, a feeling he hadn't experienced in a long time. He was free with Gaby, there was no pressure. He wondered what his life would have been like if he'd never left, if he'd stayed with her? He pushed up her flimsy T-shirt and kissed a trail down to her navel. She helped him lift his shirt over his head and saw his injury, the scar still angry and raw, and touched it lightly. "Nico, I'm sorry…"

He tugged off his pants, flinching not from physical pain, but from the memory. He unzipped her jeans, and she did the rest. The only people in sight were far out from shore on a fishing boat. He pulled her over him, taking what he wanted. Her thighs were tan and taut. His eyes burned into hers, the yellow flecks sparking with lust-filled need. Unable to break his gaze, she leaned over him and tentatively swept a lock of hair from his eyes before kissing him deeply and long. Placing his hands on her waist, he guided her onto him. She moved slowly until the pain and pleasure came as one.

He barely made out her whispered words, "I have always missed you, Nico."

He lay spent. Her hair, smelling like rosemary, fell over his face covering him in a protective darkness. A foreign sensation of contentment filled him, the first in as long as he remembered.

4

The Ducati sped down Calle Defensa. The wind whipped Nico's hair as he navigated the winding cobblestone streets. Without a helmet obscuring his vision, he took in the stately architecture of the old city. After several weeks he'd adjusted to being back home. Home. It was an odd word. More of a feeling than a place. There were the years living with his dad in New York City. Those were typically wild years with his friends in middle school and high school, cutting class and smoking marijuana. In those days Roberto owned a restaurant that was popular with the glamourous after-hours crowd. He was never around, working long hours, and he left Nico to fend for himself. The city scene infused their lives where drugs and alcohol extended to their apartment. The women flirted with him, and Nico hung around and watched as lines of cocaine were snorted and couples disappeared into bedrooms. He made a game of pilfering handbags for cash, not because he needed it, but just to see if he could get away with it. His plan was to finish high school, go to college in the city, and work with his dad in the restaurant. But his world shattered again when he learned his mother had HIV. When he graduated high school, he left New York and returned to Buenos Aires putting the plans he'd made to rest as if they had been nothing more than a fantasy.

He turned the corner and parked in front of El Federal. A comfortable feeling of reminiscence washed over him. Coming into the room from the sunlight, his eyes took a moment to adjust. It was early, and there were few people seated at the bar. The old brass cash register was still on the counter, just as he remembered it. In the dim light he spotted his old friend Mateo texting on his cell phone. It wasn't quite noon, even so a tall glass of draught beer, the foam head still brimming, remained untouched in front of him.

Mateo turned around. It must have been the flood of light through the open door.

"Hola, Nico querido. Cómo seguís? Estás mejor?" Mateo asked. He was surprised to see Nico looking so well.

Mateo was a head taller and heftier than Nico. He stood and clasped Nico's hand and pulled him into a bear hug adding several vigorous pats on his back.

Nico tensed. The friendly slaps made him uncomfortable. The wound throbbed, reminding him he hadn't fully recovered.

"Y, sigo vivo." Nico said casually with a shrug, as if there had been no question he would live. "Vos boludo, cómo andás?" He realized he hadn't seen Mateo since his mother's funeral.

Nico saw the distinguished fringe of grey at Mateo's temples, and crow's feet at the corners of his eyes when he smiled. He didn't think he looked old as much as he looked wise. Nico signaled the bartender to bring him one of the same and pulled up a stool next to Mateo.

"I'm supposed to be resting but I've been looking for studio space." He was embarrassed that everyone knew he'd been shot, and he didn't want to appear weak in Mateo's eyes.

The edge of the bar was bare where the varnish had worn off. On Saturday afternoons he'd come here with his father to watch fútbol. Maradona played for the national team, and when he was on the field everyone would go wild cheering. He was so little he had trouble climbing up onto the stool. He would order a Coca-Cola from the bartender, proud to be sitting with the men.

Behind the rows of glittering liquor bottles, he caught sight of himself in the mirror. Black leather jacket, dark hair still thick with no sign of grey. For a split second he saw himself as a much younger man, fearless and full of possibility. He looked around and thought how nothing had changed. Cigarette smoke made serpentine shapes in the golden rays slicing down through the windows. As a child he imagined the luminous cilia stirring in the yellow shafts of light were his spirit guides.

Wasting no time, Mateo asked grinning, yet in all seriousness, "So, old friend, what did you do that made someone want to kill you?"

A few years older than Nico, Mateo had been like a protective older brother. Now, he wasted no opportunity to poke fun or reproach his friend.

"Apparently I pissed someone off." Nico answered matter-of-factly. His beer arrived and both men raised their glass.

"Salud!" Mateo said grinning. They both drank deeply. "Glad you are alive, amigo. What have you been doing with yourself since you got back?"

"Nothing much…hanging around with Gaby," Nico said haltingly. He knew Mateo had been interested in her and wondered if they'd ever hooked up.

"Gabriela Perez? Posta?" The disapproval was clear in his voice.

"She used to be my girl… a long time ago." Nico defended weakly. Shifting on the barstool he looked away and stared up at a large Victorian clock, the centerpiece of an elaborately carved wooden arch mounted above the bar.

"You know her brothers are connected. Are you looking to get into the game?" Mateo asked.

"No, of course not." He absentmindedly touched his side where the bullet had penetrated.

"What will you do? Teach yoga?" he asked with a hint of sarcasm.

"I don't know…" Nico shrugged, blowing off the question. He'd grown up with Mateo and knew the taunt was meant in jest.

"I'm sure you met a lot of movie stars in L.A., no?"

"Of course. I was the best…they all came to my studio." Nico huffed. His wound was hurting again, and he stood and stretched.

"So, you are a big shot now." Mateo laughed, yet the pride he had for his friend was obvious.

Encouraged, Nico boasted, "A big director made a movie about me called Amaru of the Andes. It won an award at Cannes, the big film festival." He wasn't going to let Mateo think he'd amounted to nothing.

"Guau! That's incredible." Mateo exclaimed. "You should open a studio here. Things have changed, and people are into that now."

"I don't know. Maybe." He shifted restlessly in his seat and dragged the bowl of nuts closer and ate a few. He knew Mateo meant well, but the questions made him uncomfortable.

"You okay for money?" Mateo asked thoughtfully.

"Todo bien…. and I'm selling my house…" Nico said casually. He was sure Mateo would never believe how much money he'd made teaching yoga in Los Angeles.

"Mira vos! You bought a house?"

"Yeah, it was crazy. This prince from the Arab Emirates paid me a shit load of money to go over there and teach him. So, with the money he paid me, I bought a house in the hills outside of L.A."

"Dale, contame… An Arab prince wanted to learn yoga?"

Nico laughed. "Not exactly. These are exercises that give you psychic powers."

"Jódeme!" Mateo exclaimed. "You must teach me."

Mateo's phone began pinging and he picked it up from the

counter and began texting with someone.

Nico didn't need to ask what Mateo was doing for work. His father owned several of the underground parking garages in the city and as far as he knew Mateo had taken over the lucrative business. While Mateo was on the phone Nico sent a quick text to his dad asking how it was going with the sale of the house. He was conflicted about selling, but it was just another reminder of Élodie, and nothing had been the same since. If she had done as she promised and followed his plan, he would have the yoga center he deserved and be living in Beverly Hills. Instead, he was back home and starting over. He was even dating Gaby again. It was as though that whole chapter of his life was erased. There was no answer from his father, and he shoved the phone into his pocket.

"Che, buddy..." Mateo squeezed Nico's shoulder, rousing him from his reverie. "You'll be fine. You are here with family."

"Yeah, I know..." He knew when Mateo said family, he was including the wider circle that included his friends, even the ones who had some shady dealings. He'd left here at a young enough age to have escaped a dangerous life, yet Moirai, the Greek goddesses of fate, had pursued him.

"Look, Nico, I'm getting together later with some of the guys. You should come and hang out, okay?"

"Bueno. It'll be good to see them again." He agreed, though he doubted he would show up. He hadn't gone out since he'd come home. He hadn't really wanted to do much of anything, not even meet new women. It was easy to just hang out with Gaby.

"I got this," Mateo said, as he tossed some cash on the bar. "Meet us at Plaza Dorrego tonight and I'll hook you up, get you back to yourself in no time."

° ° °

Nico squinted as he stepped from the amber glow of El Federal into the daylight. Mateo pulled him into a bear hug saying he'd see him later. Nico fished for his Ray Bans and texted Gaby he was on his way. He'd invited her to look at spaces for the studio. So far, she had been good company since he didn't like to be alone.

There was more traffic than he expected, and the narrow cobblestone streets had cars parked on either side, making passing impossible. Nico pulled up in front of her house and tooted the horn. The Perez home had been in their family for generations, and though not as old as Nico's, was historic and sat on one of the prettiest streets in the district. When she didn't appear, he texted again. Annoyed, he squeezed the bike between two cars.

Taking the steps two at time, he went up to the door and rang the bell. Gaby should have been waiting for him in the foyer. He grew more annoyed when no one came to the door. Leaning back, he looked up at the arched windows on the second-floor French balcony to see if there were any lights on. Impatiently, he rang the bell again more persistently. Her brother Thiago finally came to the door. His hair was disheveled, and he wore crumpled boxer shorts, a sign that Nico had roused him from sleep. He grumbled and motioned with his head for Nico to enter.

"Gaby will be back soon." Nico followed him to the kitchen where Thiago opened the refrigerator and took out two cans of beer, handing one to Nico.

"She was supposed to be here…" Nico complained, popping open the tab.

"When did you get back?" he asked indifferently, tugging on jeans.

Nico shrugged, taking a swig from the can.

"You've been spending a lot of time with my sister. Are you planning on staying this time?"

"I don't have any place else to go… I'll probably open a yoga center here."

Thiago walked over to the counter and reached inside a metal canister with the word TEA on it. Feeling down to the bottom he pulled out a packet of small baggies rubber banded together. Removing one, he shoved the others back to the bottom and replaced the lid. There were no words exchanged as Thiago unceremoniously arranged the lines on a cutting board and presented them to Nico.

"No thanks." Nico said, feeling a sudden twinge in his side.

Thiago shrugged and snorted up three lines then set the board aside. Opening the refrigerator, he retrieved a container of eggs and a bowl of leftover vegetables. He emptied the vegetables into the iron skillet that sat on the stove and lit the burner.

"Gaby's running an errand," he announced. Cracking the eggs into the bowl he scrambled them with a fork. "Do you want frittata?" Tiago asked casually. He poured the yellow liquid into the skillet.

"Okay, gracias."

They had finished eating in silence when Nico heard the front door open and the sound of footsteps going upstairs.

"I'll be right down," Gaby called out. A few minutes later she entered the kitchen, took a beer from the fridge, and joined her brother and Nico at the table.

Nico narrowed his eyes at her and scowled. "Where were you? I told you I was coming by. You said you would come with me to look at spaces for the center."

"I had to go to the bank." She glanced over at Thiago and said cryptically, "The funds were short…"

"I'll take care of it later," he replied frowning.

"Let's go. I'm late already." Nico said curtly. He stood abruptly, impatient for her to join him as he made for the front door.

"I'll get my things," she said anxiously. Darting quickly out of the room she ran up the stairs followed by Thiago.

Nico paused at the front door long enough to hear their muffled voices in obvious disagreement.

"Don't be out too long. You have work to do." Tiago told her.

Nico was on his bike with the motor running when Gaby came out of the house. "Where is my helmet?" she asked. She was obviously flustered.

"I forgot. Get on," he scowled.

"What's wrong, Nico?"

"I didn't want to hang out with your thug of a brother waiting for you."

"What are you talking about? You guys grew up together…"

"I am trying to stay clean, and the asshole offers me lines of coke. That's what I'm talking about."

"I'm sorry," she said meekly and climbed on the back of the motorcycle.

Nico swerved wildly in and out of the traffic along Avenida Callao toward the wealthy barrio of Recoleta. They arrived late and spent the next several hours with a real estate agent looking at space for a studio. Nico repeated the same questions. What is the square footage and access to water for locker room facilities? The agent had become increasingly irritated when Nico did not make an offer. Gaby stood across the room looking at her phone. Nico had warned her not to show enthusiasm that would hinder his ability to negotiate a lease. After hours of going from one location to the next, she leaned on him and asked if they were done.

They entered a large ground floor space with tall windows that faced out on the avenue. The polished wood floor gleamed in the triangle of sunlight as it spilled in through the window. He stood in the center of the empty room and looked around. The space reminded him of his studio in L.A. All day he had tried to recreate his past. Feeling anxious and unresolved, Nico patrolled the room like a lion pacing inside a circus wagon. He was unable to stop thinking about the time he and Maya spent the afternoon looking at spaces in L.A. She'd worn shorts. Her legs were limber and lean, the color of burnt caramel. The bike was second nature to Maya. As a stunt person she had often driven them at high speeds. She had climbed on the back and wrapped her arms around him. He wondered if Maya had found him a studio in Beverly Hills. The light reflected off the floor. He felt suddenly vulnerable. There was no going back to L.A. He would always be looking over his shoulder.

Out on the street a couple walked past the window holding hands. Without turning around, he asked the agent the price then countered with a lower offer. The agent, appearing relieved, said he would get back to him in the morning. Gaby showed her delight, but quickly bit her lip when Nico glared at her. Grabbing her arm, he brusquely thanked the realtor and ushered her out onto the street. Gaby had trouble keeping up with him as he headed to where the bike was parked. They rode only a short distance until Nico stopped in front of the neo-classical gates of La Recoleta Cemetery.

"Walk with me," he said getting off the bike. He didn't explain but called over his shoulder for her to keep up. As the shadows lengthened, they walked up and down the grid of elaborate marble mausoleums centered around the historic Church of Nuestra Señora del Pilar. The cemetery, a popular tourist attraction, was one of the most beautiful in the world and contained the graves of the country's presidents and most notable people. He paused to read the names on the tombs, not speaking until they had covered the entire grid. The tall, weathered wood doors were open, set against the lustrous white walls of the centuries-old church. Upon entering Nico crossed himself. It was dim and quiet. There were a few people inside praying. He slid into a pew and knelt, bowing his head over folded hands. Gaby knelt next to him keeping her head down.

Under his breath, he asked menacingly, "What are you doing, Gabriela?"

She hesitated before answering. "What do you mean?"

His voice, though barely above a whisper, was threatening. "You know exactly what I mean. I want to know exactly what work you are doing for your brothers."

"Nothing. I just do some errands for them occasionally... to help them out. Some jobs are easier for a woman...You know..."

"You're crazy, Gaby. I can't believe your brothers put you at risk. They're fucking assholes who don't give a damn about you."

He sat back in the pew, staring ahead. He was unable to look at her. The auric rays of the setting sun streamed through the vaulted windows and coruscated off the ornate alter, as though touched by the creator.

"You are being ridiculous, Nico. I'm not *involved*." She voiced emphatically.

"You're an idiot. Do you think I don't know? Why are you working for them?"

She looked down at her hands. "They are my brothers. I have to."

"I am not going to do this. Not again." His said angrily.

"What do mean, again?"

"You forget... I grew up here. I would be just like them if Ita hadn't sent me away."

"I remember... it was just after Mrs. Sanchez..."

Nico furrowed his brow, wondering if she knew it had been his fault.

"I never would have come back if my Mom hadn't been sick." His voice was restrained, like a paperweight lodged in his throat. "Her death was my fault…too."

"No, Nico. That's insane to think that…"

"She sent me away to protect me. But then she became *involved,* as you put it… If she hadn't, maybe she would still be alive."

"No one forced her, Nico… You can't blame yourself…"

"Yes, I can." He had raised his voice and heads turned toward them. He rose and stepped into the aisle where he crossed himself and walked briskly toward the door.

Gaby followed, calling after him, "Nico, wait…" Standing in the last slanting light inside the church she took his arm and pleaded, "Look… Nico, take that space we just saw. I'll help you with the studio… I'll learn yoga… you can teach me. We'll be together, and I won't…I promise, I'll cut ties with my brothers."

"Gabriela, I wish I could believe you. You know, they won't let you go."

"You can believe me, Nico. I don't want this life either. I want…I just want you," she implored. Her fingers gripped his arm tightly, as if she'd fallen through the ice on a frozen pond and he were her only lifeline.

He shook her off him, ignoring the tears running down her face.

"It's this fucking place, Gaby. I can't believe I am back here. It was all happening for me in L.A. I was famous. I was making money and about to open a center in Beverly Hills. Still, the drugs, like beautiful and dangerous Sirens, lured me."

"I'm sorry, Nico. You can put it behind you." There was a long silence between them until Gaby spoke, "Do you know who shot you?"

"Gaby… I wasn't in a drug ring. It was nothing like that…"

he huffed, running his hands through his hair as though tamping down the memories.

"Then why?"

"I don't know… I guess someone was out to get me," and gave her a crooked smile.

"You haven't lost anything. You are still the best, and everyone knows that."

"I suppose so…" Nico sighed. Shivering, he zipped his jacket up close under his chin. "But I'm exhausted. I can't believe I have to start over…"

"You can do it, Nico. I know you can," she said, wrapping her arms around his waist.

"I need you with me. To help me. I'm all alone here," he pleaded.

Taking his face between her palms, she kissed him. "Of course, I'll help you," she softly consoled.

They'd walked halfway around the block and stood in front of Portezuelo where a sidewalk chalk board listed the drink menu for Happy Hour. Taking seats at the bar, Nico ordered two margaritas. Quizzing her, he asked her opinion about each of the spaces they saw earlier. Which did she consider to be the best location? Reading from her notes, she began to recite the pluses and minuses of each of the spaces. Listening to her, Nico remembered Maya's dedication to him. She'd explained why the North Robertson location was better than the place they saw on Wilshire. He knew she'd been right and chided himself for not leasing the space. Instead, he placed all his trust in Élodie to raise the funds needed for a world-class center.

"What day is it?" he asked Gaby.

"Tuesday," she said, confused by his question and the lost look on his face.

"How long have I been here?

She looked at her phone, "It's just after six..."

"I meant how long have I been home?" he snapped, his impatience smoldering.

"Um... two or three months. I think... Why?"

Nico stared blankly. He did not reply. He had an urge to call Maya. She messaged him every day, but he didn't always text her back. She never pressured him or asked when he was coming home. Home. That word again. He wasn't sure where home was anymore. He thought he should tell her not to wait for him.

"Don't you agree, Nico, that you will get a higher clientele on Callao?"

"Yes, of course. That's why I put the offer in on it." The anger in him swelled. She was trying too hard.

When the bartender asked if they'd like anything to eat, he ordered french fries. He had a penchant for fries. He recalled lunches at Stout Burger in L.A., sharing a large plate of them with Luna.

Gaby was intent on finding something in her phone and perked up when she found it.

"Nico, look. I found this article on yoga studios in Buenos Aires. The business has grown a lot in popularity in just over a few years. Several in San Telmo are listed and two in Recoleta. The author offers teacher training. I was thinking, I could take her course and become certified. What do you think?"

Visibly agitated, Nico quashed her suggestion. "I don't need you to teach yoga. I need your help with marketing and running the office. I can't be scheduling appointments myself; it doesn't look professional. And you teaching would ruin my brand."

"I'm sorry. I was just trying to be helpful. Of course, I'll help you with whatever you need. Make appointments for you…anything at all," she said. She knew he needed her to be obliging.

He smiled and his eyes flashed from under the lock of hair that fell over his face. He raked it back and looked at the bill. Pushing it toward Gaby he stood. "You're making money— you pay for this. Come on. Let's get out of here. I have a lot to do now."

Gaby quickly rifled in her wallet for cash. Tossing it on the bar, she ran after Nico who was already in the street.

"Where did I park?" he complained when she caught up to him.

"Just over there," she pointed. "On the corner by the cemetery," she said confidently. She felt it was her job to unruffle him. She finally had him back in her life. He was taking the lease on the studio. They would be together and have a family. She'd worked it all out in her mind.

He drove fast down the cobblestone streets, weaving through the traffic. He parked near the Pasaje.

As they walked through the gate he hesitated. Turning to her, he said firmly, "Let me do the talking."

"Nico, I don't want to cause any trouble between you and your grandmother…"

"You are not to take orders from those low life brothers of yours anymore. Do you hear me? They will just cause me problems."

"Okay. But what about Ita? She doesn't like me."

"When I explain you want to get away from your brothers, she'll welcome you." Taking her by the arm he reminded her, "Don't speak."

Their footfalls on the glazed tile floor echoed off the towering ceiling as they walked down the lantern lit corridor. Nico pushed opened the heavy door and they stepped into the patio just off the kitchen.

"Hola, Ita. Soy yo!" he called out to let her know he was home.

Ita answered from the kitchen. She was tending a large pot on the stove.

"Qué estás haciendo?" Nico asked. He kissed her on the cheek.

"Locro." She said. She continued slicing the potatoes that sat on the cutting board.

"Gracias, Ita. Mi favorito." He picked up the spoon and tasted the rich medley of beef and vegetables.

Lucia was sitting at the counter. She got up to greet her friend with a double cheek kiss. Gabriela looked over at Nico. The moment was awkward. She wanted to disappear.

Nico relayed the day's news. He'd found a space and would be opening a yoga studio.

"Gabriela is moving in. She doesn't want to live with her brothers, and I need her to help me with the business," he added as an aside.

Gabriela's dark eyes stared at Lucia. She raised her finger up to her lips and looked over at Ita whose back was still turned away from them.

"Here, go set the table." Ita pulled a stack of bowls down from the shelf and handed them to Lucia.

Gaby collected napkins and flatware and followed her from the room. Nico remained behind with Ita and filled the wine glasses.

"I am warning you, Nico. She will bring trouble," Ita said. Though her voice was subdued, it was firm.

"It will be fine if she stays away from her brothers." His voice was steady and knowing. "Besides, she's Lucia's best friend," he continued pleading his case.

"It's not that simple, Nico. You are bringing danger into this home."

"If I stay, then I want her with me," he said flatly.

"This is no place for you, Nico. I sent you away for a reason."

"This is my home, Ita. You're here…and Lucia…" he stressed.

"You were meant for something better, Nico. It was told to me when you were born."

The girls returned to the kitchen and Ita broke off midsentence. Handing Nico two potholders, she told him, "Take the pot over to the table."

The girls dominated the dinner conversation with pointless gossip. Nico grew impatient. When the last bit of locro had been soaked up with bread, he took his plate into the kitchen and opened another bottle of wine. Gaby offered to wash the dishes, but he sent her and Lucia upstairs. He wanted to talk more with Ita about the past—his past. He'd thought about what she said all through dinner.

"Ita, what do you mean it was told to you…?"

Her face was lined by age, and he noticed she'd become slightly stooped. Yet, she was formidable and spoke with authority worthy of her years.

"Siéntate." She waited for his impatient mind to settle. When she saw she had his full attention, she began, "My grandfather was paqo. He was a healer, one who brings balance. You know this."

"I remember you telling us stories when we were little… I suppose that's why I was always interested." Nico refilled his glass, then poured one for Ita. Though she seldom drank, she accepted it.

"Do you remember when my brother Gonzalo brought you to Q'eros? The paqos, the spiritual leaders, took you to the sacred mountain at Qoyllur Rit'i to give Karpay, a rite of passage. You were just a small child, and when you got back you made your first mesa out of the stones you collected." She smiled at this memory.

"Hmmm, I remember going to the mountains..."

Ita ignored his interruption. "The rite of Karpay planted the seeds of knowledge from your ancestral lineage into your spirit body, preparing you for when the time came to fulfill your destiny. The ceremony is of the heart, a process of becoming that ends one's relationship with time." She stopped there.

Nico didn't say anything. He'd always felt he understood the fluidity of time. He'd talked about it with Luna. When his mother died, she'd sent him a poem by the Indian poet Tagore. It was about the ceaseless journey of life and death on the river of time. It was deeper than he could understand. But even so, it was beautiful.

Ita continued, "There is a doorway between worlds, Nico. When you step through the holes in time, you will regain your luminous nature. Then you will see through the eyes of your soul."

"Are you saying this was your plan for me all along?" The weight of her words made him dizzy.

"Nico, nothing is predetermined. The rite transmits only potential. It's up to you to bring about the flowering. Follow your own footsteps. Learn from the teachers, the Apu, Mother Earth. Honor yourself and all of creation."

"I've been working towards this... well, at least I've tried," he sighed heavily, "but, it appears I've failed miserably."

She sipped the wine in her glass. Nico thought he'd never seen her drink wine. Was that true? He had trouble remembering. But then he recalled she liked a dark, bitter liqueur from Sicily. It had a wonderful complex aroma of oranges and herbs. She'd take sips from a coffee mug she kept above the stove. Looking toward the shelf, he noticed the mug wasn't there.

"Escúchame. They wove the bands of power—water, earth, air, fire, and pure light—into your energy field for protection. This ceremony revealed your essence to the paqos. Afterwards, they bathed you in the sacred lagoon at the glacier. I was told they saw your ability to direct kawsay, the life force, and this is a powerful gift that should only be used for good. Never to harm or control another."

"Si, y qué diferencia hay? I couldn't save Mami. It's my fault she got sick. Don't you see? I've done nothing right. If I hadn't been delivering the groceries to Mrs. Sanchez, and…"

Ita cut him off before he confessed to stealing money. He didn't think it was much, just a bit here and there to save for a new bicycle. Still, it had to have been his fault. He never spoke of it. But sometimes he awoke feverish, his skin burning from the memory.

"Nico, you were a child. You had no idea what kind of people they were. Gloria Sanchez was murdered because she helped her son get out of the country. He was an asset. They wanted him. They used you, and you didn't know any better. I tried to watch over you as best I could." She turned on the faucet and began to wash the dishes.

"Ita… please…" he begged, turning off the water. "Please, tell me…"

"Tell you? Tell you what?"

He hesitated. Embarrassed. But they'd come this far. "How did she get AIDS?"

"Mijo, your father never told you?" She paused as if to reflect on the memory. She dried her hands on her apron and sat down at the table. "Siéntate de nuevo."

Nico sat down beside her. Her hand trembled slightly when she picked up the wine glass and took a drink. "She had a blood disorder, something wrong with her liver. They gave her a blood transfusion, but at that time they weren't careful. The blood was infected with the virus." Her voice tightened and her eyes welled with tears.

"This country… Nobody knew." The tears fell down her cheeks.

"I didn't know. I thought…." He was aghast. All this time he thought it had been sexually transmitted. Why hadn't he been told the truth. He emptied the bottle of wine into his glass. He didn't know what to believe.

"Ugh, it is the past, Nico. We need to put it away."

For the longest time he'd held fast to his own view. There was the auspicious life that his friends and clients believed he was living, but then there was the other life, the afflicted one he saw only through the lens of his past. Everything was familiar and known to him from childhood. All of it lay behind him and yet it still existed. Reconciliation was beyond his control, like dumping the contents of a desk drawer onto the floor and trying to make sense out of it.

° ° °

In his mind he is there again. He remembers everything. The images are vivid, as if they are happening now. He is standing on a stool in the kitchen helping Ita fold empanadas, they are crimping them closed. He is stilled by the memory of Ita clasping his hand in hers as they walked through the airport to the gate. In this other life he is a young boy. The summer is ending. He remembers chasing Mami along the wide-open stretch of deserted beach, his bare feet splashing in the surf. He shrieks with joy. The light was as he'd never seen, clear and transcendent. She is smiling back at him, her hair tossed by the wind as they run along the wet sand. Afterwards they listened to the waves breathing—rising and falling for eternity. In his collection of memories, without her there is nothing. Their lives are woven together like braids of sweetgrass.

° ° °

"Ita, I promise…" He slurred his words either from being tired or too much wine.

"Mijo, don't make any promises to me."

"But..." He remembered what he said to Luna. That he would do whatever it takes. He'd lost everything and had nothing to take its place. This was his home. He wanted to stay here with Ita. Only here could he feel rooted like he belonged. Here, he could start over.

Nico shook his head to clear away the cobwebs. "I've learned a lot," he announced defiantly. "I made it big in L.A. I had rich clients who paid me a lot of money. Did I tell you? They made a movie about me. That's a big deal, you know."

"So, you want to be a big deal?" she asked quizzically.

He knew she was mocking him. "I know what you think, Ita. But why shouldn't I be commended for my gifts? I worked hard for them. I suffered for them," he boasted, but the bravado was weak and thin.

"Entonces... You think you have suffered?"

"Yes. I suffered. I was nearly killed. I had to leave just when my business was going well."

"Then, things were obviously not going well, Nico."

He put his head in his hands. "No, you're right. They weren't. This girl...I loved her. She made me promises, but she broke them. Everyone..." He looked at her fully. "Everyone abandoned me, Ita."

He blamed her, too. And Roberto, and his mother. The anger lodged in his throat like a ball of wax that he was unable to cough up. It was his fate.

"They all had their own interests." The words flew out of him, like angry bees.

"Oh si?" There was no point in challenging him. "You should go back to study with the paqos and learn the true meaning of your gifts."

"No puedo… I can't. It's too late for that. I'm opening a studio in barrio Recoleta. You won't believe it. All these fancy shops have opened, and the old mansions have become boutique hotels. It's a lot like Beverly Hills. It will be the finest yoga studio in Argentina. I'll be a success in no time. Which reminds me, I have to call the realtor back…"

Before he could step away Ita covered his hand with hers. "Nico, only you can decide how to use the gifts you were given." She didn't release him until his eyes met hers.

"I can do good work here…with you, and Lucia. Gabriela will help me."

Ita went back to the sink and turned on the faucet to wash the dishes. He went toward the stairs, then turned back to her. "Ita, I can do that… permiteme…"

"Estoy bien, Nico. Déjame."

Wrapping his arms around her from behind, he hugged her and kissed her cheek. "Te amo, abuelita."

"Enough! And watch out for that little zorra."

"Ita… Everything will turn out fine. Lo prometo."

"That is a promise you may not be able to keep."

5

Nico closed the shutters allowing only slivers of the early morning light to slip through the louvers. Gabriela's body was arranged enticingly on the white sheets, the marbled curls of her hair spilling across the pillow. He slid back into bed and pressed his erection against her back. He loved the smoothness of her skin, the curve of her spine. His need was urgent and he eased into her from behind, barely disturbing her sleep. After he finished she wriggled out from under him and turned onto her back. He looked down at her long black eyelashes resting on her high cheekbones and thought she looked like one of Goya's masterpieces of Spanish ladies. She curled into him and lay with her head in the crook of his arm. He listened to the sound of his own heartbeat. She smelled wild and earthy. Her hair the fragrance of an herb garden. The uniqueness of a woman's scent, like that of an animal.

He pictured Élodie's bisque skin, savory and sweet, and her expensive lace bras and matching thongs from the finest shops in Paris. How blindingly stunning she was. He'd been enchanted by her voice chattering away in a medley of French and English about artwork she had just sold to an Emirati collector. He didn't understand half of what she said, only the pleasurable sensation of being inside her. Every cell of his body became aroused remembering her voice until without warning a flash of images of the night he was shot nearly made him bolt upright. Suppressing those chilling, bleak thoughts, he lay still until his nerves quieted, contemplating how scent never faded from memory. Uncorked, its perfume evoked the moment, compelling him to relive it. Too soon he became restless.

"Come on woman, we have work to do today." Jumping up, he gave Gaby's thigh a forceful but playful slap.

He stepped from the shower and wrapped a towel around his waist. Studying his face in the mirror, he combed his fingers through his wet hair and pursed his lips bemoaning his misfortune. After shaving the scruff off his neck, he trimmed his beard with the electric razor to a length slightly longer than a five o'clock shadow. Gaby was still showering, and he pictured her behind the shower curtain. Still aroused by his thoughts of Élodie, he was tempted to join her under the raining hot water while she pleasured him, but he was impatient to get going. She took longer in the shower than any woman he'd known and waiting for her was already making him irritable. He'd lounged around recovering for too long. Unwrapping the towel from around his waist he examined his body in the mirror. The wound had healed and only an angry scar remained. It barely ached any longer. He'd put the weight he had lost back on, but without being able to exercise, he'd lost muscle and could no longer see the definition of his former torso. He would begin a vigorous yoga routine today. He would be back in shape by the time the studio opened.

Glancing at his phone he saw a message from Maya. He thought about answering but didn't. He envisioned Maya's cat-like body. She was athletic and flexible. But more than that, there hadn't been anything she wasn't willing to do to please him. Even when he was flying high on cocaine, she had gone all night with him. The next day, she could barely walk, but she never complained. Without a word, she would disappear when Élodie came to town, and reappear once she had left. He scoffed thinking she probably knew all along that it wouldn't work out with Élodie. He was going to have to find a way to tell Maya he would be staying in Argentina—at least for a while. He felt a fleeting twinge of guilt.

Pulling on black jeans and a T-shirt, he grabbed his wallet and keys off the dresser. He picked up the well-worn black leather motorcycle jacket that had been his father's.

"Darse prisa!" he called out impatiently to Gaby, urging her to hurry up.

As he was about to head downstairs, her phone pinged, and he saw a text from Thiago. It read, *Ven a casa ahora!* He demanded she come home at once. Nico bit down on his lip. He'd made Gaby promise she wouldn't work for her brothers. Either Thiago had ignored her, or she hadn't told him. He heard the shower stop, and the bathroom door opened releasing a cloud of steam.

"Why do you take such a long time to get ready?" he complained. "Hurry, I don't want to be late," he barked.

"Go have your coffee. I'll be right down." She chirped while toweling her hair.

He scowled. Images continuously reminded him that the past was always present, that he was never far removed from its ravages. Thinking back to when he was child, it was after his dad left them and moved to New York City that he remembered the two strange men who came to the house. When they arrived, his mother told him to go to his room while she took care of important business. From the shadows on the staircase, he saw her slip off her shoes and sit on the man's lap. He listened to her girlish laughter and the sound of ice cubes clinking in their whiskey glasses. A sadness came over him along with the revelation he wasn't enough to fill the emptiness she felt.

° ° °

The sunlight came through the conservatory windows. No one was at home. He wondered where Astro was and called his name. When the dog didn't appear, he decided Ita must have taken him for a walk. The coffee in the carafe was still warm and he poured himself a mug. On the counter a basket held biscuits and the butter in the dish was warm and soft. He thought about Ita. She had an awareness of everything around her. His eyes moved around the kitchen. He knew this room, its aromas, its meals, the play of light glinting off the tiles.

One morning before school, Ita and his mother were arguing. He thought it must have been about something he'd done wrong. As he heard more of their argument, he discovered it was about her boyfriend, the younger of the two men, and something about the bank. Ita had asked her about a pouch of money she'd retrieved from the coat closet, and she'd stormed out of the house. It wouldn't be until years later, when he was living in New York City with his dad, that he'd heard the term smurf as it alluded to seemingly ordinary people who laundered money by making frequent deposits and transfers of cash into a bank account. Ita had figured out she had been doing that at the bank where she worked.

He'd begun cutting school to tag along with his older cousins and their friends. He watched them, fascinated by the science and precision, as they weighed the refined white powder and filled the tiny baggies. He listened to them talk about the raw cocaine paste that was shipped to Colombia from Argentina. He was just a kid, but they allowed him to go with them to the lab where the paste was refined into a commercial white powder. Whereas the older boys had clients who bought the baggies of powder cocaine from them, Nico's job was to deliver the shopping bags of groceries that held the cash hidden inside. There was such an abundance of money floating around him, he never considered the danger or the consequences. It seemed harmless, and he had only taken what he assumed was his fair share. Thinking back, Ita had been right, they had been grooming him.

He remembered certain things exactly as they were. But most had been colored by time. Some were fabrications important to his story, the one he chose to believe. There was no doubt he had altered the past to fit. His mother had been dead a dozen years. He searched for answers, but with each breath there remained a hollow place that needed to be filled. He had a photograph of her wearing a flowered dress with sleeves like a butterfly. She was smiling at the camera, her eyes sparkling in the sunlight. He looked at the picture often, sure she was smiling at him.

He was on his second mug of coffee and had eaten the biscuits when Gaby came into the kitchen. She wore skinny jeans with motorcycle boots and a white top that fell off one shoulder.

"What took you so long?" he demanded. Without waiting for a reply, he grabbed the keys and headed for the door.

Gaby picked up his mug and gulped the remaining black liquid before following him. "I need to stop at my house first."

"I told you to have no more business with them." He swung around and grabbed her by the chin forcing her eyes to meet his. "No estaba claro?"

"Yes, Nico. You were clear, but…" she stopped when he flicked her jaw in disgust.

He mounted the bike and quickly started the engine.

"I need to get the money they owe me." She moved to get on the bike, but he blocked her.

"Then go," he said brusquely and pulled away leaving her at the curb.

Gabriela looked after him in despair. Half expecting him to turn around and come back, she stood waiting for many minutes before she headed in the direction of her house. She looked over her shoulder hoping he would come for her. She'd walked several blocks and stopped at a corner bodega for a bottle of water. A group of boys were gathered at the entrance. She ignored their leering eyes and pushed past them. They were the local riffraff with nothing better to do, yet she was partly flattered by the attention.

Her friends had married years ago and most had children. She hadn't made finding a husband her goal and even her mother stopped asking her about marriage. The youngest of three, Gabriela had been a senior in high school when the oil company her father worked for transferred him to Germany. The three siblings remained living in the family home, with Gaby under her brothers' protective, patriarchal care. They thwarted her dating efforts to keep outsiders from seeing their illegal dealings. She paged through her life, a murky pool of dashed romantic prospects and fading youth. Nico stirred in her a strong desire for union that she had not allowed herself to feel since he'd left. He was the only one she could trust and the only one who knew the truth. Her mood brightened at the prospect of unexpected fulfillment. She stopped and gave thought to her assurance. All her life she had deferred to her brothers, sacrificing her happiness and even independence. She doubted that could be what her parents would have chosen for her.

° ° °

Gaby stood on the street in front of her house. After all these years it was impossible for her to make her own decisions. She'd become accustomed to taking orders from Thiago. Nico was all that mattered to her now. If she weren't careful, she would lose him.

Bebe greeted her when she entered the foyer. A sturdy mix of

Shepherd and Rottweiler, he frantically wagged his tail eager for a walk. She scratched him behind the ears.

"I miss you, too, Bebe. I'm sure Nico will let you come live with us," she said kneeling down to kiss his nose. Rescued from the streets as a puppy, she couldn't bear to leave him with her brothers.

Hearing Thiago and another man quarreling in the kitchen, she snatched the dog's leash off the coat hook and darted back outside. Gaby walked the dog down the street. There was no easy way to tell Thiago she was leaving. It would also mean she would have no income. Nico had said he needed her help to run the yoga studio. That must mean he would pay her to work for him.

She saw Mateo coming out of her house and she darted behind a parked car. She knew Mateo gave Thiago cash from the parking garages to launder. Mateo had pursued her for years after Nico left Argentina. Even though he was strikingly handsome and wealthy, she wasn't interested. She had always believed that Nico would return, and they would reignite what they once had. She watched as Mateo walked in the opposite direction, and she slowly headed back to the house allowing Bebe to stop and sniff each lamp post.

The odor of burnt onions wafting from the kitchen was pungent. Thiago and Sebastian were at the table and looked up when she entered. Before she had a minute to swipe a wedge of the enticing omelet from the iron skillet, Thiago began to bark out orders, "Give these papers to Lucia. She is to open a new account today." Handing her papers with columns of numbers, he continued with the instructions.

She'd been coerced by her brothers to involve Lucia who worked at the bank. If Nico found out he would never forgive her. Everything would be ruined. Lucia never asked any questions. Either she had no idea, or she feigned ignorance. Lucia received the cash deposits and integrated them into Thiago's accounts. Given their friendship, she never made a transaction with anyone except Lucia.

Instead of taking the papers from Thiago's outstretched hand, she picked up the plates from the table and carried them over to the sink. Without sounding confrontational she explained, "Nico has asked me to run the yoga studio he's opening in Ricoleta. It will be a full-time job with long hours. I will be booking appointments, scheduling classes, and handling the business for him. I won't have time to help you…" She quickly added what she hoped would settle the situation. "and, Nico has asked me to live with him."

Sebastian looked up at her with what may have been compassion. He was about to speak but Thiago put up his hand to silence him. "Gabriela, we are family. Your role in our business is necessary. It keeps us together and provides well. Sit down. I will explain what you have to do today at the bank."

Gaby turned to him, wiping her hands on a dish towel. "I can't Thiago. I don't want to do this anymore. I want to start my own life…with Nico."

Thiago inhaled sharply and bit his lower lip, restraining himself. Squinting up at her he voiced firmly, "Don't be stupid, I won't let you get away with this betrayal, Gabriela. Quitting is not an option, you know that. You can fool around with Nico…who may disappear on you again…. Then what?" he smirked. "You will come crawling back here? No. You will continue with your duties to this family. Lo entiendes? This is not up for discussion."

"Ti, you are my brother. I love you. But this is an opportunity for me to finally be my own person. For God's sake, I want to be married and have children…as you should be doing, too."

She sensed Sebastian wanted to speak in her defense. He was the gentle one—a romantic at heart. If up to him, she knew he would set her free. But leery of Thiago's wrath, he didn't venture any response in her defense. She rested a hand on his shoulder signaling a plea for help. He kept his head down, staring into his coffee mug. When none came, she shook her head and fighting back tears walked briskly from the room.

Thiago was on her in one step. Grabbing her roughly by the arm, he spat harshly, "Don't fuck with me, Gabriela. I warn you."

"Really? Are you threatening me?"

He eyed her venomously. "You'll see what happens if you abandon our family… there will be a price to pay."

"I'll take my chances, Thiago. I want to have my own life and be happy. I'm sure you will find someone else to do your dirty laundry." Twisting away from his grasp, she stormed out.

On the street, her tears flowed freely, and she walked briskly in the direction of Nico's house hoping he would be there. She wished she could have brought Bebe with her and had time to pack some of her belongings. She'd seen Thiago angry often and knew he was quick to flare but just as quickly would regain his composure. He was quite rational after all. She would ask Nico to talk with him and smooth things over. The air was getting chilly, and she walked faster.

° ° °

Nico wasn't home yet. Ita made her a cup of hot tea which she carried up to his room. She found an old copy of Pablo Neruda's poems in the nightstand. Curling up under the covers she opened the small book. Inside, on the title page, was an inscription that read, *All my love forever, Olivia.* The American girl who had arrived after the funeral. She began reading the poems but soon her eyelids grew heavy. She awoke drenched in sweat and shivering. She'd had the most distressing dream. She was adrift in a small boat in the ocean and unable to navigate in the dense fog. She got up and walked over to the window overlooking the patio. She must have slept a long time. The winter's light bathed the floor tiles below in shadow. She expected Nico to be home soon. Closing the shutters, she went into the bathroom and stripped out of her damp clothes. Turning on the water, she waited for it to get hot and the steam to envelop her before stepping under the shower. The hot water caressed her, and she closed her eyes letting the anxiety melt away. She wanted to marry, to have her own life. She'd given up on the prospect. She thought about how much she loved Nico and how grateful she was to be starting a new life with him.

She was startled by Nico's voice when he opened the bathroom door. He was naked and got into the shower. Standing under the hot water, he nudged her to go down on him. He finished quickly and stepped out, calling after her, "Hurry. Dinner's ready."

Gaby twisted her wet hair, looping it up into a bun, then pulled on leggings and a sweatshirt. He told her he'd signed the lease that afternoon, and they would have a lot to do before opening the studio. He zipped his jeans and combed his hair back off his forehead. She smiled at him, happy to be included in his plans, promising she was done with Thiago.

He pulled her to him and acknowledged his approval with a lingering kiss and a gentle warning. "Make sure you keep to it," he cautioned.

Ita was in the kitchen. She was frying breaded fish fillets and drizzling them with chimichurri sauce. Nico came up from behind and startled her by giving her a swift kiss on her cheek. Her eyes danced as she swatted him away playfully. Nico stood next to her at the stove and spooned a serving of aromatic rice onto each plate. Gaby collected four plates and silverware and brought them over to the table.

"Where is your sister? Dinner is almost ready, and she didn't call to say she would be late."

Nico had just opened a bottle of Malbec and poured two glasses when the doorbell chimed. Ita glanced over at him questioningly. He set his glass down and walked through the patio to the front door. The muffled sounds of agitated men's voices carried into the kitchen.

Nico returned to the kitchen. His face was tight and pale. "Lucia's been in a car accident."

◦ ◦ ◦

When they arrived at the hospital, Lucia was sitting up in bed, a white gauze bandage was wrapped around her head. "I'm fine, really… it looks worse than it is," she said weakly.

Ita doted on her nervously while Nico asked her questions attempting to figure out the cause of the accident.

"Stop fussing!" she pleaded. "They examined me and I only have a small bump to my head and a few bruises on my side."

"Dios mio! Como esta ella?" Ita asked, looking at Nico. Nico spoke with the nurse at the desk and returned with a cold ice pack.

"They said I just have to stay the one night for observation." Lucia assured them.

Nico removed the room-temperature icepack from her head and replaced it with the cold one. "You need to keep icing it."

Ita and Gaby went to find the doctor so they would have a full report.

Nico stood over her, his brow furrowed. He looked into her eyes trying to assess the injury. "You fucking hit your head, Lucia. It is very serious. You could have a brain injury."

"You're exaggerating," she pooh-poohed.

"What happened exactly?" he demanded in a hushed voice.

"I'm not sure…" she muttered, pausing to consider the incident.

"This car sped up alongside me, and… They must have forced me off the road… Oh, Nico! My new car," she whimpered.

"I'll take care of the car tomorrow… and everything else…"

° ° °

The fluorescent light flickered overhead in the underground parking garage. No one had spoken since leaving Lucia's room. Nico cursed under his breath. "Where the fuck is the car?"

"I see it over there. A silver Camry, right?" Gaby said hopefully.

Ita had quit driving years ago but refused to sell the ten-year-old car. Gaby opened the passenger door for Ita and helped her buckle the seatbelt. She then sat in the backseat.

Nico's phone rang. He paused and looked at the screen. It said the call was restricted. He thought it might be the doctor, and he answered. The voice on the other end was muffled. Nico listened.

"This was your only warning," the caller said.

"Who is this?" Nico asked indignantly. He was certain he knew, but before he could say Thiago's name, the call ended. "I'll kill him!" Tossing the cell phone into the cup-holder he slid behind the wheel hurling a barrage of expletives. He recklessly backed out of the parking spot and accelerated blindly into the street. No one spoke until he pulled up in front of Gaby's house. "Get out. I don't want to see you right now."

"But Nico…" She fumbled with the seatbelt and got out of the car. "I—"

"I've had enough of your family." He cut her short and pulled the car away.

It was midnight when they entered the kitchen. Ita filled the kettle and placed it on a lit burner. The ordinary clatter of setting cups onto saucers and retrieving spoons from the drawer punctuated the uncomfortable silence. He said nothing until Ita served the tea. "You foresaw this happening, didn't you?" he asked grimly.

6

Nico sat on the bed with his hands in his lap gazing unfocused at the tips of his fingers. He wasn't meditating. He was deep in thought remembering the day Ita held his hand until he was passed off to a young, smiling flight attendant. He could still hear her soothing, cajoling voice assuring him his father would meet the plane when it landed in New York City. He saw his life as perpetually leaving. He still felt like his nine-year-old self. He was always looking back with sorrow at what he was leaving behind rather than hopeful anticipation of what lay before him.

The sun had not yet risen when he dressed and crept down the stairs, shoes in hand so no one would hear him. He had told Ita not to get up, but she was waiting for him in the kitchen. The moonlight shone through the conservatory ceiling of the patio, spilling across the tessellated floor. She held a folded alpaca poncho. On a field of stormy grey, the red outer stripes of the lista stood for the bloodline binding him to his maternal kin. For the Quechua people, a poncho's markings define who you are and where you come from. Resting on top of the poncho was a colorful chullo, a knit cap with ear flaps ending in pompoms. Both items were worn by a paqo, a medicine man, performing a ceremony. Ita handed them to Nico.

"These were my grandfather's," she said. The reverence in her voice was clear.

"I can't...They are too precious."

He choked back tears as she pressed them into his hands. The simplicity of the soft poncho didn't surprise him. It starkly represented the world as he knew it.

"Apologize for me..." he uttered, his voice cracking.

Ita nodded. "I'll explain." The fleeting moment that passed between them was more than love. It was born of deep memory.

"She will be angry," he said. The corner of his mouth lifted in a weak smile.

He hadn't the will to face Lucia, and this would be the second time he left Gaby without an explanation. Neither knew of the misdeeds for which he was ashamed, nor the danger he faced in staying. They wouldn't understand his need to return to the Q'ero to find the peace he sought after. He pressed his lips to the top of Ita's head. He lingered. Neither of them said anything for many minutes. Then, he quietly left the house and hailed a cab to Ezeiza Airport.

◦ ◦ ◦

The engines came to life and the plane moved down the runway. It picked up speed, racing faster and faster, its wings vibrating. He held his breath. Then silence as the plane became airborne, followed by the grinding sound of the wheels retracting. Higher it climbed into the heavens as the earthly lights grew fainter and disappeared. Argentina was behind him.

◦ ◦ ◦

Nico drew his jacket closed about his neck. He didn't remember it being this cold the last time he was in Cusco. The city's aged white stucco buildings capped by red tile roofs and adorned with black iron balconies, projecting like long curled eyelashes, reminded him of home. It had been less than ten hours since he'd left Ita in the cocooning warmth of his family's kitchen in San Telmo, and Lucia had already sent a barrage of text messages that ranged from angry to worried over the urgency and secrecy with which he had abruptly departed. He thought about calling her, but he still hadn't the courage. He'd nearly lost her because he'd gone home, and that was something he could never allow her to find out. He should have known he could never have happiness. It was as elusive to him as the morning mist cradled in the bosom of the surrounding hills and devoured by the rising sun. It had been shortsighted to think he could go home again. What delusion to assume he could commit to history the fear and irrational panic that plagued him. Just as foolish to believe he could carry his success from L.A. with him, like a suitcase filled with magic tricks. There was no escaping the past. It lurked in murky waters waiting to ambush him and left him no choice but to flee.

The narrow, steep cobblestone streets were lined with cafés and vendor's stalls. He was taken aback by the throng of tourists and numerous souvenir shops overflowing with colorful woven textiles, ponchos, and trinkets. After checking into a quaint colonial guest house on Pumacurco, not far from the Plaza de Armas, he walked toward where he had seen a café with outdoor seating. Climbing up the vertical steps flanking the road, he overheard Spanish blending harmoniously with an array of languages spoken by Europeans and Americans, dubbed gringos by the locals. On the corner near a fruit stand, three diminutive Quechua women wearing colorful traditional dresses crossed in front of him, leading their treasured alpacas. Arriving at the café, he took a table on the veranda from where he could look out at the mountains in the distance. Climbing the stairs had winded him, but he reminded himself the altitude was over eleven-thousand feet.

Maybe, he thought, I'll stay in Cusco for a while. It'll take some time to get acclimated to the altitude before making the trip several thousand feet higher.

Staring into the distance, he pictured the remote Q'ero village, the women and young girls laughing as they tended to their herds of llamas and alpacas. In Q'eros he had found a kinship, which he hadn't encountered before or since, working alongside the men on the stepped terraces with the heat of the sun on the back of his neck and planting corn and potatoes in the same ancient way it had been done by their ancestors, the Inca.

When the server arrived to take his order, he asked for a menu, and she pointed to the lunch specials drawn colorfully on the chalkboard. He took a moment and ordered a bottle of Cusqueña, the local beer, and a bowl of pork adobo.

What will I do if Don Castillo is dead? he worried, considering the possibility for the first time. Even if he's alive, he probably won't want me back as his apprentice.

Unconsciously, he began tapping his heel rapidly on the floor, a nervous tic he had never been able to control. Glancing impatiently toward the bar in search of his beer, he experienced a twinge of loneliness and a familiar tightening in his chest. He couldn't remember the last time he didn't have a girl with him. Companionship distracted him from the emptiness that was always present.

As if moving through space and time, he stepped back into the womblike candlelit yoga studio in L.A. The room was suffused with the rhythmic chanting of temple monks. He stood in front of the class. Their adoring eyes were upon him as he guided them through the exercises. The sex, of which there had been no shortage, was only a piece of what he needed to keep the darker impulses at bay.

It had been their allegiance and admiration that quieted his doubt.

I had fame, money, recognition, he told himself, trying to reclaim the missing pieces. But as if clutching a handful of sand, it spilled out between his fingers. Lost, like time.

Suddenly, the daydream turned terrifying. He shuddered. His heart was racing, and he squeezed his eyes closed. He felt helpless to stop himself from opening the door. There was a flash and then the pain. In that moment, everything had been destroyed. Leaving had been his only choice. At least here, in Cusco, no one knew him and that was strangely comforting.

Without thinking, he rested a hand on his thigh. He imagined it was Luna. Her hand pressed down gently on his knee to stop the nervous agitation, the way she would when they sat side-by-side. The simple touch was intimate but not enough to be sexual.

I was too hard on her, he lamented. She believed in me.

Taking a couple of long slow breaths, he wiped the beads of sweat from his brow. He was relieved when the server arrived with his order. Taking a deep swig of beer, it foamed, and he cursed too loudly as it gushed onto the table. She hurriedly brought him another, apologizing profusely that she must have shaken the case when hauling it up from the cellar. Mumbling thank you, he noticed her for the first time and smiled as their eyes met. Her skin, a creamy caramel, reminded him of Maya. He watched as she walked away, admiring the swing of her hips. He envisioned Maya, always accessible and synchronized with him.

She was blindly devoted to me, he thought, I should let her know where I am. He picked up the phone, then put it down. Forget it, I don't even know if I can ever go back, he silently bemoaned.

One small memory he could contain, but suddenly all were upon him, like a pack of wolves. He absentmindedly began scrolling through the photos on his phone. He never deleted the nude ones, though he promised he would. Entranced, his fingers caressed a stirring image of Sofia, her blonde hair cascading as she bent over him. He stopped at an artistically exquisite photo of Élodie. The first night they made love he inhaled her scent, an intoxicating medley of musk and jasmine. Like the finest Stradivarius, her round unblemished porcelain ass lifted to him, the small of her back gracefully bowed into the curve of her narrow waist, whereupon the hourglass shape tapered into her long swan neck. A warm breeze off the Persian Gulf billowed the floor-length white gauze drapes in a dance conjuring the ancient Jinn, Arabian spirits living in the unseen dimensions.

What caused the blind rage in him to percolate? Like a silo overflowing after a heavy rain, he had no ability to control himself. He couldn't remember what had caused him to hit her until she lay limp and whimpering. She was always coming and going. Work, she would say. He didn't want her to leave him, ever—for fear she wouldn't return. He needed her. And he hurt her. He thought about that night. What if it had been Élodie who shot him?

They all wanted something from him. When he needed them most to help him—to love him—they abandoned him. But he didn't… No, he thought, he couldn't accept that they loved him. Every test he gave to prove their love, they failed. He drove them away with his brutality. He destroyed everything worthwhile that came to him. It was too dangerous to surrender to love and risk losing it. He flipped quickly through more risqué photos of nude women. He stopped at a photo of himself with Luna in the park. They stood close together, their faces taking up the entire frame. She was smiling, her head tilted in toward his as he took the selfie. Luna was there when the others failed him. Holding her hand as they walked along the shore, the smell of salt water on her skin and hair. More than anyone else Luna knew his heart, or more rightly, she understood his affliction. There was no sex, no need to prove himself. Yet, he said to himself, I doubted her veracity and made impossible demands of her. I tested her limits. Now, alone in a faraway city, he began questioning if her friendship had been sincere. Frowning, he punched the button on the phone, darkening the screen. Why must I always be disconnected, he asked himself, like a forgotten balloon stuck to the ceiling?

He heard laughter. Peering down, he saw a commotion in front of the souvenir shop across the street. A film crew focused their attention on a striking woman—blonde, shoulder length hair, with sharp cheek bones. Her broad smile was both memorable and contagious. He recognized her as a well-known American actress, but her name escaped him. A scarf the color of wisteria encircled her neck and a man's straw fedora shaded her eyes. She laughed disarmingly as a Quechua woman patiently taught her how to hand spin alpaca fleece into yarn.

Another celebrity, he said to himself. The large number of spiritual tourists and gringo-operated new age retreats in the Sacred Valley offended him even though his practice had profited by offering the same transformative experiences, the despacho ceremony and mescaline from the San Pedro cactus. He wasn't, he reasoned, exploiting the indigenous culture. It was, after all, his birthright.

He finished lunch and paid the bill. The server thanked him and said she hoped to see him again. He considered getting her number but lost the will and went quickly down to the street. The general bustle of the city overwhelmed him, but he liked the anonymity. Pushing through the large crowd in front of the actress, he decided he should leave for Q'eros as soon as possible. A couple of tourists loaded down with shopping bags brushed passed him on the narrow walkway. They were talking to each other and oblivious when their bags collided with him. Fuming, he turned around, but stopped himself before cursing them out loud.

Arriving at the Plaza de Armas, he was unable to find an empty bench to sit. All around the fountain tourists were taking pictures and workers sat eating their bag lunches. Chess players had set up make-shift tables and local teenagers zipped by on skateboards. It was hard for him to imagine this ancient "square of the warriors" had been where Francisco Pizarro proclaimed the conquest of Cusco in 1533. Dominated by the imposing seventeenth century Cusco Cathedral, the square had also been the scene of the death of Túpac Amaru II, the leader of the indigenous uprising against the Spanish in 1780; two hundred years after his namesake ancestor, the last Incan monarch, had been executed by the Spanish. He'd named his yoga studio Amaru, meaning snake in Quechua, for the Inca leader and the life force of kundalini—the coiled snake at the base of the root chakra.

Nico walked across the plaza toward the Iglesia de la Compania de Jesus. Known for its ornate baroque façade, the Jesuits in the late fifteen-hundreds built it upon the foundations of Amarucancha, the palace of the Inca ruler Wayna Qhapaq. All the churches in the plaza had been built on top of sacred sites with the intention of removing the Inca religion from Cusco and replacing it with Catholicism. Adding insult to injury, they had used Inca labor as most of Cusco's population back then was of Incan descent.

He stopped and listened to an elderly Spaniard playing guitar on the steps of the church, his tobacco raspy voice wresting out a traditional song. It made him nostalgic for home. It had been Ita's brother who had taught him to play guitar. He reminded himself he ought to call her later. Nico pulled open the heavy wooden door and stepped inside the cool, dimly lit cathedral. When his eyes adjusted, he peered up at the impressive domed ceiling and towering gilded alter. It was midday and there were only a few worshipers in the sanctuary. He made the sign of the cross, slid into a pew, and lowered himself onto the kneeler. The lingering scent of incense permeating the air brought back memories of Luna sitting next to him in the Spanish church in Los Angeles. Somehow, she understood the soothing effect the ambience of an old church had on him. Years later, when he was in a downward spiral, she brought him to that same church and warned him he was destroying everything he'd worked for. She promised to see him through it if he would stop using drugs and be true to his calling. Why had he refused to listen? Instead, he'd lost everything. He sat back in the pew and closed his eyes to the dazzling gold relics. This wasn't where he needed to be. He would go back to Q'eros where the Apu, the great spirits of Pachamama, the cosmic Mother, would guide him and where he would find his purpose.

He left the church without crossing himself and hurried across the plaza. It might have been the beauty of the old church, or just the smell of it, but he felt restored. The sun had just dipped behind the rooftops. There was a chill in the air and he zipped his jacket underneath his chin and walked through the steep narrow alleys in the direction of the hotel. The walls shielding the old city mansions were claustrophobic and made him uneasy. In the thin air, he struggled to fill his lungs.

Near the hotel, he saw a street level sign advertising one of the city's oldest trek companies. He felt a tug he couldn't resist and went inside. He was the only customer in the small office. A young, attractive woman he took to be Quechua sat behind the counter. She looked up seemingly surprised that someone had walked in. There were large posters of Machu Picchu on the wall. He'd never hiked the famous trail considering it a tourist attraction. Something compelled him, and he picked up the pamphlet. He must do this, he told himself, before going to Q'eros.

"Can I help you?" Looking up, she asked in English, assuming he was an American tourist.

Unfazed, he continued in English. "I want to hike the Inca Trail to Machu Picchu." He nodded his head at the poster.

"Most people book eighteen months in advance, ya know…" she explained.

He stood silently in front of her and squinted his eyes.

She must have registered his disappointment and looked to her computer for answers.

"Let me check the calendar again. Maybe there's been a cancellation…" While searching, she continued to talk excitedly, "The best experience is the classic four-day trek. Do you know anything about the expedition?" Without waiting for an answer, she explained, "The bus ride is three hours and goes through the picturesque villages of the Sacred Valley. The start of the trail is at kilometer 82."

Sensing she would go on indefinitely, he interrupted, "Can I book a trip?" he said with carefully spaced words.

"I don't see anything available. I'm sorry. Like I said, these expeditions book way in advance."

Annoyed, he turned on his heels and walked out. Before he hit the curb, she called after him, "Wait, sir… I may have something."

He returned in a huff. While he waited for her explanation, he drummed his fingers on the counter.

"May I see your identification?" She put her hand out. Her eyes were on the computer screen in front of her.

He hesitated, then withdrew from his breast pocket a red leather case and handed her his passport.

"I have a thought… There's a small group leaving tomorrow that's not on the official calendar. It's a luxury trek and was booked privately. I can ask if you can go with them."

He looked up at the large poster of Machu Picchu and nodded.

She took the phone into the back room and closed the door. A few minutes later, she came out smiling. "Good news, they don't mind you joining their group. I explained you were a lone traveler and able to make the arduous climb." Nico hadn't yet agreed, but she just kept talking. "It's a premium booking, but I think it's worth it. I can take your credit card and issue the permit…"

"Okay, fine," he said, tossing his credit card on the counter. His head was spinning. Before he could grasp the commitment, she'd charged him twelve-hundred dollars.

"Our porters have everything you need." She handed him a folder. "Here's a packing list of the clothing items and personals you should bring. Oh, did I mention there's a private chef on this expedition? Where are you staying? I can have the van pick you up first at four in the morning, or would you rather meet the group at their hotel, Palacio del Inka?"

She spoke so quickly he was barely able to follow her and wasn't sure if she'd paused to take a breath.

She looked at him, waiting for his answer.

"I'll meet them at their hotel." he stressed, a bit too firmly.

The guest house where he was staying wasn't shabby; he thought it was charming. But his travel companions were at the Inka, a five-diamond hotel.

"Okay, you're all set. Just be sure to pack what's on the list," she said emphatically, then added, "I'm glad this worked out." She smiled. Her teeth were perfectly straight and white against her skin.

Nico nodded. "Me too…" he mumbled, rifling through the packet.

He wanted to ask about the people he would be hiking with but didn't want her to know he was nervous about spending four days with strangers.

"When you get back, stop in and let me know how it was."

Nico looked up, seeing her clearly for the first-time, and he smiled. He'd been anxious and impatient to the point of being rude, and yet she was sincere.

"Um… Okay, sure…Thanks." He heard the flatness in his voice. Showing gratitude wasn't his strong suit. But he'd meant it. He turned and walked out feeling a bit solemn. Immediately, he turned and called back, "What's your name?"

"Sabrina," she answered, a glimmer of light shone in her eyes as she smiled at him.

"Thank you, Sabrina," he stated with more confidence.

"Your welcome, Mr. Romero."

"Nico is fine…" He appeared surprised, then remembered she'd seen his passport and credit card.

After he packed, he called Ita and then had dinner in the open courtyard. Still, he was perplexed about his sudden desire to trek to Machu Picchu and curious why these strangers had agreed to let him join them.

Twilight had not yet adorned the night sky as he trudged the short walk down the narrow alley of Calle Palacio. The burnished cobblestones gleamed as if wet under the streetlights. He could barely distinguish the sky from the black undulating humps of mountains, like lumbering mammoths in the distance. His eyes followed the trailing twinkling incandescent lights of dwellings sloping up their shoulders. In defiance of the ambient glow of the city, it appeared as though a net of Christmas lights had been cast across the sky. He searched for the Milky Way and found it low on the horizon, nearly out of view. He'd seen spectacular photographs of the galaxy and its magic was one reason he'd wanted to make this journey. Inhaling deeply, he took the frigid air into his lungs and slowly exhaled to clear his head before meeting the climbing party he'd be going with to Machu Picchu.

He shifted the heavy load on his back. He had dutifully packed everything on the list, all except sunscreen which irritated his skin. But now he worried he was carrying too much. The manager of the guest house agreed to keep his other possessions and guitar safe until he returned. He had a lightweight Nalgene water bottle. In the brochure it explained the porters would provide boiled water every three hours. Nico wished he could have taken the guitar but conceded it would be too cumbersome. Everything he'd brought to Peru for his stay with the Q'ero was suitable for this trek—sturdy hiking boots, a packable down jacket, lightweight base layers, and polar fleece. He had a penchant for sunglasses and had bought a new pair of Oakley in L.A. The alpaca chullo and poncho Ita gave him were safely stowed in the pack as well. I have the perfect combination of the old and the new with me, he told himself. He was beginning to feel better about the trip in front of him.

He'd finally spoken to Ita, and she was proud of his decision to take this momentous trip in advance of his training. Although he'd been forced to leave, this time they both acknowledged the danger he was dodging. Her sight extended well beyond what she observed plainly. Ita assured him she had warned Lucia about Gaby's brothers and convinced her to take leave from the bank. When Lucia took the phone, she cried. Nico fought back tears, thinking how he'd put her life in danger by being there. Lucia didn't hang up before scolding him for breaking Gaby's heart for the second time. All he could say was, "someday, I'll tell you."

Nico combed the vehicles parked in front of the entrance to Palacio del Inka. He was early, and it appeared the van collecting them had not yet arrived. He pulled open the lapis blue doors of the hotel, once the colonial mansion of Pizarro. Walking into the reception area he was stunned by the grandeur of magnificent stone arches. The Inca had built the walls of tightly interlocked stone five centuries ago. Under the vaulted glass ceiling a regal red, black, and gold rug covered the flagstone floor. In the center, a Spanish Renaissance trestle table displayed Incan pottery and archeological artifacts reflecting the majesty of their former empire. In search of the group, he walked into a cozy inner lobby. The warm ochre stucco walls were adorned with gilt framed oil paintings. In front of the fireplace, a few people dressed for hiking were seated on the sofas. Paper cups of coffee and half eaten breakfast sandwiches decorated the tables.

"Nicolás?" a woman's voice called out.

He looked across the room and when their eyes met, she waved him over. She was the actress he'd seen from the patio of the restaurant, and the men with her were the crew who had been filming.

Skipping the introductions, she asked hurriedly, "Is the van here?" Then, without waiting for an answer, she turned to the three men sitting around her. "Come on guys. We better get going," she said with urgency.

They hoisted their packs onto their backs and began heading through the reception area toward the exit. Nico followed, flummoxed over whether he was expected to know who she was. The van, which was not there a few minutes ago when Nico arrived, was now standing with its doors open in front of the hotel entrance.

The driver came out to greet them with his clipboard. "Camille Hawks? Group of four…oh, um, it was changed to five, I see." He began loading their packs in the back, while informing them the porters, cooks, and their guide would meet them at the trail head.

Nico looked on smugly listening to the actress inquire about her demands. "I requested a personal porter. Does the itinerary say the number of porters we have?"

He referred to his clipboard. "It says here, you have nine porters going with you. Two extra were added for the film equipment you're bringing." Predicting they would expect special treatment, the driver lectured. "I'll remind you, the packs the porters carry will be weighed and cannot exceed twenty kilos. If there is anything you don't need, I suggest you leave it behind. You won't be allowed to use a tripod on Machu Picchu, you know."

"We'll be fine. The guys can manage," she said dismissively.

The burly bearded guy, Nico had seen with the camera, claimed the front passenger seat, while the other two, installed in the far back, had already pulled their hoodies over their heads and scrunched down to nap for the three-hour drive to the trail head. None had yet introduced themselves to him. Nico, relieved to at least have learned his enigmatic companion's name, climbed into the window seat behind the driver, and she slid in next to him as if she had set out to travel with him from the start.

"I'm glad you came with us. Machu Picchu has been on my bucket list," she said in a voice that betrayed a southern accent and honeyed the crisp break of day. He mumbled something about trendy buckets, but it was barely audible.

No one spoke when the van pulled away from the hotel. Other than a sporadic flicker when they passed under a lamppost, darkness enveloped them as they drove through the narrow cobblestone streets of Cusco toward the Sacred Valley. After a few minutes of silence Nico asked her, "Why did you agree to have me join your group?"

"When Sabrina asked me, I Googled you. You're a well-known yoga teacher, aren't you?" She seemed unfazed that she openly disclosed searching his name online.

He smiled at the knowledge she'd checked him out. He wondered if she'd stumbled upon an article about the shooting. It had made the local news. He didn't get the sense she had, but her self-confidence gave him the impression she would have invited him to join them anyway.

When she tilted her head at him quizzically, he smirked, "You're clever."

She bit her lower lip defensively, but her eyes smiled, "I practice yoga every day. In fact, the guys are going to film me on the hike."

He'd seen a lot of movies and still he couldn't place her. He wanted to ask her but was embarrassed.

"Have you seen *Amaru of the Andes*? It's a documentary about me and my initiation as a shaman. It won an award at the Cannes Film Festival?" It was hard to read her shadowed face in the dark of the vehicle.

"No, but I saw the link to the trailer on your web site. What does Amaru mean?" She'd turned in her seat to face him, appearing eager for his answer.

"It means sacred serpent in Quechua. The Inca drew it as a winged double-headed dragon-like serpent on the pyramid because he could slip between the spiritual realms. And, in kundalini…"

She interrupted and began talking over him. "Of course! Kundalini is the coiled snake at the base of the root chakra." Oblivious to having talked over him, she continued, "It's awakened through yoga and moves up through the chakras. I read on your website you offer despacho and San Pedro ceremony, combining Andean cosmology with kundalini yoga. I love the way you wrote about gratitude in the description of the despacho, and about opening the mind to new possibilities with San Pedro."

She is so rude, he thought, and she hadn't stopped talking long enough to take a breath. It was as though she needed to prove she knew everything about him and his business.

He turned around to check if the guys in the back seat were sleeping and saw they were folded like cloth napkins after dinner. The camera man in the front seat was snoring like a French bulldog. The long, flowing drive in the darkness eased his discomfort. He had planned on napping, but he found Camille's interest in him intriguing, even though he questioned her motives. His eyes traveled up her body which appeared slim and athletic, despite being concealed beneath khaki hiking pants and an oversized alpaca sweater with a llama motif she must have bought from one of the local women. The pale early light washed the horizon in watercolors softly illuminating her opaline heart-shaped face, and he took a moment to observe her for the first time. She wore a slouchy olive-green wool beanie the same color as her eyes, and her blonde hair swept out from the bottom in a graceful swirl around her neck. When their eyes met, he suppressed the urge to look away. She couldn't be more different than Maya, he thought. Maya hardly spoke.

After he was shot, Maya stayed with him throughout his recovery. There were nights he lay in bed waiting for death to take him. He left a mess behind him in L.A. and guilt followed close behind. He'd disgraced himself and still Maya hadn't faltered in her devotion to him. His future, if he had one, was unknowable. He shuttered with shame knowing he'd slunk away like a malnourished rat caught raiding the scullery.

He looked closely at Camille. Her lips were moving but he didn't hear a word she said. She had determination, he thought. A good quality, but he wondered about her sincerity and whether he could trust her. He pictured her as a sailing ship, undeterred by a storm that might snap her mast, yet could not sink her.

He sensed there was something Camille wanted from him. He would wait for it to reveal itself. The attempt on his life had been in the news. If she'd Googled him, like she said she had, then she must have read about the shooting. He ran his hand through his hair, pushing it off his face. He hoped he wouldn't appear nervous, or defensive. Before answering her question about the despacho ceremony, he steadied his voice.

"I take pride in performing the despacho ceremony. It's a living prayer, important for healing physical and emotional ailments. By showing gratitude and reciprocity it restores balance and harmony in our lives. As we say in the Andes, ayni—an equal exchange—like oxygen and carbon dioxide. The despacho was popular at my studio in L.A. My clients were surprised when I added candy for the sweetness of life." He laughed self-consciously. "Typically, they all just wanted positive outcomes…mostly in the way of abundance… money and relationships."

Camille seemed interested. She took a moment, as if to remember something.

"I've only participated in the despacho here in Peru," she said. "The k'intu of three coca leaves is essential to the offering. What did you use in L.A. instead of coca leaves?"

Taken aback, he worried she had some hidden agenda. He paused before answering tentatively. "The leaves are legal in South America. My sister sends them to me from Buenos Aires with mate de coca tea. Coca is a divine plant that brings clarity and connection with the sacred realms. It's invigorating and opens the chakras. The stigma is completely ridiculous. The coca plant is a gift from Pachamama—Mother Earth—and working with the leaves is a way to connect with her. Ya know, after the Christian conquest, the Q'ero began to associate coca with the sacrament."

This seeming dissertation made him anxious once he presumed everyone in the van was probably listening to their conversation. Suddenly regretting what must have sounded like a lecture, he slouched in his seat and turned away.

Camille, sensing his irritation, leaned forward and placed her hand on his knee. "What's wrong, Nick? It's just I find what you do extremely interesting."

He was startled and offended she called him Nick. No one ever Americanized his name. He found her annoying, but he was also mystified. "It's Nico. If you don't mind," he snapped.

She smiled broadly. "Sorry, Nico. And you can call me Cami, everyone does. I live in L.A. too, and I'm kind of surprised I hadn't heard of you."

"Yeah, I'm surprised you haven't been to my studio. Most of my clients are in the movie business."

"A few close friends and I did ayahuasca at the home of a producer I know in Malibu. You should come next time. We brought in a well-known curandero from the Amazon. You know, they only brew in the jungle and smuggle the finished potion into the country. It's still against the law but the officials know it's a medicine, and don't bother. Why do you perform the Huachuma ceremony which contains mescaline instead of ayahuasca?"

What was she trying to prove? He asked himself. Camille's questions made him uncomfortable. He thought she was prying into his business.

The sky was brightening on the horizon in brilliant shades of orange that gave the illusion of a tremendous forest fire in the distance. He debated whether he should bother to respond. He felt she was showing off, calling the plant teacher by its Quechua name instead of the more common Christian, San Pedro. The Spanish thought Huachuma held the keys to the gates of heaven. That's why they named it after Saint Peter. Glancing over to confirm the others still slept soundly, he thought if she were interested, he might as well teach her.

"San Pedro goes back a thousand years before Christ," he said. "He is Grandfather Wisdom, the cactus plant teacher of the Andes Mountains. Ayahuasca, or what they call yage, is a blend of two plants, the ayahuasca vine and a plant called chacruna, which contains the hallucinogenic DMT. I've never been to the jungle, but I have heard stories of bad blends by people who don't know what they're doing."

Ayahuasca had become exceedingly trendy in L.A. with affluent Hollywood types flying in shamans. He knew of one curandero arrested at the airport carrying containers of the liquid, but he had been released with a diplomatic assist from the Brazilian embassy but could have easily resulted in a prison term. On principle, he refused to pay for a shaman to bring the ayahuasca potion from the jungle when he made the cactus brew himself and charged top dollar without risking arrest. Not that there had been any raids in Los Angeles of the rich and famous seeking enlightenment. He'd taken ayahuasca once with an artist who had invited him and waived the several hundred-dollar fee. There would be an inevitable transformation with either of the plant teachers, so he wasn't surprised this movie star was boasting about her experiences.

Seemingly unaware of his agitation, she told him about her experiences. "I remember when I did San Pedro, it took my breath away. It was as if I had become San Pedro. I got these jolts of electricity through my body, and I thought I would be able to see the blood running in my veins. It was like the cactus was examining me from the inside out. Thankfully, I was with a supportive group and it was daytime. The colors were incredible…the mountains and the sky. It was fascinating. I relaxed and trusted the plant, allowed it to do its work. The overriding sensation was one of turning inward…" She paused for only a second to catch her breath. "Ayahuasca is different, it frees the spirit from the body to commune with the stars. I swear I could see the order in the universe. Everything is energy, we are all energy—connected to everyone and everything… You know what I mean? I was transported beyond my physical limitations and completely detached from my ego."

He was still affronted she hadn't let him finish. Regaining his footing he added, "With Aya you may in fact become lost in the wonder of it all. Aya takes you out of yourself. You become conscious that you, your spirit, and the universe are one. San Pedro brings the universe into the body. During the ceremony you meet yourself and meet the possibilities of what you can be. He teaches you your place in the world, putting you in touch with the creative powers you possess to direct your own life." Nico paused and looked away. He was unsure whether he should continue, that it would reveal something about him. "You know, everyone feels alone and afraid. They want to know their reason for being, what their future will be. San Pedro helps you to face your fears. He shows you the beauty of your soul. But he is also humbling and teaches you that everything is in balance…everything is equal in its importance."

Camille tried to meet his eyes. When he finally looked up, she said, "That was really beautiful, Nico." They were both quiet, watching the road as if they could see the unknown.

"I have this mission," she said. "I hope you don't think me foolish, but it came to me on ayahuasca. I've created a philanthropy to help raise the consciousness of women everywhere. It's called The Visionary Sisterhood, and its mission is to connect women across the globe and show they have the creative agency to shape their lives. We are bringing together healers, and artists to explore self-knowledge through meditation, dance, music, art, and spiritual practices like altered states using the plant teachers. You have an impressive following; you should take part in helping us."

"You'll use your fame to do this…with this sisterhood. Is that how it works?" That's it, he thought, she wants me to do something with her charity. I knew she was playing me. These celebrity types are all the same. They all have their own interest. He was growing increasingly more anxious to get to the trail head and begin their hike. At least climbing he wouldn't feel trapped by questions.

Camille told the driver to stop in Pisac. Nico felt the urge to object at the delay, but when none of her crew spoke out, he swallowed his words. In her carefree manner she asked the cameraman to document the ancient Incan ruins and stone aqueducts. While he filmed, Camille explained how they were built during the Incan empire and were still in use for irrigation. It was a picturesque village. In the central courtyard, the artisans were already setting up their makeshift stalls to sell produce, flowers, and the exquisite weaving for which they were known. A century's old outdoor clay oven was fired, and they all enjoyed fresh empanadas for breakfast. Now, back in the van, they continued along the winding road and wouldn't stop again until Ollantaytambo, which was the pit stop before the trail head. The early morning sun had risen enough to illuminate the terraced steps on the shoulders of the surrounding mountains where villagers grew quinoa, fava beans, and potatoes. He thought it weird how Camille didn't really look at him when she spoke. She was now intent on watching a Quechua woman, traditionally outfitted in a flouncy skirt and red embroidered sweater, herding a large flock of sheep across the valley. He thought she might not have remembered his question, but after a while she answered as if there had been no gap in time.

"The best way to heal oneself is through service to others. If I can reach more people because I'm a movie star, then it's my obligation to do that." She curled up on the seat and rested her head back, closing her eyes. "I think we should sleep the rest of the way, Nico. When we get to the trail head, we'll have a long climb to our campground."

8

Sleep had eluded him. The cloak of darkness under which he might have slept lifted, and a radiant sun shone on the multicolored fields in the Sacred Valley. The vehicle sped steadily along the winding road, its tranquilizing rhythm a natural sedative to its passengers. Nico glanced over at Camille; her mouth partly open as she slept with her legs folded neatly together under her poncho. Turning away, he gazed out the van's window at a flock of sheep grazing lazily. He thought about the life from which he'd been separated, and felt woefully alien, like the phantom sensation of a recently amputated limb.

It had been only a few days since he'd left Buenos Aires. He'd kissed his grandmother's forehead praying it would not be for the last time. The gauzy moonlight seeping from the patio into the kitchen had glanced off the Spanish tile floor like a silver river prophetically lighting the way. With a crushing sense of failure he'd hastened to the street.

They should be arriving at the trail head soon, he thought with relief.

He glanced at his watch. The old Rolex had been his father's. A gift given to him when he left New York in what seemed like another lifetime. When he looked up, the driver and he locked eyes for a split-second in the rear-view mirror. Nico looked away, uncomfortable at being watched, as if his soul could be gleaned through the mirror's reflection.

He'd dedicated years mastering healing powers and been rewarded with adoring clients whose recognition he believed he deserved. But still, he had been unable to restrain or willfully eradicate the demons that lurked in the shadows and crept into his tormented dreams. When he finally tasted the sweetness of his success, it grew bitter in his mouth as if he were unworthy.

I am alone again, he said to himself. They abandoned me when I needed them. What do I do now? he thought, leaning his head against the cool glass of the car window. Luna would know what to do, he told himself. Closing his eyes, he tried to focus on the humming of the wheels instead of the screaming voice in his head.

He'd never known what it was to feel safe, to be loved by someone you could trust, someone who will never betray you. Maya was the only one who remained at his side, but even she had reached out to Luna for help. She'd told Luna his darkest secrets, about drugs and the sexual preferences he found thrilling. He'd gone at her with his fists and she'd locked herself in the bathroom. He ended up crying with his head in her lap while she stroked his hair. Again, Luna had interfered and caused trouble. I warned her not to insert herself into my life, and she still got involved.

It was Luna's fault that Élodie left me, the voice in his head cried as the spiderweb widened and grew taut inside him. Élodie promised to bring him investors. She said she loved me. Lies. It had all been lies and betrayal, he told himself. The negative tape got louder, as did the throbbing behind his eyes. He was horrified by the violence that overwhelmed him and he felt the brutality of what he'd done. He knew he had a problem. He felt his heart pounding in his chest, ready to explode. The drugs had cost him time and memory. His brutality drove everyone away and landed him bleeding out on the studio floor. All he wanted now was to forget.

The vibration of the engine lulled him, and his mind slipped. It's much easier to keep moving, he said to himself. It was only when he looked back that he saw the damage. I'm such an idiot, he thought. I fooled no one, but myself. It may take my lifetime, and still I won't fix what is broken. Imminent death forces you to look truth in the face. It has a way of unearthing the past and lugging it into the present. He was here in Peru, starting his life over.

They were nearing their destination and Nico's traveling companions stirred, teased from their dreams by the mysterious water gods that raged below them. Nico looked down at the Urubamba River, muddy and churning wildly, hurtling itself over the rocks, furiously drawn to its destiny. Like the relentless waters below, he'd lived his life with the same irrepressible passion and urgency. Weary from rushing head-long in pursuit of widespread praise, he was caught between currents. For the first time in as long as he could remember, he had no scheme laid down. I left it all behind me, he thought wistfully, sweeping tears from his eyes before they escaped.

What had possessed him to join this group, to climb for days up this mountain with strangers to see an ancient site? He'd seen the advertisement in the window of the travel office and taken it as an omen. Something else struck him. The image of a serpent swallowing its own tail. Luna had drawn it in black ink on the medicine bundle she'd made him. I've been running from the monster my entire life and gone in circles.

They arrived at the trail head, known as KM82, later than planned due to Camille's need for empanadas and the bathroom. The Quechua porters greeted them at the weigh station with the equipment needed to shelter and feed them over the next four days. Nico's fluency in Spanish helped mediate the discussion that ensued with their guide, Quispe, over the camera equipment.

Once the gear was distributed, they walked across the footbridge over the swollen Urubamba river and began the first leg of the twenty-eight-mile climb to an oxygen thin altitude of 14,000 feet. The sun shone in a cloudless sky as they started the eight-mile trek that would take them to the first campsite. It didn't surprise him when Camille took the lead, and Nico stayed close on her heels as she moved quickly up the trail. Carrying only a small day pack, she gained ground while the porters and her film crew, bearing the brunt of the load, kept a slow steady pace behind them. He thought how agile she was as he watched her navigate the stone steps, her hips shifting, sure-footed and graceful as a mountain goat bounding fearlessly along precarious ledges on steep canyon trails. They passed through a forest of eucalyptus, the sun warming their faces as they climbed higher, and the river receded below them. Camille stopped to remove her sweater and hat, shoving them both into her pack and took big gulps from her water bottle. He took off his polar fleece and tied it around his waist. She hadn't rested more than a minute before continuing ahead.

Smiling, she called over her shoulder, "Have you climbed at this elevation before?" Her hair, free of the hat, glistened in the blazing sunlight as if on fire.

"It was a long time ago. Patagonia... when Lucia and I were kids...with my dad..." his voice trailed off as the memory came to mind.

"I've never been to Patagonia." She called out without turning, "But I did hike Kilimanjaro. The best part was the animals. I love Africa... the giraffes, elephants, and the herds of wildebeests..."

"I've never been to Africa. But I've been to Disney's Animal Kingdom."

Camille stopped in her tracks and turned to face him, a wide smile on her face. "You can be funny," she exclaimed with surprise.

"Since we are tossing out countries, like it's a competition, I climbed Anamudi Peak, near Munnar, when I lived in Kerala. The views are spectacular. Have you been to India?"

"Yes, but not to Kerala. I was just north of Mumbai, at an ashram." The climb was getting steeper, and she'd slowed her pace down.

"Of course you were..."

"Why were you living in India?" she asked, ignoring his sarcasm.

"I told you I lived in Kerala, didn't I? I taught yoga at a surfing resort on the southern tip."

"No—you did not," she said amused. "And you're teasing me about going to an ashram? I suppose you know how to surf?" she asked facetiously.

"I got to be pretty good, but it's been a long time..."

"Is there anything you can't do, Nicolás Romero?" she jibed, without turning around. They were gaining elevation, and there were now ancient stone steps before them that seemed to have no end in sight.

"Yes, keep up with you!"

They remained silent for a long while, saving their breath. The first day of the trek was technically the easiest, but the day's hike would take about six hours and they still had the steepest part of the climb ahead of them. The porters had the water, and he noticed they were both low and conserving what remained on them. They passed through a small village and the ruins of an old Inca fortress, Willka Raccay, came into view. Camille stopped, and when Nico came up alongside her, they gazed in awe. From this vantage point, on this brilliantly clear and cloudless day, the Urubamba mountain range was sharply visible with the impressive Mount Veronica showing off her snow-capped summit. They waited for the porters and the crew to catch up to them. While the dining tent was being erected and the chef prepared lunch, Quispe told them the fort had once provided the Inca with views up and down the river and from where they could control access to the valley. Below, on the opposite bank, was Patallaqta, an expansive terraced agricultural settlement first discovered in 1911 by Hiram Bingham when he stumbled upon what is now called Machu Picchu.

After munching on bread and cheese and fresh vegetables, the chef served perfectly ripe avocado and papas rellenas. The porters, speaking Quechua, kept to themselves. Nico thought of approaching them to ask if Don Castillo was still in the village but had second thoughts. I'm sure they wouldn't know him, he told himself. Besides, he thought, I don't want to answer any questions. Instead, he made small talk with the film crew and told them about the documentary. He noticed Camille sat alone looking out at the mountains. He was glad she kept apart from her crew, and instead chose to keep pace with him on the trail. Maybe, he thought, it was why she invited him to join her group. The break wasn't long before they refilled their water bottles, shouldered their packs, and got underway.

Over the next two hours they climbed steadily toward the evening's campsite at Wayllabamba. The crew had caught up to them hoping to grab shots of Camille who smiled as though it was no effort at all to hike in the oxygen depleted air. As the air became thinner, they barely conversed, but to his perplexity an unspoken closeness between them was forming.

Quechua families made their living along the trail selling chicha, a fermented beer made from maize. They came upon a refreshment stand in a small enclave along the trail. The children gathered around Camille who crouched down to smile into their faces, admiring their dress and hair ribbons in the best Spanish she could muster. As the cameraman discretely captured the moment, Camille enthusiastically bought two large glasses of frothy pinkish liquid, handing one to Nico.

"It smells like popcorn..." he said. He took a sip and wrinkled his nose at the tartness. "but it tastes like kombucha."

"Salud, Pachamama!" She called out, raising her cup ceremoniously to the mountains. The women laughed in appreciation. "It's interesting... a bit like hard cider," she said and licked the froth off her upper lip.

"An acquired taste." His eyes flashed with amusement as he took another sip.

The porters, eagerly anticipating the local brew, weren't far behind, and while they all took a short break to partake of the chicha, and snack on fruit and popcorn, the crew continued filming. A man leading two horses with a puppy following close upon his heels approached them, a beaming smile lit up his face as he inquired, "taxi?" to which they burst out laughing.

Nico was tempted to take the horses, but Camille politely declined the offer. While the porters and crew gathered the gear for the final leg of the journey, Camille bounded ahead, and Nico followed her. Within the hour, the porters took the lead with the aim of getting to the campsite ahead of them. When they arrived at the small village, the sun had dipped behind the peaks turning the mountains a soft shade of violet set against the blush of a pale pink sky, the tents had been erected, and the chef was preparing dinner. Nico watched as the film crew set up the shot overlooking the village with its picturesque white church tucked into the valley. Camille gave her hair a quick comb with her fingers and put her alpaca sweater and beanie hat back on before stepping in front of the camera. He thought her lackadaisical attempt at preparation admirable. It embarrassed him that he broke into a nervous sweat under pressure. He would have liked a cold beer—an impossible request, and to get off his aching feet. Instead, he watched as she confidently beamed into the camera, blessing Pachamama and the spirits of the mountains before cheerfully chronicling the day's climb.

She described the ancient worn steps built in the 15th Century to connect the vast Inca Empire, the yellow orchids growing along the trail which he must have overlooked, the welcoming indigenous women and children who refreshed them with homemade chicha. She didn't forget to mention the man with the wide laughing smile who offered them a taxi ride on his horses. The porters, she explained into the camera, were the heart of the expedition, without them none of this would be possible. After introducing Quispe, who spoke about the history of Machu Picchu, she directed the crew to grab shots of the village before they lost the light. The camera man followed as she moved to the dining tent where the chef dished up Andean corn chowder as their first course. The table was covered with a woven tapestry and set with melamine plates and clear plastic wine glasses. A small bouquet of wildflowers had been placed in a milk bottle in the center of the table. Camille removed a flask from her pack and poured a measure of amber liquid into two of the glasses. Turning her attention to Nico, she smiled, "Sit down, you look exhausted." She quipped, handing him a glass.

"What is this?" he asked, responding to the mischievous look on her face.

"Pisco, it's a local brandy."

Nico sat down across from her and inhaled the aroma, then took a sip. The liquid went down smoothly, warming his throat, and then a pleasant soft burn suffused his stomach. It could be the altitude, he thought, as a calming sensation took over his body. He nodded and leaned back in the chair. “I needed this,” he said.

Moving forward felt like sleepwalking. It was unfair, he thought, to live life and only understand it through the lens of the past. It would have been best if he had no past, and there were no memories to torment him. He knew no one here in the Andes, where a fiery sunrise over the mountains welcomed the day and where the apus, the mountain spirits, watched over the people.

The film crew drifted into the tent and crumpled into the three vacant chairs at the long table. The big fellow with the full beard, who had ridden in the front seat of the van, was speaking to Camille. His husky voice was tinged with the same long-drawn-out accent as hers. She leaned in closely, her elbows resting on her knees, and she held the cup of brandy under her chin with both hands. Nico could tell by the tilt of her head they were close, and that she trusted him. They called him Griz, and Nico thought the name fitting.

The chef opened bottles of Malbec and they toasted the first day on the trail. There was corn chowder and a basket of dinner rolls on the table that were soon scarfed down. Punctuating the silence, the syncopated rhythm of clinking metal spoons against the bowls proclaimed everyone’s hunger and exhaustion. When the chef presented a platter of steamed trout in mushroom sauce and stir-fried noodles with kale, a voluptuous sigh of approval gushed from the group. The lanterns cast a warm glow inside the tent’s interior. As darkness fell, the last of the wine was wrung from the bottles, and apple cinnamon pudding arrived at the table with a pot of tea. Camille seemed to have expected the chef’s culinary proficiency, but Nico was truly astonished by the gourmet fare that had been prepared by propane torch.

Quispe reminded everyone they had to get up at dawn. Sated and dulled by the wine, they made their way to the sleeping tents.

Nico dallied, gazing out over the valley. The mountains melted into a blue-black sky and the twinkling lights of the village merged with the stars. He said he was lonely, and though Camille stood nearby, he didn't think she heard him. He watched as she walked to her tent and ducked inside. Nico pushed his hands inside the pockets of his polar fleece jacket and stood outside her tent listening to the thud of her boots dropping to the floor after she'd tugged them off, and the sound of her slipping out of her pants. He wondered if she would wear pajamas.

"Cami…can I come in for a while?" He hadn't tried to sound pathetic, but he could hear it in his voice.

"Go to sleep Nico, you are exhausted… you'll feel better in the morning."

"Okay, night," he mumbled.

He had to urinate badly. No one was around, and he thought about relieving himself on a nearby bush, but instead went to the outhouse. He found his tent without the aid of a flashlight. In the dark, he removed his boots, and clothes except for his T-shirt and crawled into the sleeping bag. He left the top of the tent flap open and gazed out at the bottomless pool of the night sky. Against the vastness of the universe he was weighted, tethered to the Earth. Instead of feeling transported by its majesty, he was terrified. For the first time in as long as he could remember he prayed. He wondered what god it was he called upon, and if it mattered. Waiting for sleep, he lay there, unable to move a muscle listening to the whooshing of the wind sliding off the mountains. Through the little opening in the tent flap, he watched the lazy clouds drift across the moon.

It had been foolish to come back from the dead, he thought. What could I ever hope to achieve with my pointless pursuits? I've only hurt myself and others around me, he told himself, pressing his hands hard against his face. I may never be able to escape this curse. The wind picked up and the flap beat against the canvas like bird's wings, echoing the beating of his heart. This is my journey, he thought, a struggle to find direction, to separate dream from reality, and to discover what's possible. But I will never have an answer to the one question that sucks me down into the mud, leaving me paralyzed. Didn't I deserve to have my mother love me? That is the white-hot ember that sits on my heart and burns my soul. I will never again know her touch, her soft lips on my neck. Now she is gone forever.

He wondered if she were alive would she feel remorse for abandoning him. He pictured her holding his small suitcase of soccer jerseys and the worn-out Snoopy he'd had since he was a baby. Suppose she had changed her mind and refused to let him go. He imagined them together in the kitchen, standing next to her at the warm stove, his small hand clutching her apron and the smell of onions filling his head while she fried empanadas until they were perfectly golden. Gently she nudged him away, and said softly, in a way that assured him she was not scolding, "Nico, sit down before you get burned."

Can you forgive me? He desperately wishes to hear those words and considers what his answer might be. It wasn't fair to be discarded by the one person who should never have done that. I am tired of being alone, he thought. How will I acquire the strength, not just to endure the loss, but to accept the heartbreak, and even forgive the mistakes? I lost her a long time ago, and the anger and fear have never faded. I drove everyone away with my unreasonable demands and my impulsive rages. He'd been searching the sky for answers, and now the clouds had moved in erasing the stars, leaving the questions unanswered.

Earlier, Camille had asked him if he surfed. He'd told her he had become quite capable at it. He considered the relevance, and wondered if she had, too. When you surf, you learn not to fight nature. The ocean has control. It doesn't care whether you're scared, or if it kills you. When you wipe out, there are whirlpools that pull you under preventing you from floating to the surface. If you fight it, you will exhaust yourself until you drown. Under the water, in the whirlpool, you face death, get to know it, then overcome it. There is no point in being angry with the ocean. Unless you get over the fear, you will never be an accomplished surfer. He'd been fighting to control the unavoidable in his life which made as little sense as trying to control the ocean. Tormented by the monotonous brooding voice in his head, he masturbated, hoping it would relieve his anxiety and allow him to sleep.

Staring out of the triangle, he waited for the longest time to see if the stars would reappear. The answer finally comes to him. He would forgive her. He still possessed the memories, the feelings, the lost possibilities, but decided it was best not to look back at them. They held him underwater, preventing his escape. It cannot be undone, he thought, as he slipped from consciousness.

9

The rooster paraded up and down the line of tents crowing like a marine drill instructor. Nico had slept fitfully, waking repeatedly to the clamor of wind and rain. Tugging at the zipper, he disentangled himself from the sleeping bag, nearly spilling the basin of warm water that had been slipped inside the tent. Rubbing his eyes, he peered outside. The sky, barely hinting at sunrise, was still a somber shade of grey. He washed his face and neck, raking the water through his hair with his fingers, then brushed his teeth using the drinking water from his Nalgene. Rummaging in his pack, he found a fresh T-shirt and changed out of the one he'd slept in. Desperate to pee, he stumbled barefoot out of the tent and was struck by the sight of Camille in tree pose, her hands together in Anjali mudra, facing the impending sunrise. Capturing the blue hour of twilight, Griz quietly filmed her as she raised her gaze and arms upward greeting the tangerine halo rimming the mountain.

"Is that you, Nico?" Camille called out without losing her balance. "Come join me in the sun salutation."

Ignoring her, he went straightaway to the latrine. On his return, the aroma of breakfast from the cook tent was tempting, but he acquiesced, moving together with her through the poses as the sun broke over the mountains, and vibrant pink and orange hues swept through the sky like wildfire.

After the heavy rain during the night, the stream that ran

through the village had turned brown and torrential. Nico stretched his hands and heels to the ground in downward facing dog.

Camille suddenly blurted, "Starving!" Tugging at the back of Nico's pants, she pulled him to the breakfast tent where they were handed mugs of hot coca tea. The stimulating properties of the coca plant would help them cope with the altitude. Nico and Camille joined the rest of the crew at a long communal table where everyone talked at once. Without too much lingering, they delighted in a fortifying breakfast of pancakes drizzled with caramel, creamy quinoa porridge, and omelets stuffed with peppers, carrots, and cheese. The porters packed up the tents and gear. Detailing the day's trek, Quispe explained they would be ascending 4,000 feet to Warmi Wañusca, also referred to as Dead Woman's Pass. The elevation would be just shy of thirteen thousand feet, the highest point of the trek, and he urged them to take the strenuous climb slowly and steadily to avoid altitude sickness. Camille was quiet as they both gathered their packs and filled their water bottles. The chef handed them each a bag of snacks: an apple, granola bar, juice box, cheese sandwich, and chocolate saying it would provide the energy they would need. The porters led them out of camp on a meandering path that soon became steep steps leading up into dense forest.

Stopping to catch her breath, Camille gently petted the thick emerald colored moss growing on the side of a tree. "There's something about moss.... I just love the way it feels."

Nico hadn't thought much about it and asked her why.

"I remember hiking in this magical place called the Hall of Mosses, in the Hoh Rainforest in Washington State where these big-leaf maple trees and tall spruces are covered and dripping with moss, their limbs alive like giant arms reaching out for you. The intensity of the palette and smell of the damp earth, melting snow, and cedar is overwhelming...in a way that reminds me of *Lord of the Rings*. My husband and I were thinking about having a baby, and I wasn't sure if I was ready, but my clock was running out. I stopped alongside a clear glacier pond and lay down on a soft bed of moss in the warm sunshine listening to the water trickle over the rocks and asked for the answer."

"Who'd you ask?" he ventured.

"I asked my higher self, Atma, the God within us. It's the one universal spirit that is everywhere. It's our own true nature. If we listen, we will always hear the truth. We are all our own savior, after all. You must know what I am talking about…"

"Of course. Raising kundalini connects you to your higher self." He stopped. "Did you get your answer?"

"Yes." She paused, stopping to turn and face him. "I have a son. But I'm separated from my husband."

This must be the unrest he had been sensing in her. In the car, she'd been effervescent, chattering about her work, and yoga. Now, high in the Andes and enveloped in this ancient forest, a glacial stream rushing beside them, she was pensive.

"How old is he?" They were pausing every few minutes to catch their breath.

"Jackson is ten. We have joint custody, and I get along fine with his father. But Ben wanted a different lifestyle. I guess something more traditional. "I hardly saw them. I was away too often, shooting on location. But I love my work, and I always rationalized, what if this is my only chance? I admit, I neglected them." She continued walking with a measured pace up the trail, breathing hard. After a dozen steps she stopped again, and remarked, "I bought us a big house in the Hollywood Hills. At least there is a substantial investment account and a college fund." She concluded with bitter sarcasm.

"It's important to be passionate about what you do every day, then you bring that happiness and fulfillment home to your family. I'm sorry your husband didn't see it that way." He'd taken it for granted, that to become one with your purpose was to achieve true realization. He felt like an observer of himself, lonely, and separate from his connection to the universe. The thin air, the loamy smell. He touched the soft greenness. In his fear and desperation he'd lost the joy.

"I think he believed I would be a stay-at-home mom, or at least be home a lot more than I was. If our careers had been reversed, I'm fairly sure we would still be together. He's an aerospace engineer with basically a nine to five. When we got married, I had a lead in a sitcom on ABC, with a somewhat normal schedule. The show kept getting renewed, and I didn't think much beyond that. Then, I landed a lead in a hit movie and my career took off."

"How did you end up marrying an engineer? I thought most actors marry each other…for a reason."

"He's a friend of my brother, they went to Cal Tech together. My brother invited a bunch of us scuba diving in Mexico. Ben was smart, funny, and handsome. We hit it off. I liked that he wasn't an actor. He thinks about the future, and how to improve the world. He's advised Space X and given TED talks. Shit! I'm rambling… and I suppose it's obvious I regret fucking it up."

Their thighs burned as they steadily climbed the hundreds of steps that switchback up the mountain. Talking became increasingly difficult in the thin air and for a long while they listened to the stillness of the swirling clouds moving through the valley, whispering tales of the ancient ones who went before them, like the soundless echo of ghosts.

"That's it? It's fucked up forever?" he asked.

He was surprised she told him about her marriage being a failure. She was bossy and a know-it-all, which annoyed him, and yet she had no qualms about sharing the most personal bits of her life.

"I don't know..." Camille stopped and took a granola bar out of her snack bag.

Nico sat down on a rock facing the stream and ate an apple.

"I can't change my desire, my need to feel fulfilled outside of being a mother. The breakup made me think about my motivation... my reason for being. I want to open a center where people come to get in touch with their calling, their purpose in life—what the Japanese call Ikigai. It sort-of translates as, the realization of what one hopes for...or a reason for being."

"Would this be part of the Sisterhood thing you have going?"

"Sure, but it would be for everyone, especially artists, creators and business leaders who need to bring people together. I want a space where we can help people realize they are the supreme source of light and love, and to transcend attachment to outcome. Remember I said I needed to think about my motivation? I had been externally motivated for prestige and money, afraid I wouldn't be praised for my talent, instead of being driven by the joy of acting. But I did notice, when I was focused and immersed in a role, I was in the zone. What if external motivation is the problem, and we need to move people to intrinsic motivation? Have them experience being in flow with their passion, have the self-desire to try new things because they are interested, challenge themselves, and be driven by the enjoyment the work gives them without the expectation of some future benefit, but simply to experience it as the main goal."

"It's what I do with Kundalini," he said smugly. "What's the Japanese thing you mentioned?"

"Oh, Ikigai! In Japanese, iki means to live, and gai means reason. It's your reason to live—what makes you feel valuable, and your life worthwhile. The practice is about celebrating the small things in your everyday life. A cup of tea, and the morning sunshine are equally important as a compliment from someone whose praise you value above all else. And mindfulness, a big ass catch word that is thrown about a lot lately, but it means to be present in the here and now, not having an attachment to the outcome, or expectations of anyone." She stopped and gave him a look that begged his acknowledgment.

"Yeah, right… good luck with that. Not only is that not L.A., but we also all have goals and expectations of each other. Don't we?" He thought about the people who'd disappointed him. He wasn't the sort of person who could easily resign himself and accept fate.

"Well, this is the time to deepen our connection with people. Ironically, we have more access to information and each other with social media, yet people are becoming ever more detached. Don't you believe that San Pedro guides us to find our truth? It empowers us to become more loving. I want to help people find satisfaction in love, and in all their relationships, and do work that is not based solely on financial reward, or acclamation."

"Definitely. That's the nature of San Pedro, to create florecimiento—the flowering. When I conduct the ceremony, it puts the participant in a state of wonder, bringing the soul of the universe into them."

"My experience was a heightened state of awareness. You actually become connected to the universal spirit, the One. You've abandoned your ego and are no more important and no less important than anything or anyone. You see the beauty of everything around you. It becomes about knowing yourself, the true self like it says in the *Upanishads*. There's a shift in the state-of-mind where you stop struggling to control everything. The more you struggle, the more stuck you are."

"Exactly!" Nico exclaimed.

He beamed at her and thought she blushed, but then reasoned she was flushed from exertion and the altitude. As they cleared the tree line his thighs were burning. He thought it signaled their arrival at the top. He heard Camille sigh as a turquoise sky opened-up above them. Shielding his eyes from the sun, he gazed dispiritedly at the long snaking trail up the mountain toward the peaks in the distance. He stopped to retrieve the snacks from his pack and put on his sunglasses. They sat together and ate their snacks without speaking, looking up at how much farther they had to climb before they would reach the top of Dead Woman's Pass.

Nico stood and stretched his arms up over his head. Looking back, he winked at Camille and said, "We could fly up there if we were eagles."

"Don't I wish…" she pleaded and followed as he led the way. "Um, Mr. Romero, I believe it is time to bring this understanding into the world. Don't you?"

"Obviously, it was what I was doing with my center in L.A. until…"

"Until you got shot, right?" She stated bluntly.

He couldn't tell what she was thinking.

"I wasn't sure you knew about that," he muttered.

"Google, remember? But here you are, obviously to heal body and soul.

"That's the idea…" He was relieved it was out in the open.

"When Sabrina called from the travel office, and I saw the article in LA Weekly, I took it as synchronicity. You're the proverbial Wounded Healer. I had to meet you." She smiled at him, and her eyes twinkled playfully.

"Not you, too," he said cynically.

"What do you mean?"

"Never mind." He shook his head, "When we get back, I'm going to Q'eros to study with my teacher, if he's still there…" he garbled the last part.

"How long will you stay?"

"Maybe years…maybe forever. I don't know.

"So, you got shot. It's likely you pissed off someone. And now you're running away from the world?"

"That's not how I see it." He answered too quickly.

He had thought himself better than everyone. His life should not have turned out this badly. He was angry at her for making him see it.

The mountain range, in its rugged magnificence, was laid out before them. Nico put his head down and walked ahead, creating distance between them. For the next hour they hiked without conversing, only stopping to drink water and catch their breath. At the top of Dead Woman's Pass, Nico inhaled as deeply as his lungs would permit him at fourteen-thousand feet. Camille came up behind him and dropped her pack. Julio, one of the porters was waiting for them, to be sure they were okay, and to resupply them with water.

The wind had picked up and Camille pulled a long-sleeved top over her T-shirt, and reapplied sunscreen to her face. Looking back down the trail from where they came, they saw the rest of their party not far behind them. Above them the cragged white peaks seemed a post-card against the starkly blue sky.

"Should we wait for them?" Nico asked, breaking the uncomfortable silence like a welcome rain.

"Let's go ahead. They aren't far behind, and I won't be able to go fast."

Nico rummaged in his pack and brought out a small pouch. Removing a few coca leaves, he handed her a few. "Roll them up in a little ball and chew on it. It's a little bitter but you'll get a boost of energy."

"Thanks," she said, accepting the offer. "Look, I didn't mean to be insensitive before… I shouldn't have said it like that."

"You were right. It's just I've been struggling my whole life to make something. Always, when I think I finally reach my dream, it turns to dust. Whatever. There's no escaping my past."

"Whatever?" She asked delicately, waiting for him to explain.

The trail down was a long series of steep ancient stone stairs. At Julio's suggestion, Camille took the steps sideways to lessen the impact on her knees. Nico didn't object when she reached out to lean on him, thinking how she had been like a mountain goat the day before. Even going up the trail today she had been robust. But the hike down was laborious and slow-going.

"Why are you disappointed, Nico? I admire your knowledge of both yoga and energy healing."

"By now, I expected to be a famous, the most well-respected healer with centers around the world. Everyone who promised to help me let me down. Never mind—you wouldn't understand…." He turned away.

It was not that she was difficult to talk to, he just wasn't sure how much he trusted her. Yet, unwittingly, he found himself telling her more than he intended.

"Okay, I hear where you're coming from," she said, and sat down on the stone step and took a drink from her water bottle. "We all make choices based on the way we think it will make us feel. I thought notoriety and money would make me feel fulfilled. I didn't trust that I would receive everything I thought I deserved in the right time. My ego and fear of missing out resulted in the destruction of my marriage. I can't waste my time and energy wishing for a do-over. That's done and gone. It's taken some soul searching, but I learned to let go of my expectations, about how I think my life should go, and instead approach life from a place of exploration."

"I feel like I have been on this fruitless journey only to end up back at the beginning. You're already a celebrity. You have a child, a home…money in the bank. And I bet if you want your husband back you can have that too."

"If you're right about the last point, it will be because I'm more loving, of myself and others. My self-worth is no longer determined by external validation or by the movie industry."

"But it already is, you've already become a star…" he argued. It occurred to him that he didn't know her age.

"It's not about whether I have achieved my goals. You can see in L.A., you know this as well as I do, it's never enough money, fame, awards… Someone is always coming up behind you and taking your spotlight. And everyone is jumping from one relationship to the next. I'm not saying you can't enjoy success; you're just no longer defining your self-worth by it. You have to get to a place inside yourself where if you lost it all, you would still maintain your serenity."

"Are you saying having a goal is a bad thing?" It seemed to him she spoke in riddles.

"Not at all, but it's about intention. Leaving room for something unexpected. Being open and willing to go with the flow as a means to achieve something that wasn't what you had intended. Things happen for you not to you. I've learned that where I am, is where I'm supposed to be."

It wasn't that he disagreed as much as he was skeptical. She made it sound so easy. He'd worked hard, and yet failed miserably at his business, his relationships, and almost lost his life. How could this be where he was meant to be?

"Listen to your higher-self, Nico. If you are feeling disappointed, then change the way you are looking at the situation. There are only moments, pieces that eventually make up the whole. Whatever we do, even what we don't do, are still decisions. Life is about those choices we make, each one is an opportunity and reflects who we really are. Release the fear and the judgement, you don't have to have it all figured out."

He heard Luna's voice in his head, the day before he left for Buenos Aires, You pushed everyone away… "I suppose you're right…" he stammered, nodding as he considered her words.

It took them a painstaking two-hours before they got down into the valley where Pacaymayo Camp lay surrounded by lush green cliffs threaded with cascading waterfalls. The porters had arrived long before to set up camp and as tradition dictated cheered their arrival with hot tea and fudge brownies. As the sun fell behind the mountains they were overjoyed when a local villager arrived with beer. They sat side-by-side, as if in a church pew, savoring the slightly tart brew as shadow descended across the valley, like a lace mantilla falling gracefully over the sloped shoulders of a Spanish lady.

I'm a stranger here, he thought without pity, and yet, I've shared more about my feelings with this woman than with anyone except for maybe Luna. He looked over at Camille, "We're all trying to find a way out of the darkness, aren't we?"

She was back-lit against a dusky-purple sky. He could barely make out her smile. "Interesting you should say that. I saw a YouTube video not too long ago about the Andean perception of time. Are you familiar with it?"

Camille hadn't answered his question and so he didn't answer hers. However, he sensed another of her pearls about to drop.

"They believe the future is behind us, and our lives are created ahead of us from the future that has informed us from behind. I know, it's confusing, and it sounds crazy, but if we remain open to life, knowing that the energy comes from behind, flowing through us, we can have an impact on what we manifest."

"I've watched a lot of *Star Trek*," he chuckled. "Time is fluid, free flowing…an illusion, like the quantum slipstream used to manipulate the fabric of the space-time continuum." Nico saw the look on Camille's face and laughed. "It's like, I can be older than someone who is twice my age. Or a star we see in the sky today may have died a million years ago."

"That's true." She laughed at his childlike enthusiasm.

Camille paused to absorb the subtle beauty of the darkening sky over the hulking mountains. The lingering silence as day passed into night was solemn, but not melancholy.

The beckoning aroma of fried chicken and freshly cut potato chips signaled dinner was ready, and although Nico could barely keep his eyes open, he was lured toward the dining tent. After a couple of glasses of wine, more of Camille's stash of brandy, and scrumptious dark-chocolate cake, he stumbled to his tent and crawled into his sleeping bag. He left the tent flap open to gaze at the starlight unspooling, which appeared close and bright, but his eyes grew heavy. Before he could analyze the importance of all that transpired between them on the hike, he'd fallen asleep.

He dreamt she was calling him to come with her. Her voice was urgent. He couldn't see her, but he felt she was close by.

"Nico, wake up you are missing it!" she called loudly.

In his dream, he looked for her until he was ripped from slumber and grudgingly opened his eyes.

"Nico, come out here, you are missing the Milky Way!"

"What time is it?" She was far too exuberant, he thought, as he unzipped the sleeping bag. He nearly fell pulling on his sweatpants. "I was sound asleep…" he grumbled, as he stepped outside the tent. "Whoa!" he yelped as he gazed wide-eyed at the luminous band, a halo of white light and dark dust clouds made up of billions of stars and planets, ribboned across a blue-violet sky. "What the fuck?!"

Griz handheld the camera while the other guys stood around. Camille was highly charged, obviously they'd been filming a segment of the documentary while he'd been sleeping.

"It appears to us as a band because we are inside the Milky Way, seeing it edgewise from within." Camille explained.

"Shhh, don't ruin the magic…" he whispered.

The grandeur overwhelmed him. It was the heavens as God first made them, he thought. As it was at the dawn of creation. Bewildered in wonder, he allowed the grandeur to penetrate him. I am where I'm supposed to be, he thought.

"See, in the Dark Rift, the undulating dust swirl? The Inca named that one The Serpent." She announced, pointing to a distinct snake-like shape in the dark lane of dust running through the milky haze.

"This means a lot to me, Cami…"

They sat on the ground in front of the tents passing her flask back and forth between them, until their eyelids were at half-mast. He considered it strange how comfortable he'd become around her, even though she incessantly touted her theories on everything. Sharing private matters about herself, she had managed to get him to reveal his weaknesses and the sense of failure he concealed from everyone. It surprised him that after two long and tedious days together he'd become sexually attracted to her.

What is it about this woman? he pondered. Tired, and slightly drunk, he leaned back on his elbows and stared at her silhouette in the moonless starlight. She isn't exotic or seductive in the way that normally appeals to me. All those American actresses look alike, blonde with fair skin, he said to himself. I think her eyes are green, like mine. She isn't smoking hot like Maya. Élodie's French accent turned me on, besides, she was gorgeous. When Sofia took me in her mouth, time stood still. He saw himself, the way he operated. He sang, he played his guitar. He made them a part of him. He didn't feel anything except for the power. There was never a sense of belonging. He simply bound them to him. He couldn't help himself. He needed their love, their adoration, in order to breathe.

"Nico..." She shook him awake. "I'm going to my tent. You nodded off...Go... Don't stay out here all night, you'll get a chill. We better get some sleep, it's a long day tomorrow."

He wanted to lean over and kiss her gently on the lips. She would follow him to his tent, and they would silently strip out of their clothes. Naked, they'd slip into his sleeping bag and face each other, their legs entwined, and make love slowly, listening to the frogs croaking in the tall grasses that surrounded the camp. Even in his sleep-addled stupor he knew better than to act on his fantasy. He knew she would decline, and he would be humiliated. He stood, unsteady on his feet.

"Night," he murmured and stumbled to his tent.

10

"Buenos dias, señor," the porter announced, delivering the morning's basin of hot water and a mug of coca tea to Nico's tent.

He woke in the silence before dawn and watched the coming of light. It had been too cold to get out of his sleeping bag. Taking the warm mug, he held it between both hands, and studied the fading stars framed within the triangle of his open tent. The tea was hot enough to warm his bones, but after last night's brandy he looked forward to the thick, strong coffee they served at breakfast. A misting rain saturated the air. The mountains were shrouded by clouds, and the temperature would remain near freezing until the sun rose over the peaks. He washed quickly, then put on a polar fleece over a long-sleeved T-shirt. Zipping up his rain jacket and pulling on his alpaca chullo to cover his ears, he braced himself against the weather and headed to breakfast.

Camille and Griz were huddled together looking at film clips. Nico slid into the chair next to her and poured himself coffee from the thermos. The chef placed a steaming bowl of oatmeal in front of him and returned quickly with scrambled eggs and bacon. The porters had already taken down the tents, and he ate hurriedly sensing they were eager to get going. With over six miles to cover, the porters called the day's hike the gringo killer for the steepness of the descent, but there was the promise of spectacular views and ancient ruins along the way.

° ° °

The rain had made the rocks slippery. By the time they descended to the small ruins of Runkurakay, Camille was halting in her gait. She didn't complain, but he saw her rub her knee when they paused to look back and admire the view of last night's camp, now touched by the morning sunlight. "It's like a postcard," she remarked, gazing at the village nestled in a verdant valley. A glacial waterfall cascaded from the snow-covered peaks above. The ancient steps, slick with wet moss, made the trek down treacherous and Camille, clearly in distress, sat down on the stone to rest. Taking a granola bar from her pack, she looked at him with pained eyes.

"This sucks," she said, making light of her discomfort.

"We don't need to rush, Camille, they'll have to wait for us. Take some Advil, and I have a knee brace in here, you should put it on…" He rummaged in his pack and found the pill container and a well-worn compression sleeve. He fumbled with the child lock on the bottle, then tapped out two red tablets. She swallowed them while he undid her boot and rolled up her pants. Then he carefully eased the brace over her knee.

While lacing her boot, she looked at him with a mischievous smile. "See, you are the ultimate healer to the rescue." She stood, and a worried look crossed her face. "I hope I can make it. The going is much tougher than I expected. It's probably my old volleyball injury from college acting up."

"Volleyball?" he laughed. "I would never have taken you for volleyball."

"I excelled at sports, and they gave me a partial scholarship if I would play."

"Where did you go to college?" he asked. She always had some new bit to add about herself that perplexed him.

"Duke, in North Carolina."

"I thought I detected a southern accent."

"I didn't expect you were keen on the various dialects in the United States. I grew up in Virginia. But I'm sure North Carolina didn't help. Did you go to school in Argentina?"

He hesitated before answering. He'd lied so often he would forget what fabrication he'd told. His favorite charade was to say he'd graduated from the School of Medicine of the University of Buenos Aires with a degree in Ayurveda. No one ever questioned its authenticity. Or, he'd say that he'd gone to Oxford to study biology but had to leave when his mom got sick. That lie also drew sympathy. In his mind, it had been vitally important to impress his clients and the women who were in his thrall.

He surprised himself when he replied to Camille, "I didn't go to university. I came here, to Peru for a while…and then went to Kerala. My training wasn't something I needed formal education to learn." He paused, feeling embarrassed. "Did you study acting?" He wished he'd never admitted his lack of education.

"I majored in philosophy. But I joined a theater group and took acting classes." She stopped speaking as she carefully navigated down the steep irregular steps.

"Slow and steady…Go sideways and lean on me going down. Philosophy, huh? I guess that makes sense… kind of going…how do you say…back around again."

"You mean, full circle. Yes, I've considered this. And I expect it's age as well."

"What do you mean, age?"

"I think at a certain age, you reevaluate what's important and where you would like to end up. I mean at the end of your life."

"Geez…. I'm just trying to get from one day to the next without going backwards all the time." Having been preoccupied with the constant push for success he'd never imagined it was possible to think differently.

"Well, maybe for me. At forty-five and with a ten-year-old, I've stopped to think about all of it."

"I wouldn't have taken you for…well, never mind. We both agreed, there is no such thing as age and time…right?" He thought she was much younger.

The clouds settled around them as the tall grasses gave way to forest. She smiled down on him, as she leaned her weight on his shoulder and proceeded cautiously down the uneven hand carved steps tunneled into the mountain. He could tell her knee was giving her trouble, the Advil hadn't helped much, if at all.

"I am going to open a center in L.A. this year. I'd like you to be a part of it. Will you be going back? After your stay with the Q'ero, that is…"

"I don't know Cami…" He paused to give it a moment's thought. "I may have burned too many bridges."

"I don't believe that. You're just self-focused on what happened to you and have created all these negative thoughts and feelings. Don't assume others give it the same importance, or for that matter even remember."

"Someone came into my studio and shot me. I don't think I've made too big a deal out of it," he snapped.

"And you don't have a clue who it was?" she asked skeptically.

"It could have been any number of people. Like I said, it wasn't just one bridge I burned."

"Are you saying it's not safe to return?"

"I don't know…" He didn't intend to give her the impression he was afraid, but that was how it sounded, even to himself.

"Let's go over the possibilities. We have nothing else to do but climb up and down these godforsaken stairs. I feel like Sisyphus…" she said.

"Who?"

"The god Zeus punished King Sisyphus by consigning him to an eternity of futility and frustration by making him push an enormous boulder up a hill, only to have it roll back and hit him."

"What was his crime?"

"It was for thinking he was cleverer than Zeus."

"Was he?"

"He was known for being arrogant and deceitful. He betrayed Zeus and pissed him off."

Nico was quiet for a long while as they navigated another set of punishing stairs. They came out of the forest to a panoramic view. Below, hidden within the landscape, was Sayaqmarka looking out over the valley from its commanding position. As they descended the trail, the ruins became increasingly impressive. Camille limped up the irregular stairs to the thick wall built precariously into the cliff face.

"I'm Sisyphus," Nico said despairingly, looking out over the valley. The colors intensified under an awning of low hanging clouds. Far in the distance, a cloud forest indicated the outermost edge of what would eventually lead into the Amazon rainforest.

"I see… You believe you are being punished for all eternity?" Camille asked.

"I am always starting over… I told you that," he stressed impatiently.

"You feel constantly defeated by the empty quest?" She pressed, even knowing it would rankle him.

"What's that supposed to mean? Empty quest," he rebuffed. "You're starting to piss me off." He walked away. When he looked back, he saw her limping.

"Why don't you let me look at your knee?"

She sat on the stone floor of the veranda and leaned her back against the perimeter wall while he rolled up her pant leg. "Shit, Cami, your knee is all swollen, and look… filled with water."

"It hurts, but there's nothing I can do," she shrugged. "I'll have Julio take a look at it. But listen, I didn't mean to get you riled. Let me explain what I meant."

Nico sat on the ground next to her. The warmth of the stone soothed his back, and he closed his eyes against the sun. "Okay, explain."

"An empty quest is one you believe brings enduring happiness—like power, or prestige…or money. But these acquisitions themselves don't provide meaning in life. In the absence of a spiritual life, the sense of emptiness is the result of the preference for having over being. The shattering of this illusion is why you read about rich and famous people with addiction, depression, and even aggression."

"But I've healed my clients. The practice of Kundalini Yoga and opening their chakras changes their consciousness and unlocks their potential. Having a bigger center, and publicity with a book deal and a TV show—I could help more people. Isn't that what you want to do, too?"

"Yeah…but it always points back to the relationship between meaning and motivation. Hedonic motivation strives for maximum pleasure. The other motivation is what Aristotle called eudaimonic, meaning good spirit. He believed happiness was a common or low-minded idea, that not all desires were worth pursuing, and though some may provide gratification, they would not produce well-being. He said happiness is found by leading a virtuous life and doing what is worth doing."

"And isn't that what I do? Even without knowing all that high-minded Greek philosophy."

"Yes, Nico. And if I didn't think you were an accomplished healer, I wouldn't have invited you to come with me. You haven't been completely honest with me about what happened. But that might not be a fair statement since you don't know me."

"So, tell me more about the meaning of a life quest. Do you think I've done everything wrong?" he said sharply.

He was interested in her theory but irked by her criticism. His conversations with Luna pissed him off at times, and he would cut her off, sometimes for months. But Luna had been close to him. He didn't know Camille, and he hadn't expected her to get under his skin.

"As I was saying, in striving for a fulfilling life, the aim is not for pleasure, nor for the thrill that comes with recognition, power, and money. On the contrary, the work may be stressful, uncomfortable, and even hard. But it's where you rise to a challenge and strive for something bigger and contribute to something outside of yourself. By doing this, and sticking to universal values, like love and relationships, you find meaning in life."

She turned her head to look over at him. His eyes were closed, and he didn't respond, not even in defense. After a moment of silence, feeling the sun on her face, she nudged him.

He picked up his head and looked her in the eye, silently questioning her sincerity.

"Are you saying if I work with you, in this new center of yours in L.A., then this will alter my motivation, and I can stop pushing that rock up the hill?"

"Possibly. By assigning a greater meaning to the work outside of your self-interest, it would increase the level of meaning in your life. You might begin to look at this Sisyphean feat as a gift. As Camus suggested, the struggle may be enough to fill a man's heart."

"The practice of doing my work, healing others, should have been enough, I know... You remind me of an old friend... Luna would send me quotes by Yoda, from *Star Wars*. She said I should do the work every day and not strive for external validation, that it would be my undoing. She was right."

"Nico, there have always been iconic stories espousing moral lessons. As a yoga instructor, I would expect you're familiar with the *Bhagavad Gita*. It's one of the oldest epic stories. Lord Krishna teaches Arjuna about our relationship to friends, family, and the community as well as to the gods. It's a guide to spiritual development. For thousands of years yoga has enlightened us that life is the repetition of breathing—inhaling and exhaling. Itself, the concept is quite Sisyphean."

"How is it you know so much...?"

"I read a lot," She teased sassily, smiling at him. "You're not mad at me, are you?"

"No...I suppose I am only angry with myself. I pushed too hard, for what I thought I deserved...and believed was important. But I guess it was my pride."

"Ego... I think you mean your ego..."

"Huh?"

"Well, pride is a sense of accomplishment, a sense of joy. It more likely brings humility. You know the expression, a heart swollen with pride?"

Nico nodded but looked confused.

"While ego is self-importance that leads to arrogance, pride is self-satisfaction. Ah, but prideful is showing arrogance."

"Fine. I get it, I used the wrong word. But you interrupted me when I was trying to explain myself, and you went around the block and changed the subject." He pouted and turned away.

"I'm sorry, Nico. You're right. I interrupted. It was rude."

Taking a deep breath, he refused to look at her, but continued, "I was saying…there were people who cared about me, and I didn't have faith in them, or believe them. I got mad and did things I'm not proud of." He fell silent, still unable to look at her. He didn't want her to know about the drugs. He wished he could leave and get far away.

The crew and porters finally arrived, and it was agreed to break for lunch. Julio created a hot poultice made with coca leaves and covered her knee with plastic wrap to seal in the heat. They gathered at quickly erected tables for lunch. Nico could tell Camille was in pain, but it hadn't diminished her hunger. With her leg elevated, she ate the hearty of meal of quinoa soup, tuna, and bread with cheese. Afterward, coca tea and honey served with ginger cookies supplied the energy needed to continue to the next camp. The porters talked among themselves, concerned about whether they would need to carry her, but she made light of the situation.

After an hour's rest, they descended into the thickening foliage walking a path covered by a mat of miniature bromeliads to Chacquicocha campground where there was a tiled washroom. The coca leaf poultice had reduced the swelling, and determined to complete the trek, Camille asked Griz to set up the camera and film Julio applying a fresh hot poultice while explaining the benefits of coca leaf. A misty cloud forest clinging to the shoulders of the mountains was a stunning backdrop as the villagers gathered to watch Griz and the crew document this segment of their journey. Camille's spirits lifted when the women and children tending to their llamas gathered around them. As if familiar with the camera, one curious llama approached the lens and licked it, providing much needed laughter to what had been an arduous afternoon.

Camille insisted she was ready to continue to the campground, another two hours hike. When they left the village, most of the porters moved quickly ahead to arrive in advance at the final campground. Only Julio stayed behind to walk with Nico and Camille. When they said it wasn't necessary, he smiled, and walked several paces behind them. The vegetation had become increasingly wild with giant ferns, a bounty of orchids, stands of bamboo and masses of bromeliads growing out of the trunks of trees. Turning a corner, imposing stairs led to a narrow tunnel cut through the mountain, an image they could only liken to something out of Middle Earth. They rested frequently to admire the jaw dropping majesty of the Andes decorated with whipped cream clouds on top of towering peaks, looming over a blanket of green velvet. In the distance was a barely visible red flag marking Machu Picchu situated between two distant peaks. As they climbed, they chewed on the coca leaves for energy, while Julio told stories about battles that took place five-hundred years ago between the Inca and Spanish conquistadors. They stopped often to rest and eat chocolate—a gift from the gods according to Julio. Arrowhead shaped agricultural terraces cut into the hillside that had seemed diminutive in the distance were steep and wide, evidence of how large a crop had been needed to support the inhabitants of the ancient city. Julio sat at the top of the circular staircase, stubbornly refusing to go further unless he could carry Camille, who balked and said she would rather crawl down than be carried.

While descending the formidable moss-covered steps, Nico pretended to be Indiana Jones, grabbing onto the over-hanging vines, as he called out playfully, "Snakes, why'd it have to be snakes?" Camille, laughing at the movie reference, squealed, "Indy!"

All the while they bantered, with Nico calling her Marion, and quoting lines from *Raiders of the Lost Ark.* When they arrived at Winay Wayna, their final campsite of the trek, they were greeted with cheers and high fives. The tents had been erected and the cook was busy preparing dinner, which would be served early because of the four o'clock in the morning call time to arrive at Machu Picchu before sunrise. Camille went directly to her tent, while Nico took advantage of a hot shower before dinner. He arrived at the dining tent and for a while made small talk with Griz and the crew about their plans for filming at Machu Picchu. They drank the plumy red wine and dunked the warm dinner rolls in the hearty Inca vegetable soup.

Camille still hadn't shown up for dinner, and Nico thinking she may have fallen asleep, poured two glasses of wine and went to her tent to check on her. He called out to her before pulling back the flap and ducking inside. Camille lay on her back on top of her sleeping bag and didn't acknowledge him as he entered. Even in the dusky light, he saw her eyes overflowed with tears, skirting her ears as they fell, dampening the small pillow. He sat on the floor beside her cot and gestured for her to take one of the glasses.

"Here, this should help," he said encouragingly.

She sat up and smiling weakly took the glass from him.

"I didn't think I would make it, Nico. I was in agony." She sighed deeply. "If it wasn't for you making me laugh, I wouldn't have." Taking a large gulp of the wine, she whimpered, "I just want to stay in bed. Will you bring me some food? I don't want to see anyone else."

"Come on Camille. Cut yourself some slack. You made it—without Julio carrying you." He winked.

"It's the guys, Griz mostly. I don't know…they all look at me a certain way and having Griz see me as weak would change our relationship. You know what I mean?"

"I suppose. Look just put on your pajamas and a sweatshirt and come to the tent. You'll feel better. The soup was delicious," he coaxed.

"Ugh…I suppose it's easier to eat at the table, anyway…" She sighed. I'll just go like this, and then take a shower after dinner. The hot water will feel amazing." Acquiescing, she leaned on his arm to stand up. "I better ask Julio to make another compress."

"Do you have more of that brandy?" he asked earnestly.

"Enough to get us home, I hope." She smiled weakly.

When they entered the tent, Griz jumped up first, then the others all gathered around her. He picked up the camera, making a fuss over her entrance, and filmed Julio and the rest of the team clapping as she waived them off.

Griz let the camera roll as Camille praised the soup, then dug into a medley of eggplant and rice, all the while describing with apparent glee the challenging day of gringo killer steps and magnificent ruins. She blessed the food bestowed by Pachamama, the Earth Mother, who presided over them, and the mountains, and the benevolent coca leaf whose medicinal properties relieved her swollen, aching knee.

Nico sat back and watched her. She's a damned good actress, he thought, you'd never know she had just been crying. He admitted to himself that he envied her determination. Why, he asked himself, when things don't go my way, do I feel irrevocably destroyed?

I'm ashamed by my weakness. I abused myself with drugs and they nearly killed me. I blamed everyone else for my failure and for betraying me. Maybe, I have no right to resume my training. What teacher would accept me now that I have broken every promise, every oath? All the loss I brought upon myself. It's time to bury it.

Camille was still in pain. Yet, she didn't complain. Look at her, he said to himself, smiling at the camera, laughing, and telling her fans about Julio's coca leaf poultice. He snuffed, and then caught himself. Even when I foolishly tore my hamstring playing soccer, I blamed another player for passing the ball poorly.

Can I trust her? he asked himself. She said she was embarrassed, but I don't think that's it. She doesn't want them to worry about her. She's acting, he thought. Full of opinions about life and how I should live mine. It was a mistake to come on this trip.

"Nico..."

"Huh?" he uttered, ripped from his reverie. "Sorry... I was thinking..."

"Here. Have some brandy," she said and handed him her flask. "Julio said he'll wrap my knee again, but first I'm going to take a hot shower."

"I'll see you later then?" he asked haltingly. He was exhausted but knew sleep would evade him.

"I'm just going to pass out, Nico, besides, they'll be waking us early to get to the Sun Gate before sunrise."

"Oh, right..." he conceded, not wanting to sound disappointed. He hesitated, looking at her and thinking of what he might say. But nothing came to mind. "See you in the morning then...early..." He paused, still looking at her expectantly. "Thanks for the brandy."

"Get some rest, Nico. You look as tired as I feel." She placed her hand on his bicep and gave it a gentle squeeze that sent an arousing tingling sensation through his body.

He shuffled away, wondering if anyone was still in the little concrete concession that also functioned as a bar serving the local beer. He opened the door and looked in. A couple of hikers speaking German were sitting at a table. Two locals were leaning on the bar drinking beer, but he didn't really feel like talking to them. The atmosphere made him feel lonelier and more depressed. Why, he pondered, did he feel the need to be with Camille? He turned away from the concession and headed to the row of tents pitched along the rim overlooking the Andean range; the cascade was awash in gradients of grey. The stars had not yet risen. Against the nightfall he saw a lantern shining from inside the porters' tent which was set off to the side away from his.

He ducked into his tent and got undressed, leaving on his boxer briefs, and slipped into his sleeping bag. He lay awake thinking about Camille. At dinner, she'd made a speech, on camera of course, thanking the porters and had each of them say something about themselves—how many times they had hiked the trail, and what it meant to them. He thought they would be embarrassed, but she'd made them comfortable, and their faces beamed with the attention paid to them. It's customary to tip the porters on the last night, and Nico could tell by their reaction she'd been generous.

Gazing out through the open tent flap, he saw a solitary bright star, or possibly it was a planet, appear in the now almost dark sky. He began counting the stars as they appeared. He opened the flask and took a long drink of the brandy, savoring the taste and the comforting burn as the liquid hit the back of his throat. He doubted he would see Camille again once the trip ended. He lay thinking about what she said, about working together. He didn't take her seriously. Everyone lies, he reminded himself. He'd learned that. Besides, he couldn't go back to L.A. He'd been destroyed, but maybe Cami was right, he shouldn't be too quick to concede defeat.

11

A steady rain hammered the roof of the tent. It was still pitch-black outside when the porter arrived. Nico slept with the wool chullo on his head to stay warm, but he had also hoped to gain insight from its visionary power. He drank the warm tea anticipating the coca's stimulating effects. Snapping his rain jacket shut, he pulled the hood over his head and darted across to where breakfast was being served. Rivulets of water shimmered on the tents. Hearing Camille's wholesome laugh from inside he stopped mid-stride. Remembering they would part ways at the end of the trek, he felt a familiar feeling of loss. Everyone leaves, he thought.

Camille looked up and greeted him with her eyes. He took a mug off the table and filled it with coffee from the thermos.

"I can't believe this rain. I thought this was the dry season," she said to whomever was listening.

He didn't feel the need to respond to her statement. Having served himself a large portion of oatmeal, he sat off to the side. When he finished, he refilled his coffee mug and left the tent to collect his backpack. They bid thanks and said their goodbyes to the porters and chef whose services were no longer required. Camille imparted heartfelt gratitude to Julio for his healing powers.

With Quispe's headlamp lighting the way, they began the descent in the darkness through the cloud forest along an ancient stairway hanging off the steep side of the mountain. The guide no longer pointed out the various species of orchids growing through cracks in the stone. He kept them moving at an undistracted steady pace to assure they would arrive in time for sunrise. Walking single file, they hugged the mountain treading carefully over slippery moss-covered roots that protruded from the uneven paving stones, like groping fingers with malicious intent to cast them off the cliff.

Nico, following Camille's footsteps, kept his head down, the rain and mist enveloping his melancholy as they made their way in silence to the Sun Gate. Suddenly, Camille tripped, and stumbled toward the precipice. Nico reached out and grabbed her before she fell.

"What the fuck, Cami, you have to watch where you go…you could have fallen!" Terrified, he gripped her arm tightly, his eyes glaring in fury and fear.

"I'm fine, Nico. I wouldn't have fallen, it wasn't that close," she assured him, although clearly shaken.

"You're an idiot! You were half over the cliff!" He reluctantly released her, whereby she moved herself closer to the mountain.

They hiked the remaining distance in silence. As slivers of light gradually appeared in the sky and views emerged between the trees, they saw the staircase leading up to Inti Punku, the Sun Gate. The fifty stone steps leading to the gateway are vertical, and they crawled more than climbed to the top using their hands. It was a sacred moment, and their silence contained mounting anticipation of the magnificence they would soon behold.

Standing at the top, Camille took his hand. "It's breathtaking," she said, her voice choked with tears.

The sun had not yet crested the distant peaks, its pale light softening the edges. The stones of the Citadel shone like amethyst and the surrounding terraces were a verdant green. The only living creatures were the llamas apathetically grazing, and Camille couldn't help but laugh through her tears.

"Look at them Nico. They are so peaceful…timeless. There were moments I didn't think I would make it."

"I knew you would," he stated solidly. "There's nothing holding you back."

The words as he spoke hit hard, burying him like an avalanche beneath a reality he could not rise above, regardless of the effort. He always held back. No matter how much he pushed for love or to succeed in his work, he became immobilized. Camille easily expressed her joy. But as he gazed down at the grandeur of Machu Picchu, he was speechless. It was as if all the silent souls throughout the ages spoke to him.

Magically, the rain had stopped and left behind billowing layers of cumulous clouds. Neither spoke as the watercolors in the sky mushroomed into a swirling froth of luminous yellow and orange, turning the scene before them into a romanticized painting reminiscent of those by Albert Bierstadt. Tourists standing nearby gasped as the sun illuminated the ancient city. A group of Buddhist monks began to chant. Camille reverently began the postures of the sun salutation. Nico joined her. This was what she had intended. Biz filmed them, just as he discreetly had in the dark along the trail and climbing the steps to the Sun Gate. After repeating several rounds, they stopped and descended into the sacred city. Quispe led them around the ruins expounding on the Inca history, as Griz and the crew filmed them, and Camille bubbled with enthusiasm.

Nico followed a few paces behind them. He listened, keeping his distance, as the guide explained Machu Picchu, meaning Old Mountain, was a spiritual center believed to have been home to the Virgins of the Sun, women chosen to dedicate themselves to the sun god. He was in awe that these were the remains of an architectural wonder that had been one hundred and fifty structures with an underground irrigation system of water canals. Nico watched as the sun crept over the top of Wayna Picchu, bathing it in a surreal saffron glow. The holy mountain, containing a hidden shrine called Temple of the Moon, stood guard over the Inca city. He was humbled by its magnificence. For hundreds of years ceremonies had been performed here, he thought. The mountains were guardians of the spirits, the city an astronomical observatory mirroring the heavens and deepening the worshiper's relationship to the Earth.

Camille talked with Quispe while the crew filmed. Nico stood off to the side and watched the light change over the Citadel. He was humbled and overflowing with conflicting emotions. He'd made the spiritual journey and he felt hopeful. Here was an ancient city and a culture that survived and remained deeply committed to living in harmony with the Earth. In this place, under this sky, he felt there was an honesty, a living truth he'd never experienced.

From his pouch he removed the three coca leaves that Quispe had given him days before. He didn't remember the prayer in Quechua, but he said his own version in Spanish. He asked for the wisdom of the Apu to guide him. Turning in all four directions he blew on the leaves. It wasn't a proper ceremony, but he did it with his heart.

He looked over at Camille. She talked animatedly and gestured with her hands as if she were dancing. She was comfortable in her body. Over the past four days she'd spoken openly to him about herself. In a way, they were stories that made him think about his own life. She was a lot like Luna. Sometimes it was annoying to be around them, these philosopher teachers that always seem to have all the answers. Life came easy to them, whereas for him it was always a struggle. Like Luna, Camille said things to him that scorched with a painful truth. He still didn't trust her, but he was drawn to her. Now that the trek had ended, he became increasingly anxious about what was to follow.

In the coming days, he would need to find his way to Q'eros and to his teacher. The crew packed up the equipment and their group was the last to leave. As they made their way out of the ancient city, he kicked the stones on the path and thought about Maya and his studio in L.A. That was the thing about Maya, she would already know he wasn't coming back.

° ° °

Nico gripped the seatback in front of him, his head splitting from the grinding clash of gears as the bus lurched down the perilous winding road to Aguas Calientes. In hindsight he wished he had hiked the two hours to the village instead of inhaling the nauseating fumes that belched each time the bus driver downshifted. Camille's film crew was catching a plane back to L.A. from Cusco, but she decided to stay a few nights at Inkaterra, the luxury spa in Aguas Calientes. Extolling the benefits of soaking in the hot springs after their four-day trek, she insisted he stay as well, instead of taking the train back to Cusco. He'd given her a questioning look at the invitation, but she smiled enigmatically and said not to worry about it. When she described the benefits of a hot stone massage, he agreed, and she laughed, her eyes crinkling up in the corners. They were almost to town, and Nico glanced over at her, thankful the whine of the engine prevented conversation.

° ° °

The hotel porter escorted them along a stone pathway in the jungle-like setting to a remote casita. Along the way he praised the resort's historic bird sanctuary and the world's largest orchid collection, reciting the hotel's amenities which he'd learnt by rote. Standing awkwardly in the foyer, Camille discreetly rolled her eyes at Nico while the porter flipped the lever on the chimney flue, then made sure there was an abundance of logs and matches for the fireplace. When he handed Camille the key, she tipped him generously. With the porter finally gone, they exhaled a unified sigh of relief as they dropped their backpacks on the floor.

Nico remained standing with his hands at his side, embarrassed by his scruffy appearance and dirty clothes even though he surmised they weren't the only weary travelers arriving off the trail. Reluctantly, he followed Camille through the sitting area and into the bedroom with its king-size bed. He was uncomfortably aware of being with her. Not too long ago, flirting and charming women to him had come easily. He recalled Maya standing in front of him at his studio, as he eyed her body. Within minutes her arms held him tightly as she rode on the back of his motorcycle, and soon after it had been her legs wrapped around him as he fucked her.

He knew he was different. He'd changed since the shooting. The trauma forced him to question the truth, to choose which memories were his. He wasted too much energy analyzing the fragments of his life, conjuring ghosts from the past. Camille's self-possession, her certainty, made him feel as if he were drowning, sinking like a rock in the water. He was frightened that she would see him as damaged, that it was an enduring wound that would not heal. It was as though he were naked, facing himself, questioning what it all meant. In that moment of panic he saw the opportunity to change course, to cast off the cloak of fear.

Averting his gaze away from the large, looming white coverlet conspicuously dominating the room, he opened the sliding glass door and stepped onto the patio overlooking the garden. The lush tropical plants gave cover to a private heated pool that beckoned after strenuous days on the trail. Nearby stood the outdoor shower and he stepped into its seclusion and took off his clothes. He turned up the hot water and lathered himself with a body wash that tingled sensually and with the aroma of mint and eucalyptus. He inhaled deeply, attempting to cleanse his mind from its tortuous self-abusing thoughts. He reluctantly turned off the water and realized he'd forgotten a towel.

When he stepped naked from the shower Camille was there waiting, wearing a plush white robe provided by the hotel. He imagined making love to her in the shower, but he turned away and slid into the pool. He sidled up against one of the water jets and rested his head on the ledge letting the force of the water massage his back. He seemed not to take notice when she dropped into the pool next to him. The scent of honeysuckle hung in the moist air. He was entranced by the chirping of tree frogs and the gentle tinkling of a waterfall. He slipped outside his body and hovered just above the pool. The blueness of the rippling water glimmering beneath him. It was a curious feeling, but it didn't frighten him. Instead, he thought it a pleasant release from the constraints of the earth. A lone native quetzal perched on the branch of a thick-leafed palm tree ruffled his green iridescent feathers and called out to him seductively. Are you mocking me too? He thought. The distraction returned him reluctantly to his body, deepening his feeling of isolation.

He was tired of searching for love. He'd set it up in his mind as the ideal state of being, but it was an unattainable illusion that kept him prisoner. An overwhelming sense of loss that he'd held inside for a long time engulfed him, and he let himself be swept away, beyond his control. He didn't try to stop it. It occurred to him he would never be free. Since the shooting, he'd become numb, deadened to the passion of life. It was as though he carried a weight that filled him like river stones.

He shook his head, as if to jog his memory. He was unsure whether he wished to forget or to bring clarity to his life. He was nearly forty-two and had wasted so much time trying to contain and control everyone and everything. He let his thoughts unravel, revealing moments of terror and ecstasy. Images rushed at him like muddy water through an arroyo after a downpour. His mother at the beach in Pinamar, laughing gayly as she carried him over the breaking waves, her hair tossed by the sea breeze. Ita holding his small hand tightly as they hurried through the airport. His sister, in the hospital bed, assuring him the accident was nothing. He shuddered. It seemed ages ago, though it had been little more than a week, that he'd sat in Ita's warm kitchen in the hour before dawn. She'd handed him his ancestor's chullo and poncho. You think too much, you fool, he said to himself. Then again, he wondered, I have no understanding of fate, but there must be a reason I was brought here.

"I'm thirsty," he managed to say.

His voice was languid. His eyes were closed, and his hair was slicked back and glistening in the aureate light. The image was like the conjured spirit of an Incan god. He'd been dreaming but stirred at the perfumed scent of wood burning and opened his eyes to half-mast. Camille was no longer next to him in the pool, but she'd left a robe for him on a nearby chair. The last sliver of orange could be seen lighting the edges of the mountains as it slid behind them, and a snake-like wisp of smoke uncoiled from the chimney and dispersed in the cool air.

He walked into the villa and was struck by the warmth and the yellow glow that washed over the room. A tray of fruit and a bucket of champagne was set on the table near the lit fireplace. Camille, wearing black leggings and an oversized white T-shirt printed with a colorful parrot on the front, looked up from her cell phone when he walked in.

"What are you wearing?" he asked in disbelief.

"Something clean. I hope you don't mind I dropped our clothes off at the laundry, and I went to the gift shop," she drawled, her accent slightly pronounced. "Here…" she said, handing him a shopping bag.

He looked at her wide eyed and bit his lip, displeased she'd rifled through his pack. "The giftshop? You're kidding, right?" he asked, as he pulled sweatpants and a sweatshirt from the bag. He held it up examining the artfully illustrated graphic of Huayna Picchu circumscribed with the logo of Machu Picchu. "It's a nice memento, thank you." He leaned in and kissed her cheek. The gift made him feel sentimental, and a bit homesick.

Camille shook her head as he discretely turned his back to her and tugged on the new sweatpants, then shrugging off the robe he pulled the sweatshirt over his head.

She gave him the once over, making a show of admiring him. "You are easy to please," she said, handing him an effervescing flute of champagne. "To the Inca Trail," she touched the rim of her glass to his.

Lifting his glass, he nodded solemnly and drank the contents in two quick gulps. The bubbles tickled his nose making him want to sneeze, but he refilled the glass and walked out to the garden.

It was dark now and the first stars were appearing. The pool lights under the turquoise water lit up the trees giving them a commanding stature they hadn't held in daylight. Strolling the walkway encircling the pool, he told himself his reason for returning to Peru was to continue his training with the Q'ero. But there had been a series of seemingly coincidental occurrences that landed him here with this know-it-all actress he found annoying, but with whom he was strangely attracted. It was true he'd come here to restore himself after being shot, but there were deeper reasons he hadn't shared with Camille that plagued him. He finished the champagne in the glass but decided not to go back inside just yet.

He thought about the prestige he'd achieved in L.A. Everything had been exciting. It had been easy, too easy. When touched by fame, the world was brighter, more colorful, and his perceptions were sharper. All doubt and confusion evaporated, and the sorrow that pervaded him disappeared. When he possessed fame, his magic was increased. The women, and even the men, were completely enthralled. But it had all been an illusion. He destroyed himself and everything he worked for. Every gram of cocaine had delivered a serenity that subdued the nagging anxiety and desiccating thirst that inhabited his very being. The peace it brought was always temporary. Every time he binged to tranquilize his inner loathing, he despised himself more.

I said too much already, he thought. My mind is clouded. I've lost time and memory. Cocaine will do that. Then I remembered and was ashamed. It happened with Luna. I would think, I must have told her. I'd forgotten that she knew everything. Camille said the same thing as Luna about my obsession with wealth and celebrity. Camille called it an empty quest. But who would take me seriously without those markers of achievement? Luna warned me. I hadn't done the work and wouldn't be able to handle success. If you aren't prepared for the responsibility, she said, you will be lured away from the path. Even though she wasn't religious, she quoted verse from the bible and explained its universal teaching. In Matthew, Jesus was at a spiritual high point in his life. It was now that he faced the pressure and was being tested. The devil has no power over us, she explained, when we come to the intersection of desire and opportunity, it is our choice, and ours alone, to listen to the One who is in us, our higher self.

I didn't understand what she meant at the time, but she was right. Sometimes, he thought with sudden clarity, it's impossible to see things clearly on your own. Sometimes, you need someone else to show you.

It was impossible to comprehend his life when his memories confounded him. He searched for the truth in the spider webs. He was angry that his mother got herself mixed up with those thugs—drinking, and drugs. Could it be why Papi left us? The memory of her was unsettling. There were too many unanswered questions. He remembered the money pouch hidden in the coat closet. Sometimes, I'm certain I know why she sent me away. He imagined her life after his father left, trapped, and trying to eke out just a bit of happiness before she grew old.

In New York, his father had the restaurant, filled with celebrities and party girls, and after-hours soirées at the penthouse where the cocaine was plentiful. I remember the women in fur coats and stiletto heels. I was no more than fourteen, but they would flirt with me. They never saw me reach into their handbags. I never stole much, just a few twenties they wouldn't notice were missing. I learned too young how to scratch the unsettling itch to escape, he thought, recalling the red head who took his hand and shushed him into the bedroom. Her tight dress, and the soft curve of her bare shoulders shone like pearls in the darkness, illuminated only by lights from the skyscrapers outside the window. She unzipped my jeans and sat on me; her dress pushed up around her waist. It was my first time, and I came hard and fast, hidden behind the mountain of coats on the bed. The memory caused tremors in his legs, as if he were standing in electrically charged water unable to move.

He sat on a chaise lounge facing the pool, mesmerized by the sparkling water. I wasted my life, he thought, shaking his head in self-recrimination. It had been one long party with hot girls, the cocaine flowing on the dance floor and hookups in the bathrooms of the trendiest nightclubs. The past caught up with me, he conceded, feeling the anxiety climbing like a cresting wave. Now all I want is to disappear from the world and from whoever wanted to kill me. If Ita had tried to protect him by sending him away, it hadn't done much good.

"Nico, I've been calling you," Camille said with some insistence.

Suddenly, Camille was next to him. He took her in with his eyes before speaking.

"It's beautiful out here… I'm just listening to the frogs…and thinking. What do you think I should do?" he asked.

"You mean tonight? Or, with your life?" She glanced at him as if judging.

"I'm being serious. Why do you always mock me?" he challenged, certain she wanted to make him uncomfortable.

"I don't think I do…at least it's not my intention. But you puzzle me. I suppose I'm trying to find a way in…there." She poked him in the chest, next to his heart.

"Ow! Watch it… I'm a wounded man, remember?"

"Yes." She sighed. "You certainly are…"

He held her gaze and saw she was serious and no longer being playful.

"What?" he probed. He needed to be fearless in her eyes.

"A friend of mine came by to drop something off for us." She paused, intent on peaking Nico's interest. "San Pedro. I am hoping you are willing… He cooked it himself…"

"I make my own. I don't trust anyone else," he snapped. You've got to have your own relationship with San Pedro, to empower the medicine with your intention. Who's this friend?" he asked, suspiciously.

"Someone I've known a long time," she said with assurance.

"Are you sure it's pure? The way I make it, you don't get sick."

"He's a curandero from the valley. I've taken ayahuasca and San Pedro under his guidance."

"Is he here? I'm not doing…."

Camille, hearing his agitation interrupted, "No, he went to the village. But he said he'd come back if we need him. With you going away…to Q'eros… I thought San Pedro would tell you what you need to know."

He narrowed his eyes without answering. He'd taken San Pedro many times, but he hadn't taken a drug since he'd left the hospital. He wasn't sure he was ready to alter his consciousness. What if the plant teacher didn't accept him? What if the lesson was a punishing one?

"Please don't take offense, Nico. I just thought it would bring your life into balance after your ordeal."

It took him a while before he spoke. "I'll do it." He nodded. His lips pursed as they did when he contemplated.

San Pedro makes you face your fears. If all goes well, he thought, I'll learn what I'm supposed to do next.

"But I insist we do all the traditional rituals first. It's not for recreation, you know?"

"Of course not. Never. You will be our curandero." She smiled. Glad to have won him to her side.

"We'll do the ceremony out here under the stars, the darkness offers a peaceful blanketing feeling that I find comforting. The pool will act as a crystal ball, and the moon will rise soon. As for the mesa, we'll have to use what's available." He felt better knowing he had taken charge.

"It'll be magical out here. I'm glad we're doing this together," she said.

Nico looked up at the sky and shrugged, as though shaking a burden off his shoulders.

"I've performed this ceremony for my clients. San Pedro has opened my eyes and shown me many truths. It has taught me to experience the world as divine. I know we have the power to manifest anything we choose... But..." He stopped, considering how much to share with Camille about his fears and about what brought him this low.

As if reading his mind, she said, "Nico, there's a tremendous amount to learn from the plant teachers, especially San Pedro whose healing is deeper and on an unconscious level. Our thoughts have the power to heal or destroy. You've been through a lot. The trauma of being shot and almost dying was not just physical. It took a toll on you emotionally. There's a lot you haven't told me about your past. Whatever you suffered, San Pedro will cleanse away your fears and the bad energy that has dogged you. I just know it will rekindle your love and enthusiasm for life. You'll see." She spoke with an openness, a familiarity he wasn't accustomed to hearing.

He thought her too opinionated and her boldness off-putting. He felt the need to tell her, but he couldn't think of anything to say. He pushed his hands deep into the pockets of his sweatpants and looked down at the orchid plants lining the pathway. His life had been a fiction. He'd grown accustomed to telling lies. The lies he'd told himself. The lies he'd told to everyone. It had come easily to him. People looked at him differently. He became someone other than himself, someone important and successful. Without the lies he didn't know who he was.

The aching emptiness inside him was an inexorable hunger to be whole, accepted, safe. The emptiness, he always felt the emptiness. When this demon clawed at his insides, raging, and demanding to be fed, he could not contain it. When the words came to him, they sounded to his ears like they belonged to someone else.

"I feel as lonely as an orphan. Homeless. Abandoned. I can't trust anyone, everyone betrayed me. I can't explain it…but I just can't seem to…breathe… It's as if a heavy fog is smothering me, sitting in my chest, preventing me from breathing. These negative thoughtforms are like evil beings in my soul that have crippled me. I have not been… honest or respectful…what if San Pedro punishes me?"

"That's not the way of San Pedro, Nico. You know that." She didn't attempt to touch him. She hoped the compassion in her voice would be enough.

"I can't believe I'm saying this…. But… I'm frightened."

"He will show you the way home with love. San Pedro teaches compassion and to find the light within us. You will see again through the eyes of the teacher, Nico."

He exhaled sharply, mollified by her gentle reproach. He didn't recall telling her how he went off the path, broke with the teaching, and it didn't matter. She would help him get back on. He had embarrassed himself with his despondent outburst. His dark moods had always come upon him without warning. He got hold of himself quickly.

"Then let's build a mesa. I'll collect stones from along the path, and I saw wildflowers near the waterfall. I don't suppose we can pick some of these orchids," he said with more enthusiasm than he felt.

"Uh, no. Not a good idea." She insisted with amusement.

"I'll go pick some flowers at the falls. You go to the gift shop and buy sage; they may have a smudge stick. Oh, and candy, something colorful like Mentos or Skittles. And don't forget tobacco. A pack of cigarettes will do."

° ° °

Nico dragged the white coverlet off the bed and laid it on the ground near the pool. He arranged the stones in a vertical row to represent a spine and the body's chakras. At the position of the crown chakra, he placed the flowers to symbolize the flowering of consciousness.

Cami returned with the items she was tasked to buy and handed the bag to Nico along with two vials of the San Pedro potion. Nico scattered the colorful candies across the white coverlet. "We should drink the potion now because it will take a while before we feel the effect. I'm okay drinking it in one shot instead of making tea. It's still bitter as hell."

"I'm okay with the shot, too." She rolled her eyes and held her nose preparing herself.

"Okay then," he sighed. Let's just meditate on what we are asking San Pedro. I know, I have a lot to reflect on." He let his voice trail off to thwart any further commentary from her.

They sat facing each other, the vials between them, and closed their eyes. After a few minutes they drank the bitter green juice and grabbed up some Skittles, popping the sweet candy into their mouths while pretending to gag.

"I think we are starting out with mindfulness, don't you?" She smiled and squeezed his arm.

"I just know I need answers. I think it no accident I find myself here…with you," he said in a soft voice.

He was embarrassed to look at her. He continued to distribute more of the colorful bits across the white cloth. Nothing else mattered right now. He unraveled the cigarettes and placed the loose tobacco next to a cup of champagne as an offering.

"I wish I had my guitar," he said wistfully. He still hadn't looked at her.

"Would a flute be alright? I actually brought a traditional wooden flute with me."

"Do you play?" He would have liked to play his guitar, something to ground him.

"I can play some folk songs."

"Okay, sure. Why didn't you play it on the hike?"

"There wasn't really any opportunity..."

She was headed inside when Nico called out to her, "Oh, do you have any perfume?"

He was anxious about taking San Pedro in a strange place with someone he hardly knew, but surprisingly he'd begun to accept her, and might even like her a bit. Nico lit the sage bundle and began to wash the smoke over his body. When Camille returned, she had the instrument and a small bottle of lavender oil she'd brought with her on the hike. Nico smudged her, passing the smoke over her head while he chanted a blessing in Quechua. Lastly, he dabbed them with the oil at each pulse point and they inhaled the fragrance to balance their energies. He took the cushions off two of the lounge chairs and they sat on the ground next to the mesa.

Camille began to play the flute, and Nico was rapt, dazed by the sound of the rich mournful melody. He thought he'd heard it performed a long time ago, either at church or it might have been the score to a movie, like *Lord of the Rings*. He closed his eyes to the pleasing chorus of tree frogs. Their chirping was in harmony with the soothing woodland tone of the flute. As Camille played their song grew louder. The medicine hadn't taken effect, yet he envisioned himself with Lucia as children decorating the Christmas tree in San Telmo. His parents were there smiling, handing them ornaments to hang on the tree. He heard his mother tell him to help Lucia clip a bird ornament to a branch. His first impulse was to block the vision, afraid it would plunge him into a sadness from which he wouldn't be able to climb out. He stopped resisting and allowed the memories to infuse his mind and for the medicine to show him the truth and set him free.

The chirping of the frogs and the water faded away, and his breath slowed until she stopped playing.

"What was that piece? I'm sure I've heard it somewhere."

"It's Bach's Adagio in D. I tried to learn it on the flute in school. I was never any good. But it's pretty, isn't it? Hearing it played on the cello will make you weep."

"Please, play it again."

She began the adagio again, slowly, barely a whisper. Each note recalled the pain of the past, the loss of love, and the loss of relationships. Still, the song of the flute was healing, it brought him peace. He felt the effects of the San Pedro growing. The sounds amplified and colors became more brilliant. The chorus of tree frogs resumed and another memory appeared. It was as if he were there, sitting with his family around the big table in the dining room. His father stood at the head carving a fresh ham. The room, softly lit by tall taper candles in the antique silver candelabra. Ita had made Locro, a tradition at Christmastime, and proudly carried a large tureen to the table and set it down on the white tablecloth. The steaming corn stew looked festive, yellow sprinkled with green onion and drizzled with red sauce. He'd helped Ita make bread, and through time and memory he smelled the pungent aroma of the live yeast as he kneaded the dough, placed it in a pottery bowl, and covered it with a tea towel. When she'd brought the golden loaves to the table and given him the first piece, he'd felt proud. It was as though he were experiencing it right now. He could taste the bread; it was overwhelming. The crust perfectly crispy and the inside soft and moist. The visions felt real and the colors were vibrant. Lucia wore a red velvet dress. His mother tried to tie a bib around her neck, but Lucia tugged it off.

It was a happy time, he thought. He felt safe. But everything had fallen away, and now there was no one. He had thought he was special, better than everyone. He'd been revered, sought after. The images turned grim and he tried to push them away. But it was as if a caravan of thunder clouds had rolled in and let loose a torrent, leaving in its ruinous wake mud and darkness. He pictured his mother when she became sick, the darkened bedroom heavy with the smell of death. The passion that had once illuminated her eyes had become a molten puddle from which no light shone. He became frightened and focused his mind on the water. The visions intensified. The swimming pool became filled with the almond shape of her sparkling eyes repeated on the surface of the water. He watched them smiling at him in the moonlight.

"Cami, can you see her eyes?" he called out.

Camille stopped playing and reached out and took his hand. "Tell me, what do you see?" She gazed into the shimmering pool.

"I see my mother's eyes. They are smiling at me and she is laughing."

"I see eyes everywhere!" she exclaimed.

"You mean you see them too?"

"Yes, of course..." she replied with conviction.

"Then it's real. She is real... not just in my imagination." He sighed, and the tension left his body. "She is watching over me... I had thought I lost her. But she has always been here, inside me. Her light shines on me wherever I am."

"Yes, Nico, I have been trying to tell you, but now you see for yourself." She squeezed his hand and let it go. Without him noticing, she took a photograph of the pool's glittering water and slid the phone back under her seat cushion. "San Pedro opens your eyes to what is already there."

"I think I have been exiled from the whole universe." His eyes remained fixated on the water. "Life, as I understood it, has vanished. In its place is a gaping wound of abandonment, of profound aloneness. But..." He stopped midsentence to formulate his thoughts. "These are the limits I have drawn for myself."

Camille shimmied closer to the water's edge and leaned over to scoop the water up into her hands allowing it to spill through her fingers. She did this repeatedly. Nico watched closely, mesmerized by the ripples propagating outward as each droplet fell.

"The water is purifying, isn't it, Nico?" she asked without waiting for his answer. Her subtle drawl in a voice filled with exuberance. "It can heal all our wounds. It is life giving. We can rebaptize ourselves right here, can't we? I know... it's Christian, but it's also contained in the four sacred elements. Fire, Air, Earth, and Water. You can do a clearing ceremony...to open our heart chakra, purge ourselves of what is holding us back."

"What did you ask San Pedro for?" Nico asked, watching the droplets, like diamonds, fall from her hands.

"I asked to free myself from the illusions I've created around myself," she said. "The voices in my head that won't allow me to forgive myself. I suppose I carry a heavy burden. I feel guilty." She stripped herself of the T-shirt and leggings and dangled her legs in the water. "What did you ask for?"

He looked in the pool, contemplating. His thoughts reached backwards, deeply regretting. Luna had warned him. He could hear her voice. You push everyone away, she'd said. How angry he'd become every time she criticized him. He felt guilty. He pulled away because he never felt like he really belonged. He yearned for a place where he would be irrevocably connected and loved.

"I asked for a home...but I am home, right? It's always here, in my heart. I just have to trust it."

Camille slipped into the pool, standing in the waist high water. "It's warm…are you coming in?"

Nico stripped off his sweatpants and sweatshirt and quickly dropped into the water, dunking himself fully under. He emerged from under the water with his hair plastered down his head and combed it back with his hands. His wet eyelashes glistened in the light. He appeared as a shimmering sorcerer. He captured Camille around her shoulders and swept her under the water.

"Baptism," he began. "This is the moment of your baptism, your transformation into a being of light and pure consciousness. We reconnect with the Earth, our Mother. No separation between us. It's a gift we give ourselves. Let San Pedro expel the negative winds…the bad energy, wash away the grief we hold in our hearts."

A cloud passed across the moon which had grown much larger in the sky.

"Nico, I don't want to go back…either…" Camille whispered. "Let's stay here and open a center."

She floated on her back, barely supported by Nico's hands. Her hair splayed out around her head like a halo of golden wheat waving in a blue field.

"That would be nice, wouldn't it? But if I recall, you accused me of running away." Her pale skin looked iridescent. The way she floated, with her eyes closed, reminded him of Ophelia from Shakespeare's play *Hamlet.*

"I think we would make a fine team. Maybe I was wrong to think we had to do the work in Los Angeles. It's probably the medicine talking, but I feel the energy tingling through my arms." she said swaying her body in the water.

"I'm sure it's the medicine. I feel the life flowing back into my body, and the heaviness of the world that was sitting in my chest has floated away, like a balloon into the sun."

"Nico..." she uttered his name again, as if to say amen, a benediction conferring her solemn blessing. "I have the keys to the heavens. Do you know what I'm saying? It's clear to me now. I had doubts. I believed I had to live a certain way. But now, I want to engage with the world in beauty. Let's stay here in Peru. We can open a yoga, meditation and healing center in the Sacred Valley."

Nico shrugged. Releasing Camille, he gently pushed her away, like one might shove a canoe from the shore. He floated on his back mesmerized by the pure light of the cosmos. He studied the heavens and was able to make out the edge of the Milky Way.

"I have nothing left to lose. Everything I created, and everything I believed was duradero...enduring...was destroyed. I killed myself. I'm invisible." His voice was without hope. After a moment of contemplation, he questioned her. "Camille, tell me the truth. Why did you let me come with you?"

It could be intuition, or the medicine making him feel paranoid, but he wanted to know if she could be trusted. She didn't answer right away, but she moved further away from him and stood by the wall.

"When Sabrina asked if you could join us, I felt something... intuitively. I don't know what it was exactly. I read about the shooting, and I sensed you were on a journey to heal your wounds—physical, emotional, and spiritual, too. You'd reached a level of renown that suggested you are a skilled healer. In one sense, you have returned home, not run away from it, as you believe."

The morning sun through the window had made the room unpleasantly warm. Nico kicked off the comforter and untangled himself from the bed sheet. Opening his eyes, he saw Camille curled beside him, sleeping, her blonde hair spread over the white pillow like an angel's wing. Her breathing was a soft snore, like the purr of a kitten. Last night they'd been intimate. She possessed a confidence fitting with her celebrity, that he did not share. He'd become insignificant. He slipped from the bed and cranked the window open letting the cool mountain air into the over-heated bedroom. Walking to the bathroom, his bare feet squished into Camille's wet underwear lying on the floor, a reminder of last night. Glimpsing himself in the mirror, he was startled by the wild tangled tufts of hair framing his scruffy face. The watery blue tiles pulsed like jellyfish contracting and relaxing in a steady rhythm. After relieving himself he gulped cold water from the sink before remembering he should have drunk bottled water. Splashing the water on his face, he ran his fingers through his hair, and he felt the earth beneath him. His thoughts began to organize themselves. Each time he'd taken San Pedro it was as though it was the first. The vividness of colors had decreased, and he was no longer seeing geometric patterns repeating on the walls. He gargled with minty mouthwash provided by the hotel, took bottled water from the mini-fridge, and returned to the bed. Camille stirred, and he placed the cold bottle against the back of her neck.

"Mmm," she hummed.

He rolled it down her spine until she turned over. "How do you feel?" he asked, as she squinted into the light. He twisted off the cap and handed her the bottle.

"Thanks," she said huskily. As she sat up the sheet fell revealing her naked breasts. After quenching her thirst, she nodded. "I hate the thought of going back to L.A. I should open a center here in Peru."

"My intention was always to stay here, with the Q'ero, at least for a while. Does your plan still include me?"

"I should think so." She blinked at him, trying to block the sun from her eyes. "I can't possibly do it all alone. Besides, I like having you around." Her hand slowly emerged from beneath the sheet and softly closed around him. Her expression remained impassive as she gazed up at him, as if it were the most natural thing to do.

The overt action confused him. He was unsure of her, as he should be. She was a married woman with a child. During the climb she hadn't once flirted with him. She'd confided in him about her personal life, but mostly, she was judging him.

Her thumb pressed along the ridge, as though smoothing a scar, and he began to swell. He slid his hand behind her neck and into her hair. Her eyes, greener than he remembered, flickered playfully. He held her gaze, wishing he could admit to her that he liked having her around, too. She desired him, he thought. But he couldn't be sure. He'd come to Peru, and unforeseen he met this woman, and she made him feel new. The fear that had been gripping him was lessened by her presence. Her mouth parted slightly, and he kissed her with a hunger he'd been suppressing. He lingered briefly on her lips feeling her awaken.

Breathlessly, he whispered near her ear, "I've never met anyone like you…"

She traced her fingers down his spine, the slight gesture was enough to draw him closer to her. He had the sense of moving in slow motion, as if sleepwalking, without the impatient urgency he normally possessed. It must be the lingering effects of the San Pedro, he thought. Her breasts were small but round and firm, and her nipples responded under his touch. Wordlessly, she guided his hand down. He positioned himself between her legs feeling her open to him like a night flower. Her skin glowed, translucent as a firefly, and she arched her body melting into him. He listened to the birds conversing in the trees outside the window. He moved slowly. She was trembling, like a frightened deer. In that moment, a disorienting strobe-light flashed in his mind's eye of Maya dressed for a fight scene, her supple body flexing underneath him. It's the San Pedro causing visions, he told himself. A voice called to him, hauntingly. It was Gaby, asking when he was coming home. Home. He took a deep breath and exhaled slowly. Ita's weathered face appeared in his mind and called his name. No es tu culpa, it's not your fault, she said. Not my fault. Not my fault, he repeated almost aloud, until he pushed the visions away.

"Cami…" he whispered. "The San Pedro… it's playing with me…."

"I'm here, Nico." She held his face in her hands. "It's okay, just look at me…" she murmured, her warm breath on his neck gave him goosebumps.

Her fingers, gentle and unhurried, sent him beneath a sea of white light where the timeline between reality and dreamscape collapsed. He focused on her as wave upon wave rolled into the shore.

"Stay with me," he uttered huskily.

Their bodies were slick with sweat and cum, and the musky, primal scent of sex hung thickly in the room. She moved out from under him, and he rolled onto his back uncomfortably aware that he'd been holding her tightly. A wetness was on his cheeks, then saltiness in his mouth and he realized they were his tears falling like fat rain drops from a pregnant storm cloud.

° ° °

The rain. He remembered the rain. The San Pedro was still sending visions, pulling him back in time, forcing him to remember. He'd ridden his bike over in a rainstorm and carried the heavy grocery bag up the stairs. The vision was as clear as a movie. The red and white Campbell's soup cans had torn through the melting wet brown paper and he clutched the bag tightly to his chest and knocked on the door. Mrs. Sanchez smiled when she saw him. She wore an apron over a floral dress, her dark hair streaked with grey was knotted in a bun on top of her head. The water dripped from his hair and his wet pants clung to his legs. She invited him in to wait out the rain. As always, there was a place set for him at the kitchen table—it was chrome with a yellow Formica top and matching vinyl covered chairs. She gave him sweatpants and a T-shirt that had been her son's and put his wet clothes in the dryer.

He thought to himself but dared not speak out loud. I can still taste the creamy tomato soup with little crackers floating on top. I couldn't hold my eyes open, and she said to go in the back room and nap while my clothes dried. I could swear he'd been there, a tall boy, much older than me standing in the doorway, unshaven with unkempt hair that needed a wash. The voice came from an adjacent room, "So you're Nico?" he said in a menacing tone. I don't know how long I'd slept. I stumbled into the kitchen and called out, but Mrs. Sanchez didn't answer. The dryer had stopped but was still warm. I changed into my dry clothes and rode my bicycle home. The next day Ita told me Gloria Sanchez had been murdered. I couldn't breathe. In two days, I was in New York. It had to have been my fault, he thought, his heart pounding loudly in his ears. But...there was something else. A secret I am not brave enough to tell anyone. Not even Ita.

° ° °

"Are you okay, Nico?" Camille's muffled voice drifted through the fog.

"That was intense," he stammered, pushing his way back to the present. "The San Pedro gave me flashes. I remember..." He managed to swallow a lump of emotion.

She sat up and placed her hand on his cheek. "You will be fine, Nico. Come, let's take a shower, you'll feel better."

"Wait." He grabbed her arm a bit to firmly. Releasing her, he sighed, contemplating the escaped tendril snaking along her jawline. He leaned forward, inches from her face. "I need to ask you..." he murmured, tucking the hair behind her ear. "People need a place where they belong, don't they?" He wouldn't show his fear, but the thought of her leaving was distressing.

"Yes, I suppose they do..." She responded thoughtfully. "The feeling of being connected to family, friends, or something greater than us provides a sense of identity."

"I've never had this... connection." He stretched out that last word for emphasis. "Every time I thought it might be there for me, I lost it—like sand through my fingers."

"Nico, we all lose things we treasure." Her voice was measured. Consoling, like speaking to a child. "People become lost to us, same as opportunities we can never get back. The sum of life is loss. But we have our memories. They live forever... like the library at Hogwarts," She added playfully.

"Now you are making fun of me." The humiliation made him

angry and he turned away.

"Nico..."

"Forget it," he snapped. "You could never understand..."

Taking his hand, she quickly assured him, "I just meant...to fill our hearts we have to write new stories for our personal library." Playfully, she pressed her foot against his thigh. "Come on, we have to get going."

Ignoring her, he asked, "Are memories that important? I would rather forget the past."

"I think they are the most important thing we carry with us. You can't change what's already happened. It'd be like trying to lasso the moon."

"I don't trust them," he scoffed.

She turned to face him, and her voice softened. "I want you to remember me."

"I don't think I could forget you." There was a dose of sarcasm in his voice. He wanted to take her picture, but he knew she wouldn't let him. Studying her face, he added, "There isn't anyone I can count on. When I leave Q'eros, I have no place to go back to."

"Look Nico, I meant what I said about us working together, and if we are together in other ways... that's fine too." She got up from the bed. He lay back on the warm sheets allowing the sun to bathe him. He could be content with this woman beside him, imagining a new world opening to him.

Trailing her to the bathroom, he called after her, "Are you saying you could fall in love with me?"

"It's easier to be with someone you don't love romantically." She didn't sound cynical. Rather, it was a plain statement of belief.

"I thought you believed in love?" he said. Her statement seemed incongruous with everything she'd been touting.

"I do. But falling in love is like Narcissus infatuated with his own reflection, searching for the missing pieces of himself." She'd turned on the faucet. If she said more, he didn't hear her.

He listened to the falling water. Was there a meaning to what she'd said? He yearned for something deeper but each time he'd seen a glimmer off to the side it had disappeared like a mirage in the desert. He thought about the ripples in the pool. He'd been mesmerized watching them travel out from the center in ever-expanding circles traveling outward, searching. Trying to fill the empty space.

He stepped into the shower and watched her massage the shampoo into her scalp. She kept her eyes closed, and he admired the gentle curve of her ass as the soapy water ran down her pale unblemished back. Without a word, he placed her palms against the tiles and parted her legs, arranging them with care. She reached beneath to guide him, and he entered her thinking he wanted her to remember him, too. She's famous and can have anyone she wants, he thought. Yet, she's given herself to me with such generosity. She'd told him she hadn't had sex in over a year. Regardless of her fame, he thought she was lonely. He held her close to possess her more fully. He was proving how much he desired her, making her his own.

∘ ∘ ∘

Camille stepped out of the shower without a backward glance. Taking a towel from the rack, she left the bathroom. He was unable to stop thinking about the impossibility of their paths converging, a random collision of planets spinning into each other's gravity. I never met someone whose desires and dreams aligned with mine, he thought, as the hot water and steam enveloped him. The others had their own interests. They all lied to me and betrayed me. I'm alone again, always alone. Doubt filled him. Why should I think this will be different? She'll use me like the rest of them. I won't allow myself to have hope. What did Cami call it? Ikigai. She said it was your reason for being. I know my purpose in life. I'm a healer. I lost what I had—the studio, my clients. I had to leave L.A. But I am still the best. With Cami, her money, and her connections, I can make it happen.

Toweling himself off, he heard Camille call out their clothes had come back from the laundry. He brushed his teeth, shaved, and combed his hair back off his forehead. A package of new boxer briefs from the hotel store sat on the top of the bundle of clean folded clothes. The thoughtful gesture confounded him. In the week they'd traveled together, he'd come to know things about her, things she had told him. But you can't know someone's thoughts. He kissed her forehead. "Is there anything you don't think of?" he asked, as he dressed, then shoved the clothes into his pack.

"I imagine it's because I'm a mother," she said, not giving his sentimentality much significance.

He watched Camille wrap her flute in a scarf and place it within the stack of clean folded clothes in her backpack. The attentiveness she paid to small details reminded him of Luna. He remembered how Luna had organized his dresser drawers. She said external disorder reflected internal chaos.

A jasmine scented breeze floated in the open window, and the hairs on the back of his neck prickled with the memory of the visions from the previous night. He wanted to forget the culmination of his painful past. His brow furrowed. Stalling for time, he knelt to tie his boots, shielding his face from Camille. He hated the thought of parting from her. He swallowed hard, and still his voice cracked. "I have to go back to Cusco to collect my things. Are you taking a car back?" He stood and fiddled with the buckles on his pack.

She looked over at him, hesitating, but he didn't meet her gaze.

"I'm not going to Cusco. You'll have to take the train." She crossed the room placing more distance between them.

"Are you going back with your husband?" he blurted, unable to conceal his confusion.

"Not exactly… I have something to do. You're going to Q'eros, aren't you?"

"Yes, but…" A palm leaf tapped the window, startling him. When he looked back, she had left the room. He should say something. He wanted to convince her to take him with her, but the words wouldn't come. He slung the pack across his shoulder and went to where she stood reading something on her phone. Coming up behind her, he brushed her hair aside and kissed her neck. He wanted to hold her the way he would the memory of their days together, but something prevented him from it.

"I'm sorry, Nico. I need to be alone now."

He nodded and walked to the door. He wanted to ask her when they would see each other again. The question welled up inside him, making it difficult to breathe. He looked back and asked, "When…will I see you?"

"I was afraid… and I made choices that hurt me and my family. It's something I have to live with." She hesitated, then added as an aside, "I need to find the missing pieces of myself."

"But… where are you going?"

"I'm going to Iquitos."

"Shouldn't I go with you?"

"I thought about it, but no. You are too much of a distraction." She tilted her head slightly to one side as if reconsidering. "Besides, you have to find the strength to grapple with your affliction… this burden you haul around. Come to terms with your mistakes."

"I know," he mumbled reluctantly.

"Do you?" She smiled as though she held a secret.

A sudden weight pressed down on him, and without answering he walked out. Again, I'm alone, he thought. He barely recalled the taxi ride to the train station. There were families with young children pushing carts piled with old luggage. Hikers were waiting for the train. Some sat on the platform and leaned against their heavy packs. They looked tired having just returned from Machu Picchu, their clothes soiled and with the damp, gamey odor of sweat. He made his way among them to the ticket booth; the line to buy tickets was long. After buying the ticket to Cusco he stood on the platform and looked down the track. The cloud forest tumbled over the mountains and through the streets, pouring itself into the river. Machu Picchu was falling away. She had taken him there. He wouldn't forget. The train didn't depart for over an hour and an impatient tightness gripped his chest. Propping his pack on a bench as a pillow, he lay gazing up at the colorless sky, his mind racing with worry. Will Don Castillo be there? he asked himself. I am certain he will not take me back, he thought. After all, he'll know I failed, violated my oath...misused my power.

He shifted back and forth on the bench. "Mierda!" He pressed his hands over his eyes blocking out the light. "Dios ayúdame," he whispered softly.

He sat up and rubbed his thighs with his hands to keep from fidgeting. I wish I weren't alone, he thought. But you are alone, he agonized, his anxiety percolating, and you have only yourself. He heard pigeons cooing and watched them competing over breadcrumbs being tossed to the pavement by an old man on the next bench.

"Fight for it, pigeon," he said to the bird beating his wings to keep the others at bay.

Just beyond the station he saw a sign for Hostel Amaru and smiled inwardly at the irony. An omen, he thought. I will have my studio back, hopefully soon. He picked up his pack and crossed the avenue feeling only mildly encouraged. The café had a large snakeskin tacked to the wall. He walked up to the bar, ignoring two guys playing billiards and ordered a bottle of the local beer.

"Is that an Anaconda?" he asked.

The bartender looked at it as if he'd never noticed it and shrugged. He saw himself in the foxed mirror behind the bar, shadowed and older. There was something Luna had written to him from the bible. He'd read it over and over to gain its meaning, For now we see through a glass, darkly... He understood his life only in part. There were times he remembered clearly, other things, the meaning of his existence was lost to him. Everything he'd believed, it had been clouded by desire.

He took the beer over to a table in a dark corner of the room. He listened to the soft click of the billiard balls. The room was rich with the odor of tobacco. Taking a long pull on the bottle, he considered texting Luna but didn't want to face the rejection if she didn't respond. Instead he texted Maya.

Are you okay? She responded within seconds.

He was on the verge of sobbing, but wrote, *I'm tired.*

I've been worried... Where are you?

Waiting for the train back to Cusco.

Are you in Q'eros?

I told you I was going to Machu Picchu. You never listen.

Nico, if you told me, I would have remembered. Are you going to Q'eros?

Yes, of course. Don't be an idiot. I'm going tomorrow. His leg bounced rapidly as he punched the keys. Damn, I forgot, he thought. I need a guide. There was no immediate reply. Then it came.

I miss you…

He sighed. There were moments he missed her. She was easy to be with. She never challenged him. He ignored the words on the screen. What am I'm doing? he thought. Resting his head heavily on his hand, he pounded the keys with one finger. *I have a lot on my mind, Maya…*

I found a place for the studio…just off Wilshire. I sent you pictures.

The train is coming. I'll call you from Cusco. He chugged what was left of the beer.

Nico… I love you.

I have to go.

Despite a chill in the air, beads of perspiration peppered his brow. Hands resting on the table, he stared at the phone's screen until it went dark, feeling as depleted as the empty beer bottle in front of him, a metaphor for his life. He lived with an aching feeling that he'd done something wrong, as if he were bad and deserved to be unloved.

"Secuelas," he muttered aloud. No one can undo the past, or escape the consequences of their actions, he thought.

He closed his eyes and the room spun as visions appeared. He was with his mother on the beach in Pinamar. He smelled the sea and listened to the waves lap the shore.

How could she leave me if she loved me? he asked himself.

For the first time, I don't know what I want, he thought. Camille had said, "I want you to remember me." Yet, she left her family, her son, the people she loved. Time is a trickster and her words felt hollow. It hurts to remember everyone I've lost. I'm caught between two worlds. Like Orpheus, once I leave, I can't look back.

° ° °

Outside was too bright, and it took a minute for his eyes to adjust. He watched the train come in, listening to the clicking of the wheels on the rails as it lengthened down the platform, the vivid blue color of the locomotive magnificent against the looming mountains surrounding the village. His body grew heavier as he walked to where the conductor was collecting tickets.

On board he found a seat and lifted his pack onto the overhead rack. The seats in the car filled, and he was relieved the seat next to him remained vacant. He looked over across the aisle to where a couple sat holding hands. Honeymooners, he thought. On the rack above them were two matching orange backpacks that looked brand new. A group of teenagers, most likely on break from school, sat a few rows away. He couldn't make out what language they were speaking.

He looked out the window at the corrugated roofs of souvenir shops and beer stalls, crowds of tourists haggling with street vendors. He heard the doors close, and then a hiss and groan when the train began to move. The buildings began to slide away as the train gathered speed, and an emptiness in his chest gnawed at him like a dog on a bone.

Suddenly, he missed Camille. He regretted not insisting he go with her. Through his own reflection he watched the Urubamba River rush alongside the tracks, light glinting off the water, much the same as when he had arrived. The train switched back around the curves, and the village passed smoothly from sight. It was another ending.

His memories were a blur, like the landscape through the train window. From his pack he withdrew a small leather journal, a gift from Luna. Inside the flyleaf she had written, *Bring forth what is within you to save you.* It was from the gospel of Thomas, she'd told him. Until now, he hadn't thought about what it meant. He pressed his hand on the window in benediction to the mountain spirits as they disappeared behind him.

The monotonous churn of the engine and rhythmic rocking of the train car carried him mercilessly closer to the unknown. The track curved away and the sun peeked out from behind the mountains illuminating fields that had endured for millennia. Swaths of iridescent green fused with the majesty of plum-colored peaks against an azure sky until his eyes closed.

In his dream he walked hand in hand with his mother on the beach. The salt air carried no sound other than the sigh of the tide cresting and falling to earth, its breath slow and meditative. Her hair is gathered at the back in a ponytail, and she's wearing small diamond earrings that sparkle in the windless autumn light. She looks over at him with eyes timeless and serene, and doesn't say anything. When he woke, she was gone, like a ghost at dawn.

In Ollanta he took a taxi to Cusco. Near the hotel, a colorfully dressed Quechua woman crossed in front of them, her shawl draped casually behind her guiding the energy forward. She knows the future comes from behind. Time is fluid, flowing through us. It was time to create a new story, one of his own.

The early morning sky was as pale grey as the frost on the window. The mist cloaked the mountains, like a weathered old woman wrapped in a shawl, and a whiteness spread into the distance merging with the sky. In the hotel lobby, a carafe of burnt coffee hissed, and Nico filled a large to-go cup before stepping into the street.

Standing under a halo of yellow light cast by the streetlamp, he watched two wiry stray dogs dash across the deserted cobblestones in search of breakfast. The crisp air crackled, and he tugged his chullo down over his ears. The dew crunching under his feet left footprints on the green as he crossed the plaza. Turning the corner, he saw the darkened windows of the travel agency, and he kicked the curb. Pacing in front of the shop, he checked his cell phone and looked again at the sign on the door.

The wind gusted and he cursed under his breath. He wished he had a cigarette. He often dreamt of smoking and of being high and wondered if the craving for tobacco and cocaine would ever subside. His nose was cold, and he nuzzled his face down into his scarf. It was the scarf he'd bought with Camille when they stopped at the market in Pisac. He leaned against the stone wall as shelter from the wind and drank the coffee, its subtle warmth flowed down his throat spreading into his chest. His mind drew a blank when he tried to remember the name of the travel agent. To pass the time, he ran through the alphabet in his head, and when he finally got to the S's he said aloud, "Sabrina."

From the shadows he saw her unlock the gate and go inside. The lights went on and he waited a few minutes, not wanting to appear eager. At the sound of the door opening, she looked up.

"Mr. Romero! It's nice to see you. How was the trek?" A knowing smile spread across her face.

The temperature in the room wasn't much warmer than outside and she was sitting behind the counter still wearing her coat.

He thought he should be angry with her for concealing the identity of his famous traveling companion but admitted to himself he was no longer annoyed.

"It was an adventure. But I'm sure you already knew that."

She stepped out from behind the desk and hung up her coat. At the coffee station in the waiting area she picked up a white mug with the illustration of a black llama on it and the words, DALAI LLAMA. He thought it was funny, and that she had a quirky sense of humor for having it. He still held the paper cup from the hotel.

"I just made coffee. Do you wanna refill?" she asked

"Sure. Just black…" He handed her his empty cup and shifted impatiently as he waited.

Her back was to him, and he studied her long black hair, thick as a horse's tail, falling to her waist. She wore a wide-neck embroidered white blouse that emphasized her bronze skin-tone. Her Quechua countenance was more apparent than when he first met her. He felt uneasy. Not from anything she said, only her apparent confidence. He envied her ability to gaze in the mirror and know her identity, her place in the world. Though curious, he curbed his desire to inquire about her heritage to discourage her from questioning him in turn.

"I need my coffee in the morning, and you're at least one cup ahead of me." She handed the steaming cup back to him.

"Thanks," he whispered, careful not to spill the brimming liquid. Noticing a thin gold band on her ring finger, he looked away intimidated by her openness. He dreaded asking her to help him get to Q'eros. He searched for the words, but they lay beyond his grasp.

Thinking back, it was as though it had been someone else's life. He must have been around twenty, he thought, escorting tourists up to Q'eros. The altitude had made him light-headed after living at the beach in Kerala. But the sight of the Quechua girls laughing gayly, their colorful skirts like parasols twirling as they danced during the Festival of the Sun had elicited the same wonder and simple contentment he'd felt in India. A darkness veiled his eyes picturing Nitya during Holi, her beauty unrivaled, wearing a white linen tunic drenched in the vibrant colors of joy. Suddenly, he missed her terribly. Why was he always trailing ashes, unable to mark his place in the world? He couldn't recall her voice and felt regret. She'd be married with a family by now, he thought. For a moment, he imagined himself happy in India with Nitya, forgetting he had felt trapped, unfulfilled, and with a compulsion to escape that was too strong to ignore.

In Q'eros he had felt free, withdrawn from the world. There had been other young people his age studying with the paqos, but he believed he was superior. It had been the beginning of his life as a healer. Performing the despacho ceremony had been spiritually intoxicating, and he'd been impatient to make a name for himself. He thought he'd forged his destiny, but now realized he'd only stumbled into his fate, compelled to repeat his discontent under different guises.

Camille was right, he was like Sisyphus pushing the same rock uphill for eternity. Ha! he said to himself, I'm afraid because I've been here before. Somehow, he thought, the past I've neglected must be reconciled. Every time I'm on the verge of making something happen for myself, it never works out. What if I don't fit in? What if the paqos don't accept me? He'd been pacing the little travel office deep in thought, and Sabrina was looking at him with curiosity.

"Sit, Nico. You're makin' me nervous." She'd made herself comfortable on the sofa as if she had all day to visit with him.

"It's nothing. I have a lot on my mind. I was gone too long…" He ran a comb of fingers through his hair then sat in the hard chair across from her. She stood no taller than his chest, but her presence was formidable.

"I had a feeling you and Camille would hit it off."

"Why'd you think that?" he said. He was careful not to show his fondness for Camille.

"You were disappointed when I said we were booked up. And, well, Camille Hawks… It was easy to figure her out. You know what I mean?"

"No. Tell me…"

"We get a lot of movie stars who trek to Machu Picchu. They're all searching for answers." She shrugged.

"Well, you know she's separated from her husband and having a difficult time." He was surprised he came that quickly to her defense.

"Then it was kind of you to accompany her," she said.

He was not sure if she'd intended sarcasm. It took him a while to gather his thoughts. He stared out the glass door. The sun had erased the low hanging grey clouds and a yellow ribbon had unfurled in the street.

"I wasn't much help. She's stubborn and bossy," he said.

He recalled Camille telling him to leave, she wanted to go alone to the jungle. I should have insisted on going with her, he said to himself.

"I wouldn't be so sure." Again, her mouth curled up in an enigmatic smile.

"What do you mean?" He leaned in. "Have you spoken to her?" He hadn't meant to sound as unnerved as he did.

"No, I only meant it takes a while to appreciate the effect people have on each other. Will you see her again?"

He didn't know the answer. He hoped he would. He was inclined to say yes but couldn't be sure. "Probably…" He shrugged as if it didn't matter to him.

"What's next? Will you be staying in Cusco?"

He'd been waiting for this opportunity. "Actually, I was hoping you can help me get to Q'eros."

"Oh, really? I have a seven-day tour to Q'eros with a Huachuma ceremony at Lake Kinsacocha leaving on the weekend."

"No, I need to get there directly. I hope only one-way."

Her dark eyes narrowed. "Have you been invited?"

He shook his head. He could feel his jaw clench, evidence of his unease. He hated relying on her, but he had no choice.

"Then you'll have to be escorted." She paused. When he didn't respond, she continued. "I might be able to arrange it. First, tell me why?"

He bit his lower lip. "I died. Well, almost… If you Googled me. Camille Googled…" They were words he had never spoken. Having almost died didn't really convey how he felt. It was as if his body slowly surfaced from the depths of a black sea.

"Well…" she nodded despite being perplexed. "Camille told me you'd been shot. But you certainly didn't die…" Her voice trailed off in disbelief.

A pained expression contorted his face.

"Coming back from death is a gift. It's like being struck by lightning," she said. She saw a flash of recognition on his face.

"Possibly..." He nodded. "In any case, I can't go home," he said through a clenched jaw.

"I'm sorry, Nico," she said sympathetically. "They never caught who shot you? Do you wanna hide out in Q'eros?" Her tone was honeyed though she remained unconvinced of his dire straits.

He stood and angrily tossed his cup into the trash. The remaining dregs of coffee spattered the wall. "Forget it, you wouldn't understand." He went for the door.

"There, you're doing it again." She looked at him with disapproval.

He stopped and turned to face her. He let out a long sigh that would blow at least the first pig's house down. "What do you want me to do?" he pleaded, hoping she had the answers to the questions he'd sought his entire life.

"Tell me why you need to go to Q'eros."

He paraded the room. His words, train cars slamming into each other piled up in quick succession. It took a minute for him to sort out what he wanted to say.

"As a child I was taken to Qoyllur Rit'i and given Karpay. My grandmother said it's in my blood—I'm a healer. Just before I left to come here, she told me I have ancestors who were high paqos." His voice was clear and without underlying desperation.

When Sabrina didn't respond, he continued, "Years later, my mother became ill. I went to Q'eros to learn how to heal her. But I haven't been back there in twenty years." He sat back and put his head in his hands. His shoulders slumped in dismay.

"What's troubling you, Nico?" She tilted her head.

"What if they won't accept me?"

"Is there some reason they shouldn't?"

He bounced his knee and slowly released the breath he'd been holding.

"I studied under Don Castillo." He stopped and looked at his hands folded in his lap. When he looked up, their eyes met. "I thought I was ready, that I could heal my mom. I shouldn't have left when I did. I was there less than a year. I know I'm not worthy."

An uncomfortable silence ensued. Sabrina finally spoke. "Admitting you aren't worthy is a good beginning."

Nico said nothing. He gazed unseeing out the window behind her, his face unrevealing.

"Were you able to heal your mother?"

He jolted to attention. Her words stung like angry hornets. He glared at her to see if she'd meant to hurt him, but she showed no sign of malicious intent.

"She died…" He breathed as though in prayer, closing his eyes to lock in the tears.

"I'm sorry." She didn't move to console him, but the compassion in her voice was enough.

"Look, Sabrina…" He stood and paced the room like a caged lion anticipating death or freedom and welcoming either. Raking his hair back off his forehead he blurted, his voice dripping with desperation. "You read what happened to me… My luck is over. I fell off the path," he confessed. "Until I am reborn, I can't begin de nuevo… anew."

"I'll get you an escort, Nico. When do you want to leave?"

"Tomorrow morning," he said with relief. He'd lost everyone's respect, but he wouldn't disappoint his grandmother.

° ° °

The Jeep had been waiting in front of the hotel since sunrise. Its motor sputtered roughly. Manuel frowned and looked at his watch again. It would be a long enough day without a late start. Strumming his fingers on the steering wheel, he calculated the drive to Paucartambo. Just under four hours if the road was clear. Half an hour late, Nico appeared muttering about being over-charged. Laden with his pack, duffle, and guitar case, he lumbered toward the car trying not to spill a precariously balanced cup of coffee. Leaping to Nico's aid, Manuel made a hasty introduction while tossing the luggage in the back.

Nico paused and surveyed the Jeep skeptically. Dead on the highway, he thought, considering the timeworn vehicle on a hazardous road.

"Estará bien," he assured him registering the trepidation on Nico's face. With a grand flourish, he opened the passenger door as if it were Cinderella's carriage.

Manuel introduced himself emphasizing the proper Spanish pronunciation even though he was sure it was unnecessary given Nico was Argentine.

"Nico," he shrugged, shaking his hand. Shoving his daypack on the floor beside his feet, he slid the seat back to accommodate his long legs.

Manuel removed a brown paper sack from a basket and offered it to Nico. "My wife made empanadas," he said. "She learned from my mother." The pride evident by his broad toothy smile.

"Thank you." Taking the golden pastry from the bag he took a bite, savoring the flavors. "Mmm, similar to mine. The roasted corn complements the chicken and cheese."

"You are a cook, señor?"

"At home..." Nico said. The words caught in his throat. "In Argentina. I learned from mi abuela. We make meat empanadas with onion, and chimichurri."

As a child he'd trailed Ita around the kitchen, dragging his little wooden stool up to the counter so he could see. She helped him spoon the filling into the center of each circle, then fold them in half. He carefully crimped them closed with the tines of a fork. Afterwards, they each ate one. He was proud when she nodded her approval.

I can't bear the thought of losing Ita, he thought. How could I leave her? She's old. I'll call her when we get to the town, he said to himself.

"There's more in the basket behind you. Help yourself. It's a long drive."

The white buildings were in shadow. Manuel downshifted and they wound their way out of the city. Nico clamped the headphones over his ears. He hadn't slept well, and he pulled the hood of his sweatshirt up shielding his eyes to curtail further conversation. The battery wouldn't last long, but for now the exotic, passionate sound of India flooded him as the Jeep bumped over the cobblestones lulling him to sleep.

He pictured himself back in the studio, the rows of women in designer yoga outfits moving through the postures, all eyes upon him. Limber bodies in downward facing dog, their butts in the air. Long blonde ponytails and chestnut brown curls tumbling onto the matt. Sofia, her skin pale as bleached bone. Maya, her tawny legs wrapped firmly around his buttocks. He'd taken it all for granted.

The monotonous drone of the Jeep's engine became a comforting velvet curtain shielding him. Outside the city, the thudding tires gave way to humming like a hive of bees. A milk-white sky had opened in front of him. They drove through villages dotted by thatched roof structures. Women tended to sheep in meadows, and a barking dog chased the Jeep until it was safely away from the herd. For long stretches the land was barren and brown, then terraced and green, lush with the promise of a harvest.

"We'll spend the night in Paucartambo." After driving for hours, Manuel announced the plan leaving no room for discussion. "It's the festival of the Virgin del Carmen. There will be food and drink, and certainly the paqos will be there to give despacho to the tourists." Again, there was that wide toothy grin to which Nico released a sigh of acquiescence.

He skirted the city, driving through the backstreets, until they came to a stop in a narrow carport attached to a traditional white stucco house on the Mapacho river. A youthful woman came out of the house and cheerfully greeted them. Manuel introduced her as his niece, Tica. She obviously had been expecting them and carried Nico's bags to a converted guest room off the kitchen that may have once served as a food pantry. The small home was cozy and inviting in the folkloric style of the town with woven textiles adorning the sofa and table. Especially enticing was the aroma of roast pork cooking on the stove.

"We are missing it!" Tica hurried them out to the back porch overlooking the river, dazzling in the sunlight. A short distance down river was an arched stone bridge, the jewel of the city, built in the late eighteenth century. On the bridge, in clear view, was the procession of the Virgin being carried atop a platform to her temple.

"Come, come." Urged Tica, as the effigy passed from their view. "You are later than expected. Everyone is in the square."

14

Spectators overflowed the cerulean blue balconies of the colonial town. They leaned over the railings as they cheered the troupes of masked dancers in colorful costumes parading the cobblestone streets. Winding their way to the square Nico and the others were jostled and carried by the throng. The air was clear and the sun warm, but it was the press of the crowd that caused Nico's heart to race and rivulets of perspiration to run down the back of his neck. In the plaza, musicians and actors performed slapstick mock-battles emulating the ancient wars during the time of the Incas. Nico retreated from the bustle and leaned against a pillar. Panic crept in slowly and took hold of him by the throat. The feeling was well-known to him. He thought himself foolish and breathed slowly to get his bearings. His mouth was dry, and he looked about hopefully for something to quench his thirst. As if answering his silent plea, Manuel appeared at his side and handed him a cold beer.

"Thanks, man…" he nodded gratefully. He took a long pull on the bottle and felt the tension leave his body.

There were children playing nearby, shrieking as they chased one another. A man wearing hiking shorts and a woman wearing a baseball cap to shield her face from the sun were taking pictures with their cell phones.

With Manuel standing beside him, Nico's anxiety subsided. They watched the dancers amidst the cacophony of music and revelry. The Saqra dancers—tricksters in animal masks, their costumes a rainbow of multicolored ribbons—performed daring acrobatics and leaped from the rooftops into the street to tempt the faithful to the dark side. Some wore gloves with claws, reaching into the crowd to abduct one of the devotees. Nico gasped and jumped back when one of the dancers, a devilish character with horns carrying a trident, tried to snatch him from the sidelines before spinning away to engage in battle with a dancer wearing a bird-like mask.

"Those are Tica's kids." Manuel laughed heartily and nudged Nico.

"What is the meaning?" Nico took a big step back from the dancers.

"It is simply the dance of good and evil."

The fierce dancers, in a parody borrowed from *Dante's Inferno*, tormented the Spanish conquistadors in a battle that signaled an end to the hostilities. The war against the demons was finished and the faithful emerged triumphant.

If only I could scare off my demons forever, Nico thought. Sorrow filled him. It felt familiar. It was as if he relied upon this sadness to know himself.

Their shadows grew longer as they walked back to the little house on the river. Tica's husband, Emilio, still wearing the kilt of the Virgin's honor guard, carried a tall crown of feathers in the crook of his arm. Together, their laughter echoed off the buildings. The two teenagers had removed their frightening masks and Nico saw they were brother and sister, possibly twins, now playfully chasing each other down the lane toward home. The air felt heavy as the light went down on them, like a grey wool blanket. Hearing the river, he lifted his head. A lamp had been left on in the living room, its warm glow a welcoming sign.

Removing their shoes at the door they gathered around the table. Tica served bowls of pork and potatoes while Emilio handed out beers from the ice chest. Nico picked up his fork then set it back down, remembering his manners. Looking around the table, it occurred to him no one knew who he was or what he had been. Everyone was talking over each other, laughing as they replayed the day's festivities. He bowed his head studying the meal in front of him. Gracias a Dios, he said to himself. It was one of the rare moments in his life when he didn't feel alone.

Nico turned when a hand rested on his shoulder. "Are you okay, my friend?" Manuel's brow furrowed with concern.

"Just tired." Nico smiled weakly.

After dinner Nico stepped out onto the back porch. He wished he had a cigarette. Across the river a yellow light coming from the church blinked intermittently like a beacon, an illusion created by the movement of trees. Far off in the direction of the square someone was playing a flute; the melody was of piercing beauty. As night fell the water blackened. The moon had yet to rise. He stood silently in the gathering darkness and listened to the river. The water chuckled, mocking him. You are nothing, she burbled, rippling over boulders and branches, her lips softly kissing the stone retaining wall.

You are right to laugh, he thought, it's a cruel joke life has played on me. The stone bridge now in shadow was like a charcoal drawing against a sumptuous purple sky. I am caught in a maelstrom. Nothing I longed for has come to pass, he said to himself. There's a vast divide between what I want and what I have. He tasted the bile of bitterness in his throat. I deserved greatness—to be rewarded for the work I do.

Touching his shirt over the place where the bullet had entered, he tried to recall that night and what had come before, but the memory dissolved like a snowflake in the palm of his hand. He thought of the women he'd trusted, the ego-glorifying acclaim for which he had labored. There grew in him the awareness that he could no longer recognize the truth. His past had become unknowable, a myth from which he could draw no conclusion. Go ahead—laugh at me, he scoffed at the all-seeing river. He thought of Sisyphus, the futility of all his effort. Was it the trying that made the failure inevitable? You win, he mouthed to the river. I want nothing at all.

The screen door creaked as it swung open then bounced twice as it slapped shut. Nico heard the clinking of glass in the ice chest. Manuel approached with the hushed stealth of a hunter and handed him a beer. Neither man spoke for a considerable length. They listened to the river, its nocturnal breathing, unfathomable and deep. A haunting murmur darkly chronicling her unending story of general despair and hope.

"Why Q'eros?" Manuel asked, his voice a whisper as you might use to subdue a skittish horse.

"I promised my grandmother I'd complete my training." Nico leaned on the railing and sighed. He dreaded having to explain himself. "I spent time in Q'eros. I can't remember the year, but it was just after I returned from India. I suppose I was twenty or twenty-one. There were other young people, grad students from the university… I don't know what Sabrina told you." A weariness came over him.

"Only that you'd been there before…and your ancestor was paqo."

"It was when my mom was sick. I thought if I learned how, I could save her." He felt small under the night sky, insignificant. "I know I should have stayed, but my mother needed me."

He looked out over the river. It seemed to wink at him, knowingly. He didn't want to think about her. He didn't trust his memories. But the veil partitioning his past from the present was gauzy.

An image appeared in his mind's eye, startling in its clarity. She wore a black one-piece bathing suit and stood over him smiling. Her chestnut-brown hair was tied back calling attention to the graceful curve of her neck as she inclined her head toward him to inspect what he had brought her. He was a child, probably four or five years old. In the palm of his outstretched hand was a seahorse he'd found in the sand. His hair, bleached by the sun, lifted in the ocean breeze. The sand was hot under his feet, and the blue sky touched the sea all the way to the horizon. The white foam of the waves curled and broke on the pebbled beach, the effortless repetition as reassuring as it was timeless and eternal.

In the vision he'd noticed his eyes, they'd gleamed with pure joy, and it surprised him to know he'd been happy. He was uncertain whether he remembered this moment or if it had been a photograph he'd seen.

"But she didn't make it." His voice faltered. He suspected Sabrina must have told him.

"Mi pésame." Manuel nodded in sympathy.

The crescent moon had been sleeping behind a cloud and was now visible. A sliver of its cold light glinted on the surface of the water.

"The training requires patience. It takes time…commitment…" Manuel said slowly.

"I'm ready. I know I won't fail."

"Sabrina said you practice the healing arts, that you're a shaman." The uptick at the end of his statement formed a question.

"It's true. I work with the plant teacher, huachuma." He used the Quechua name for San Pedro. "Most of my clients are celebrities. They may be rich and famous, but many suffer from anxiety and depression. The ceremony is a way for them to explore their inner psyche. After the experience, they feel a sense of oneness with the universe, and a connection to their divine selves. I say it is like a flower blooming."

"Then, you have been doing the work of a paqo in Los Angeles."

"Yes, but…" Nico's eyes narrowed. "I'm committed to the work," he said defensively. He needed to make it clear and not let him think he was a charlatan. "I've healed people all over the world. A sheik in Abu Dhabi paid me a hundred-thousand dollars to work with him. They made a movie about me…" He heard the boastfulness in his voice and realized he sounded foolish and desperate.

He is testing you, the river chuckled again softly, he thinks you are smug, too confident. Worried he'd already said too much, he rubbed the back of his neck to relieve the crawling sensation. He suddenly felt adrift, unable to sense what Manuel was thinking. He'd always been adept at detecting what others thought and felt. It was a psychic ability he'd nurtured and utilized to his benefit. But he'd been stripped of all sense of perception.

Manuel pressed the beer bottle to his lips and looked up with interest as a cloud passed over the moon, like a Viking ship sailing across the sky.

"Fame. Money. This is not the way of a paqo," Manuel muttered.

The river agreed. Tsk tsk tsk she smacked her lips in disapproval.

Someone turned off the light in the kitchen and stillness settled around them. With it came an asphyxiating loneliness, like smoke under the door. The shame pressed heavily upon him. It filled his chest making it difficult to breathe. It was the wanting. To want and never have was unbearable.

The women had been his creations. He'd cultivated them and made them his own. He had awakened them, but they betrayed him, abandoned him. They'd had their own interests, even Luna—especially Luna. The loss and the hurt had been too heavy to shoulder. He'd been ruined and made a withered barren husk. Then came the cocaine. He despised it but couldn't live without it. He imagined it as a creature, its shifty eyes always stalking him. The clawing need inside him with its grip around his throat. Its sinister seduction unrelenting. At the same time, it made him feel powerful. It lifted the smothering haze he hid beneath. After the glow diminished, he felt remorse, wishing he'd felt nothing at all. All that remained was his broken self, like debris washed up on the shore after a storm.

There was power in the silence that lay between them like a sleeping lion. Manuel's eyes shone, a reflection pool of tranquility. It was as if he were sheathed in solitude, protected by its deafness. Nico sensed they saw life differently. He is observing me while I am naked, transparent as a ghost, he thought. Was there any truth to reality, he asked himself, or was it all subjective, a series of self-made illusions? To him, life was a succession of punishments. He saw his desires and his fears as though he were standing outside himself, an assemblage of faded memories and the ashes of dreams. A life of desire. An empty existence.

Had it been the plant medicine, or something Camille said that had shifted his ability to interpret the world around him. He squinted at the river wishing it would help him see the truth. Blindness seized him. He was unable to decipher the vision before it faded and then vanished, like the mist in the morning. This was his last chance to prove himself worthy. If he didn't deserve it, then at least he owed it to his mother and his grandmother to try. Nico wanted to say something but couldn't decide what it would be. He stood gazing out across the water.

"When I lived in India…" Nico began tentatively. He coughed. The words, like cardboard, caught in his throat which suddenly felt dusty and dry.

"Where in India?" Manuel asked. His tone was encouraging.

"At a yoga retreat in Kerala. I worked with kundalini energy. It's a powerful force that awakens the senses, opens the mind," he told him.

"Kundalini…. The sleeping serpent. A powerful energy indeed," he said as though he were remembering an old friend.

Nico noticed a flicker in Manuel's eyes. He reminded himself he was a kundalini master; the serpent energy was clay in his hands. He needed to reclaim his power while remaining humble.

"When harnessed it transforms and expands consciousness. Awakening this psychic energy, winding it up through the chakras…" Nico paused unsure if he should continue. "It can be manipulated. Its power wielded."

A sharpness pierced the air like a prophecy unfolding.

"Always a paqo is mindful. Misusing the power is dangerous." Manuel's words, though gentle, were serious. "His heart must be right before Pachamama and the spirits. His only thought is to use his power for ministering to the needs of others."

Relieved for the cover of darkness, Nico pursed his lips impatiently. He thinks I'm a novice. I know all this already, he told himself.

"Yes, of course. I've studied the teachings," Nico said, wishing he could escape. What am I doing here? he thought, closing his eyes against the world, attempting to reconcile the person he once was with the hollowed-out shell he'd become.

Manuel continued speaking as if to the river. "Some healers

use the plant teachers while the traditional paqo journeys into the spirit realm of the Apu, the mountain spirits, to divine the cause of the affliction in the body or the soul. He is one with the living energy. In both Hindu and Andean spirituality, the shaman channels Serpent Power to open the energetic centers, weaving them together to bring inner harmony."

Manuel's face was only barely visible, but Nico saw wisdom in the lines that had accumulated around his eyes.

"My yoga studio was called Amaru, named after the serpent." Nico gave a slight smile and hoped it won him favor.

Manuel nodded. "Then you know, the chakras are the energetic belt in Kundalini Yoga, and in Andean spirituality we call this energetic belt the chumpi, the eyes to the soul. Each chakra has a corresponding power stone, call a khuya, that the paqo keeps in his medicine bundle."

"I have my khuyas…" Nico announced at the mention of the stones. "I was given Karpay at Apu Qoyllur Rit'i. My uncle took me when I was just a boy." He hoped mention of this honor earned him the credibility he sought.

A shadow fell between them. Nico felt his grasp on reality slipping away, the slow unspooling of his power. He recalled the vacant reflection in the mirror the morning after taking San Pedro with Camille. Nothing made sense. He'd been laid waste. He couldn't remember what he needed. The studio and his followers had been his identity. He was nothing without their devotion and respect. They were proof that he existed. Then he remembered he'd squandered it all. He was no longer the master. Why had he deluded himself, refused to accept blame for his failure? He'd held on to the belief out of fear, but it had been a long and agonizing downfall.

"How the stones came to you is one thing." Manuel's voice had taken on a deliberate tone, confident and commanding. "The power they have is given to them by the healer, accumulated over time. In yoga this is known as samskaras, the thoughts and impressions of our past actions practiced repeatedly until they are a habit, an expression of ourselves. Your stones hold the intensions behind all your past actions. The righteousness we do in this life creates positive samskaras and likewise the harm we do creates negative ones. It's up to us to decide how we wish to live."

There was quiet in the house. For a moment he imagined he heard Ita. She was inside doing the dishes. Manuel's judgment, like Artemis's arrow, was mortal retribution for his sins—pride, greed, lust. Nico's face burned from the indignity.

"I was chosen for this path. I've devoted my life to this work," Nico said defensively, tugging his fingers through his hair. "We're wasting time," he mumbled under his breath. "How far is it to Q'eros? Will it take long to get there? I need to find my teacher."

"Patience, my friend. The road is open tomorrow. Besides, you don't know if he's there."

"Where would he be?" he blurted. "Do you know him? Is he here in Paucartambo for the festival?"

In his mind, he heard Luna's voice. You are too hard on everyone, Nico, she said. He reminded himself everything depended on this moment. Manuel was offering to help him, and instead of being grateful he was angry. He is questioning my intentions. He thinks I'm not worthy, he told himself.

He felt helpless and vulnerable. The night air closed in around him, damp and oppressive, as if it were as ancient as the land. He stood still, staring out over the water, and wondering where it ended. As much as he wanted to get back on top of his game, he didn't believe he could. Fear began to grip him.

What if Don Castillo won't take me? The voice in his head hollered. There was ringing in his ears. His chest hurt, and a shooting pain ran down his arm. He rubbed his hands together to relieve the tingling in his fingers. He thought he'd been in control. If he were rich and famous no one would leave him. He would be loved. He would be respected. Now, he didn't know himself, and he wished he could disappear under the dark water.

He turned to Manuel. "I've learned a lot," he pleaded. "It's not too late, is it?"

Nico was losing patience and the desperation was evident in his voice. Then, he reminded himself he was nothing, a fraud. He hated himself.

"It's never too late," Manuel said. "Following the path of light can overcome even the darkest influence. A spiritual practice with prayer, meditation, and selfless service can eliminate the negative samskaras of bad deeds."

For a long while Nico was quiet. He seemed about to cry. He'd placed his trust in people and each time he'd been betrayed. He'd sobbed when he lost Sofia. Then, when Élodie betrayed him, he thought he had none left to shed. He'd shut each door behind him, closing himself off from everyone and obliterating any chance at happiness. He'd worked hard to eliminate the memory of them, erase their faces. Now they appeared first as fragments then entire scenes, like a movie. It was as if Manuel ran the projector. He thought of himself as battered and desiccated. The wind might simply carry him off in the next gust. This, he said to himself, is being alone and broken. This is his punishment for depending upon them.

Manuel was silent for a considerable length of time.

"Have you heard the saying, *Know Thyself?"* he asked.

When Nico shook his head, Manuel went on to say, "It's an ancient Greek aphorism, one of the commandments given to Apollo by the Oracle of Delphi. Knowing and understanding ourselves gives meaning and value to our lives. I believe we know ourselves best through our relationships with others."

Nico listened to what Manuel said. He didn't want to be reminded of what happened. At the same time, he envisioned what it would be like if his life had meaning.

"I know myself," he said with conviction. "I thought I was destined to be a renowned healer, but whenever it's within reach... somehow it escapes me."

He needed to explain himself, prove he was ready to become a paqo. He just wanted to rest his head and close his eyes. His ego and his actions had led him to feel shame and remorse; happiness remained elusive, too abstract to hold in his mind.

A wobbly bench, the paint blistering with age, was propped against the house. He sat there with his head in his hands, too tired to continue.

"Sometimes, we only think of changing direction when misfortune is upon us," Manuel said. He waited for Nico to reveal his thoughts, but there was only the river. He continued undeterred by Nico's silence. "What are you seeking in Q'eros?"

"When I find my teacher I'll finish the training. Then, I'll open a center in the Sacred Valley or possibly go back to Los Angeles," he said with some arrogance. It was important he sound like he had a plan.

"Nico, the teachings are based on integrating the true self with the Absolute. They are about following a spiritual path to self-knowledge. Remaining in ignorance of yourself, you repeat negative patterns that lead to failure and the very thing you fear.

"I lost sight of who I am... I destroyed everything." He turned away, unable to face him.

"Failure is the greatest teacher." Don Manuel paused, leaving space for consideration. "Creating meaning and purpose in life is not based on what others think, or whether it serves your ego, or sense of destiny. It's about doing the right thing no matter how big or small and living each moment being true to yourself. The darkness has no power over the light. No matter how faint the flame, it is bright in contrast to the shadow. Hope is never lost when you have faith, Nico. The will to find meaning in your life is strong enough to overcome all the negative influences."

"I'll do better this time." He wanted to believe that what he said was true.

Nico thought about all the events that had led him to today. His mother had let Ita send him away. The afternoon in Mrs. Sanchez's kitchen, her son had been there. Nico was sure of it.

"I'm ashamed. And I'm terrified," he mumbled, tripping over the words before regretting he had said them.

"Never be afraid of who you are." Manuel said. He hesitated then continued, "Sabrina said you were looking for Don Castillo."

Nico looked up, startled. He hadn't recalled telling her. But thinking back, he'd told her more than he should have, including his fear of not being welcomed.

"I'm sorry, Nico. Don Castillo isn't well. He's living with family in Cusco. But when I told him you were seeking his teaching, he asked if I would meet with you."

"Did he remember me? I don't understand…"

"Leaving your training incomplete has made you vulnerable to negative influences. Your gift is strong, too powerful to remain untutored."

"If not Don Castillo, then who…"

"Don Castillo asked me to guide you. He is one of the few remaining Altomesayok. This is the highest level of paqo, a mystic who communes directly with the Apu, the spirits of the mountains. They are thought to be extinct, but there are several who have met this calling after being touched by lightning. As a small boy, I was also chosen by lightning and became Altomesayok."

"You will teach me?" Nico asked, unsure if he understood what Manuel was offering.

Manuel didn't answer the question directly. Sometimes, he believed, a story was a better way to explain what he wanted to say.

"As a young man, I didn't see myself in the circle of esteemed paqos. I would often go alone up into the mountains. It was there I would listen to the voices of the Apu. There was one voice unlike any other. A woman's voice as candescent as molten gold and as fiercely commanding. Apu are typically male, but this spirit when she revealed herself was tall with pale skin and yellow hair. She told me I was a bridge between worlds. I knew then to follow my heart. I chose not to live in Q'eros. There were many in the community that thought my gift wasted in the pursuit of higher education."

"What do I do now?" He'd grown accustomed to facing a closed door in a dark room, feeling for the edges of the frame and then the knob. For him, time had run in reverse, and he'd chased it, closing himself off to eliminate any chance of escape, blaming everyone for his failure, the walls closing in until he suffocated. Now there was a door that had opened a crack and a wedge of light seeped in.

"Tomorrow we'll bring supplies to Q'eros."

15

The Jeep climbed slowly up the winding dirt road kicking up loose stones as Manuel downshifted. They'd been ascending for three hours through a barren rocky landscape bejeweled with waterfalls. The cliff-hanging road narrowed to single file. There were no guardrails, and as they took the next hairpin turn Nico looked down the drop of several thousand feet. Dreading a *Thelma and Louise* off the cliff, he slid the headphones down around his neck and wondered aloud what would happen if someone came from the opposite direction.

"Today's Monday. The traffic only goes this way." The confidence with which he stated this seemingly indisputable fact made it sound impossible some rule breaking idiot wouldn't come barreling down the mountain.

Volunteers from an NGO were meeting them in Q'eros. One of the projects was to build a bath house where the villagers could take hot showers. In the back of the Jeep were solar panels and Nico thought back to the lack of electricity and running water he'd experienced when he'd last been there. At the time, it had seemed bucolic given their pastoral lifestyle, when in truth he had been romanticizing their hardship. He recalled clear, crisp nights skinny dipping in a luminous lake with girls from the university, shrieking as they plunged into the icy water. There had been a sense of timelessness under a sky ablaze with stars and the hazy band of the Milky Way close enough to touch. Someone had told him the Greeks called it a river of milk. One of the girls was from either Denmark or Sweden, her skin lambent in the moonlight, and her hair, a pale blonde like liquid silver poured down her back to the top of her buttocks. She had plunged headfirst into the water without hesitation, like a mermaid. He followed, but yelped at the frigid temperature, his eyes widening. Laughing at him, she'd covered her mouth with her hand to hide her slightly bucked teeth. In playful revenge, he'd taken her into his arms and sucked mercilessly at her nipple while she giggled and squirmed like a fish desperate to return to the water, ceasing only when he moved his mouth to her lips. From then on, she was his, and they found each other nightly and made love, warming their bodies with the heat of passion.

Nico plugged his phone into the portable charger, hoping to play his downloaded music. Since leaving Cusco he had been anxious about the lack of communication with the outside world. But as they drew closer, he began to look forward to the isolation and comfort of anonymity, of being off the grid where no one could find him. He remarked how Q'eros must have changed, acknowledging the advantages of modernity, like satellite-based internet for the students. Manuel had been stern in saying Q'eros was far from having what it needs. He recounted, as if to a group of tourists, that the Q'ero people were descendants of the Inca Empire and had survived the Spanish conquest by retreating high into the mountains where the weather is severe. Each year, there were those who died prematurely from lack of basic services and medical attention. These days, few families stayed year-round growing potatoes and corn and tending to the herds of alpaca whose yarn is essential to their economy.

"So, we're helping by bringing solar panels," Nico said

thoughtfully.

"The volunteers who've come to Q'eros have been careful to protect the culture while improving living conditions in such a remote and inhospitable territory. There's also the risk of exploitation. It's a mixed blessing. The internet has improved education, allowing the children to share their way of life with the outside world. But it's also internet drawn attention to the Q'ero people. Paqos travel or move permanently to Cusco and the Sacred Valley where boutique hotels and retreats have become a destination for ceremonies. They generously share their tradition with others, and spiritual tourism has provided an appreciable income to them and their families."

As they climbed into the clouds the fog thickened. Nico felt the pressure in his ears and chest. At this altitude, the damage to his lung from the bullet made breathing more difficult. He could barely see a car's length in front of them, but Manuel didn't seem concerned.

Do you think you'll go back to Argentina?" Manuel's eyes didn't leave the invisible road.

"No. Well, yes. Maybe. Ita is old… and alone."

"And you have a girlfriend there?"

"Not anymore."

The cloud forest enveloped them in its dreamlike cocoon. The world as he saw it was white, vacant. The road disappeared and a strange isolation enfolded him. Ita had been right about Gaby, he thought. He was caught again in the repeating pattern, and yet another door had closed. Nico rested his head against the side window and shut his eyes, his mind muddy from lack of sleep.

Last night he lay on top of the covers in the tiny bedroom. The uncertain future filled him with dread. In the early hours after midnight, he woke in a sweat after a dream so lifelike it was many minutes before his racing heart eased. In the dream Ita had been kidnapped by the drug cartel and he was frantic in his search for her.

He sat up on the side of the bed, the small room close around him, and listened to the silence in the house. He worried the dream was an omen. Outside the window the leaves on the trees flickered like fireflies as the moonlight caressed them. Unable to fall back sleep, he called Ita and let the phone ring until she answered. He whispered her name careful not to wake the sleeping household. He told her about the climb to Machu Pichu and that he was on his way to Q'eros. Ita said Lucia admitted she'd made deposits for Gaby but hadn't wanted to get her friend in trouble. She knew she'd put them all in danger and went to stay with their father in California. Speaking in a low authoritative voice, he said he was coming to get her and they would go to Los Angeles.

"Chit!" Ita shushed him. "No seas boludo. It's not safe to go back to L.A. where they shot you. Nico, Estoy bien," she'd gently scolded, as though he were a child. "You should know I'm protected."

"Who's protecting you?" he asked skeptically. He regretted being so far away, unable to help her.

"The spirits of the ancestors have always watched over me," she said calmly.

Though fear still consumed him, he blew kisses to her through the phone. After they hung up, he wept as if purging the grief he'd held inside for his lifetime. Still furious by what he'd heard, he called his sister and listened to her tearful apology.

"Who's going to take care of Ita?" he hissed and hung up without waiting for an answer.

Sleep would not come. He kept the light on afraid the dream would return to reveal its fatal outcome. A noise outside drew him over to the window, and he saw himself reflected in the glass. Looking back at him were his mother's eyes, dark green with yellow flecks that glinted when she smiled. They looked at one another across time, and though he wanted to turn away she held his gaze. Unnerved, he pushed his hair back off his forehead, and she did the same. Waves of dark hair fell softly along her long neck. She tilted her head, and the eyes that held the secret of his fate twinkled mischievously. He wanted to reach up and caress her cheek but knew she existed only within the frame of the window. Behind her shoulder the moon passed between the branches creating a halo around her figure that resembled The Virgin of Guadalupe. He felt a gentle breeze in the room despite the window being shut, and there was a faint scent of lilies. Her perfume. In the empty space between them and eternity, he asked her what she wanted to tell him. He didn't breathe or blink for fear she would disappear even though he knew it was his own image he saw. The wind outside gusted, rattling the windowpane. His vision shifted. In the silence, only the river's never-ending story remained.

He knew she possessed the answers to his past and would certainly know his future. How would have his life played out had she not died? Always, in his dreams she was happy. Laughing as she ran along the shoreline, her hair blowing as she glanced back at him chasing after her. In every dream he was ageless, breathless, stumbling, and unable to catch her. He sensed her presence long after he turned off the light. Through the blackened windows, the trees swayed like silhouetted giraffes against a starless sky.

It rained during the night. The pat, pat, pat of heavy drops hammered the roof. He was oddly soothed by the continuous pummeling that slowly eroded his anxiety. In the predawn sky the dark clouds were eerily lit. He thought again of Ita, her long grey hair twisted in a chignon, reading glasses hanging from a cord around her neck. He imagined his home in San Telmo filled with heirlooms and the heady fragrance of cumin spiced empanadas. The scent of brine in the air at the beach in Pinamar. Indelible memories, like scratches and dings engrained in furniture that prove the existence of those who came before.

As much as he wants to forget, he can't put the past behind him. It's a fiction he tells himself. A myth that shapes him. There is a fatality to it all. Still, the dread and fear follows him. Everything he's done and become has been laid down like layers of silt, one upon the other. He might as well tell that river outside to change her course.

The clatter of dishes and voices coming from the kitchen dragged him from the past into the present. From across the river he heard church bells, angels announcing their presence. Inhaling the woodsy aroma of roasted coffee, he thought he was home and Ita was preparing breakfast. He attributed the haze and dull ache behind his eyes to whiskey and too many beers the night before. Edges of sky framed the trees outside the uncurtained window. What was it, he wondered, that she tried to tell him? He quickly showered and shaved knowing Manuel would be waiting to get on the road.

After a hearty breakfast to sustain them on the long drive to Q'eros, Tica filled their thermoses with coffee and a hamper with empanadas. Their goodbye hugs felt like family, but Nico questioned whether he belonged. He couldn't see himself clearly. He was no longer his old self, but he had not been remade. When he fled California, he went home to what he knew, where he came from. It occurred to him that he confused the memories of his childhood with home. He was on a journey, a homegoing to find meaning. Home with the spirits of the mountains and with the immortal river. Home that needs no place, like mist rising from a waterfall. What lay ahead scared him. He feared the loss of control, his grip on the world as he knew it. In the face of the unknown he was powerless. Then and now were woven, like a burden basket, with the relics of the past and an uncertain future.

Climbing further into the clouds, the mountain cliffs fell away. In the luminous whiteness was silence. He let go and experienced a freeing sense of acceptance. The past had evaporated and the unknown future pointless. As he was in the moment, it was gone, replaced by utter solitude, aloneness. He reached inside the hamper for an empanada but came up empty-handed and he finished the remaining cold coffee in his thermos.

The car jerked when Manuel downshifted. "Sorry, this last stretch is steep for such a heavy load."

"Will we be there soon?" Nico asked, bracing himself against the back of the seat.

"Less than an hour once we are above the cloud," Manuel said.

"How many of these did we bring?" said Nico, fidgeting with the solar pack Manuel had given him.

"A dozen. They will come in handy at the school and medical center."

"I can't believe how much has changed. But I suppose the entire world has changed."

They rode in silence for several miles, Manuel focusing on the barely visible road ahead. At fourteen thousand feet, a shroud of mist hung heavily over the leaden summits who stood like mystical wise men in dusky hooded rain cloaks. Upon rounding the next turn there was a parting in the cloud forest. Appearing in the distance, on the shoulders of imposing mountains, were undulations of green hills bestrewn with the thatched roof stone huts of the village.

Nico sighed, and Manuel looked over at him, a smile in his twinkling eyes. The Jeep bumped over the rugged terrain as the rough, newly made gravel road gave way to a worn dirt track where few vehicles tread.

"This road has only been open a couple of years." Manuel said. Just then a herding dog bounded toward them barking and nipping at the tires.

"Yeah, I remember going in on horseback," Nico said, taking hold of the grab handle above the door.

They rolled up in front of a construction site where people were eating lunch at a picnic table that had been carried outside into the sun from the community center. Two men sat on a stack of lumber. Manuel turned off the engine and stepped out of the car. One by one they called out, "Don Manuel!" Greeting him with wide smiles, handshakes and clasping his shoulder, they showed their affection and reverence. He seemed pleased at the warm welcome and respect given to him but his shy smile showed only complete humility.

Speaking in Spanish, Manuel brought Nico into the circle of his friends. Nico felt self-conscious as he shook hands. He thought he should be angry at the deception. He'd spent days with Manuel not knowing the man was a high paqo. It had been a test. He also didn't know if he had passed.

Besides the Q'ero people from the village, there were others who had come to volunteer. Two fair skinned young men wearing army style jackets got up from the table and offered their seats to them. An elderly Quechua woman wearing a colorful skirt and shawl welcomed them with bowls of a hearty stew and potatoes. She said nothing but her eyes were shining. It wasn't Ita's locro, but the sweet and tender meat was comforting after the long trip. He watched the university students eating together, smiling, and talking. It was a reminder that at forty-one he was no longer young, and he feared not fitting in.

A tall, fair skinned woman unfurled blueprints on a table in front of a team of workers. Nico guessed she was around his age, possibly older. He thought he heard something of an English accent. Don Manuel stood off to the side speaking with an older man in Quechua. When he finished eating, Nico placed his bowl in a large wash pan and walked over to them. The sound of Spanish and Quechua blending with both American and British English approached symphonic. He hoped for a beer, but a young woman handed him a tin cup of steaming coca tea. He inhaled the aroma. It brought back memories of his yoga studio in Los Angeles, all of which was now lost.

"Are you going to work on the bathhouse?" A young woman's voice interrupted his thoughts.

She stood at nearly his height and their eyes met before she cast her's down. He couldn't guess her age. Eighteen perhaps. Her skin was pale as porcelain, her hair the fairest blonde, and her eyes a watery shade of blue. The accent wasn't any dialect of American he'd heard. It had a cultivated sound like too much education. An American wouldn't be as shy, he thought.

"I guess so. I'm here with Don Manuel. We brought solar panels and batteries."

"Don Manuel…." She looked up and smiled. Her admiration of him was transparent. "He always manages to procure what we need most. I hope you both will be staying for a while. We can use the extra hands."

"I want to… at least until the project is completed."

"The work here is never finished. You must know that if you drove all this way with Don M." she grinned as he approached them.

"I thought I heard my name." He gave the young woman a kiss

on both cheeks. "I see you've met Rumi."

"Not exactly," he said, extending his hand. "Nico Romero."

"Um… Nice to meet you." Shaking his hand her cheeks colored. "Sorry… my aunt is waving me over. I better get back."

"We'll come with you. I need to speak with her." Don Manuel said. They walked toward Saskia who was standing in front of a partially framed out structure.

"Rumi's here with her Aunt Saskia who came from Denmark to help us," he said to Nico. "She's known for her work in green development, and she generously donates her services here and to other indigenous communities. Rumi is following in her footsteps studying sustainable architecture at Delft in the Netherlands."

It appeared to Nico that Manuel knew everyone in the village. He listened to him switch fluidly between Quechua and Spanish and then back to English. Nico's Quechua had been limited to the recital of ceremonies he'd memorized, but he remembered a few words of Quechua. Hoping his pronunciation passed muster, he greeted one of the elders, "Allianchu," bowing his head as he shook the man's hand and was pleased with himself when he heard "Allianmi" in return.

Saskia had finished detailing instructions for the completion of the structure and the group dispersed. She turned to Don Manuel, "I'm so glad you're here! And not just because you bring batteries and solar panels!" She kissed him on both cheeks. "We're behind schedule, as you can see." She turned to Nico, extending her hand. "Saskia Hansen."

"Nico Romero." He returned the smile noticing a glint in her eye when she glanced over at Manuel.

"Given the terrain, we're going with an above ground water harvesting system with gravity feed. We should be able to collect enough rainwater and snow melt off the roof for bathing. There's a group working on the bathhouse, but Rumi and I can use your help on the tower."

There was little conversation as they worked. Nico thought how short of breath he was, then remembered it was the altitude taking its toll. He watched Manuel, who he'd decided must be a decade older and was able to haul the lumber and carry out Saskia's instructions for measuring and drilling after driving for hours. They were still working as the sun dipped below the mountain. The light had fallen when Saskia tapped Manuel on the shoulder, "Go get settled before sunset. I'll see you at dinner."

16

Nico unrolled his sleeping bag on the pallet nearest the hearth. In preparation of honored guests, Ch'aska, the daughter of a high paqo, had meticulously prepared their quarters. She'd swept the earthen floor and lit the fire where two large kettles of hot water awaited them. Don Manuel filled a basin and stripped off his work clothes. He washed and changed into a fresh button-front shirt and khaki pants for dinner. He looked like the college professor he was.

"This house was built for Don Castillo and his family many years ago. But it's ours for as long as we're here," he said, laying his sleeping bag on the pallet across the room from Nico. He withdrew from his pack a knife with a bone handle, his medicine bundle that held his khuya stones, and a clear quartz crystal and arranged them on the side table. Nico observed his movements, the deliberateness with which he performed the simplest task was ceremonial.

Nothing was as he remembered it, Nico thought. Time had passed. He'd escaped death. He hoped there might be the chance to become someone new. I want to fit in, he admitted to himself.

They set out after sunset with Manuel holding a lantern to light the way. They walked past the stone huts, each alike with a perfectly thatched roof and encircled by a stone corral for the animals. The low moan of the wind as it swept down from the mountains sent a chill to his bones, and he pulled his jacket collar up over the back of his neck against the crisp night air. In the dining hall, the benches at the long table were packed tightly, but everyone shuffled closer together to make room for them to sit. Unlike the homes, the hall was a newly constructed building of irregularly formed cinder blocks with a corrugated metal roof. Inside, instead of the common packed earth, the floors were wood. Nico heard Don Manuel's name called out and others rushed to greet him. Nico was introduced, and he smiled shyly as he shook hands.

It was loud in the dining hall. There was the clatter of plates and everyone was speaking at once. The mood was joyful and invigorating. The room wasn't what Nico expected. He could tell that it usually functioned as a classroom or community center. A large bulletin board displayed notices with posters and artwork by the children. A whitewashed wall had been stenciled along the top with geometric designs. Across the width of the room hung a banner that read: Sulpayki - Gracias - Thank you.

While the men had been working outdoors on construction crews, the women had spent the day preparing a banquet in gratitude to the volunteers. There was trout from stocked alpine lakes and fresh vegetables grown in the newly built greenhouse. Guinea pigs, a Peruvian staple called cuy, had been domesticated by the indigenous peoples of the Andes somewhere around 5000 BC. They were now being farm raised in the village as a sustainable source of protein to improve nutrition. These developments were the largesse of non-governmental organizations dedicated to helping the Q'ero people thrive in the modern world while sustaining their culture.

Nico scanned the room studying the faces. They'd come from all corners of the globe to this remote village. He noticed a large white board across from them.

"Is that a Smart board?"

"Yeah, and there's one in the schoolhouse, too."

"That's incredible. It sure is different from when last I was here."

Nico looked toward the door as Saskia and Rumi entered. His stomach tightened, and he unconsciously fiddled with the fork in front of him. Coming back was probably a mistake, he thought. They walked toward where he and Don Manuel were sitting. Nico wished they would sit somewhere else. He was afraid of what they might ask him, that they would find out he was a fraud. He was accustomed to lying. He'd done it effortlessly his entire life. For one reason or another, he hadn't felt the need to embellish or lie to Manuel. There was nothing he could say that would impress him.

Saskia wedged in next to Manuel. The young men in the army jackets waved Rumi over, and she went and sat with them. Across the table the Americans were having a friendly debate with the young British fellows. They were speaking loudly. Students, he told himself. The Latinos were likely from the education institute. How short is memory? he asked himself, watching the descendants of Spanish Conquistadors in lively conversation with the Incas, their acrimonious history set aside.

Don Rafael and his wife Alma stood at the head of the table. Platters of fried trout and roasted guinea pig were spread in front of them. The room hushed when Rafael said grace and then a blessing in Quechua. The meal began with steaming bowls of potato leek soup and fresh bread baked in a large masonry oven. Hunger temporarily supplanted Nico's distress. He picked up his spoon prematurely, quickly setting it down to wait for everyone to be served. Someone had donated cases of Pilsen, a popular Peruvian beer, and Nico was grateful for the cold brew to quench more than his thirst.

Manuel slathered a generous layer of queso fresca on a piece of warm bread. "Que rico!" he said and piled the soft cheese on another piece of the crusty bread and handed it to Nico.

"Mmm, riquísimo!" Nico said with his mouth full.

He was feeling better but still dreaded questions from Saskia. He fretted about what he should say. He assumed Manuel knew he'd been shot. Camille would have told Sabrina. It upset him to think they had spoken about him and judged him.

The platters of cuy were passed down the table. They'd been roasted over an open fire and seasoned with a traditional cream sauce made with huacatay, a mint-like herb from the marigold family. There were empanadas stuffed with beans and cheese. Pan fried trout was served with rice and quinoa. Lettuces and French beans were from the new greenhouse. It was a feast by any standard.

Nico served himself a large helping of aji verde, a spicy green sauce similar to the chimichurri he favored at home. Slipping from his seat, he collected another beer from the ice chest. Surely, he said to himself, everyone would find out his secret. It would take more than one beer to quiet the voices in his head telling him he wasn't good enough, that he'd never be good enough.

He turned his attention to the plate of food in front of him and listened to the conversation between Manuel and Saskia. He only heard pieces, but they were talking about Rumi.

"New departments and faculty are available to her that didn't exist when I was in school. Delft is at the top of climate-responsive design and green building. She's passionate about saving the planet, and it's kids like her that will do it," Saskia said. It was clear she was proud of her niece.

Don Manuel nodded and asked, "Remind me, did you also go to Delft?"

"No, I went to The Bartlett School of Architecture at UC

London."

"Ah! London's my favorite city."

"You graduated from Harvard. Philosophy, right?"

Nico wished he could disappear, blow away like a shriveled leaf in winter. All these elitists, he thought, with their fancy education. He kept his head down and drank another beer, wishing for something stronger.

Don Manuel nodded. "My doctorate is from Harvard Divinity. I teach theology and philosophy. My focus is on the cultural and political forces that shape religious traditions, like here in Q'eros."

I'm surrounded by philosophers, Nico thought. Camille, and Luna's husband teaches philosophy, too.

Saskia nodded, "Q'eros Nation is important to all of us. Right, Nico?" She leaned in to draw him into their conversation.

"Uh, yeah, of course." Try sounding more enthusiastic, he told himself.

Don Manuel interjected, "This isn't Nico's first time here. He studied under Don Castillo for a short while."

"Oh, really?" She looked with interest toward Nico.

"It was a long time ago." He gazed beyond her into the distance. "My mother was sick, and I'd hoped to heal her." There was a pause before he continued. "She has since died." He looked down, twirling his napkin around in his lap.

"I'm sorry for your loss, Nico. When were you last here, in Q'eros?"

"About twenty years ago." He blanked on the year and was content to be vague.

"You might have met my sister, Kristen. She studied anthropology at Boston University. It was Don Manuel who developed the study abroad program for Q'eros at BU when he taught there."

"Maybe..." He couldn't remember.

"And you've come back... Why?"

"I'd like to continue..." he sputtered, having trouble answering. She is asking too many questions, he thought. He suddenly felt hot and his faced flushed.

Again, Don Manuel answered for him. "Nico 's grandmother recently told him about his paqo ancestry."

"I see... Are you Peruvian?" she asked. She seemed pleasant enough, as if she were merely interested, but it made him uncomfortable.

"No. I'm from Buenos Aires. My grandmother has a gift—she sees things. She told me stories about her grandfather, that he was high paqo, a mystic." He wished he'd asked Ita more questions. "When I left, she gave me his chullo and his poncho. I brought them with me," he said reverentially. He'd just shared something that was singularly important to him, yet Saskia hadn't reacted the way he thought she would.

He'd come to Q'eros anticipating the fulfillment of his grandmother's expectations. Where he'd been was not a place he could remain. His hope was wed to his desire to escape, though he didn't know what awaited. The image she'd created for him inspired his yearning. It didn't matter that the vision was second hand, seen through her eyes, it was just as potent. She'd instilled in him the belief that this journey, a healing journey, would be his salvation. He'd come to this long-imagined place in search of himself. What he hadn't expected was a return to the past, a reckoning with the truth.

Turning her gaze back to Don Manuel she asked, "Will you be

taking Nico under your wing? I mean… with Don Castillo away."

"For now."

Saskia continued, her eyes still on Nico. "Well then, Don Manuel is high paqo, a mystic. You're fortunate to have him to guide you."

"Nico's been giving despacho in Los Angeles," Don Manuel said.

Ah, Nico thought. I shouldn't have told Sabrina that.

"Oh, really?" she said with astonishment.

"I own…Well, I used to own a yoga studio…until recently. It was… I mean, I was…" God! Spit it out man! He upbraided himself. He wanted to say it was well-known, that he'd been himself a celebrity. He chose not to mention he'd performed ceremonies with San Pedro, the plant teacher called huachuma in Quechua.

She brightened at this information. "I practice yoga, and so does Rumi. Will you lead a class while you're here? Rumi would be delighted."

"Sure," he managed to squeak out. "I teach Kundalini Yoga," he added nervously, tripping over his words, "to raise consciousness by working with the breath."

"I love that. You must be passionate about it."

He stared at her. "I'm not sure anymore." It was the only thing he could think of to say.

He noticed that while they were talking their dinner plates had been removed and trays of flan custard and chia seed cakes had been set on the table. Nico wondered if a dinner like this would be served every night while the donors were there. At that moment, Don Rafael got up to speak. He thanked the volunteers by name. Then, he made a special announcement welcoming Don Manuel, saying the revered paqo would be conducting a despacho at sunrise and for everyone to attend.

After the speech, Saskia turned to Don Manuel, there was an urgency to her voice. "There are lots of projects that can use your help. I hope you are staying a while."

"We're here—at least for as long as the weather holds."

Saskia sighed, "We have some funding now. I hope it will continue. You can see from tonight's meal what we've been able to accomplish regarding nutrition. I want you to meet a friend of mine who has just arrived. He's helping with internet connectivity."

"You've done so much, Saskia. All the money you've raised, and now the solar shower. We're all grateful."

She turned to Nico, "You know it isn't easy living up here, but I hope you'll stay and learn."

"Yeah," he nodded. "I'm kinda looking forward to being off the grid." That was a dumb answer, he thought, sweeping his unmanageable forelock back.

No one was in any hurry to leave the dining hall. Jugs of pisco, the same local brandy he had drunk with Camille, were delivered to the table. He wondered if Camille would find him, and if she would still want to work together. He looked around the table. Everyone was enjoying themselves. He questioned if he would really be able to stay and if he would ever fit in.

As if on cue, guitars and flutes appeared and the hall became charged with music. Manuel hadn't told him to bring his guitar to dinner. He'd ask if he could bring it tomorrow. Playing guitar empowered him, the instrument was a shield. If he learned the songs, they might accept him and he would become part of their world.

The women began a local folk dance. They encouraged the guests to join in. Soon everyone was dancing. Nico, keeping to himself, feasted his eyes on their colorful skirts twirling and radiant smiling faces. He watched Manuel and Saskia. It appeared to him they'd danced together before. Nico thought how impossible things happened, how odd it felt to be back here, like his future self was revisiting the past. Manuel swiveled his hips as he maneuvered Saskia. It was hard to believe this philosophy professor was high paqo, a mystic able to commune directly with the Apu, the spirits of the mountains and Pachamama. He wondered if he could develop that ability. It was in his blood after all, woven like the poncho and chullo into his personal history. It was possible he had the gifts of an Altomesayok. If only Don Manuel would teach him.

The years in India shaped him. He was fearless then, in possession of his life. It was a strong belief in his purpose that animated him and first brought him to Q'eros with the assurance he was a shaman. The past lives in us, he thought. The ghost of it is still within reach, like petroglyphs on a cave wall. What remained now was uncertainty, a present filtered by what had gone before. Memories rewritten. Truth dissolved like soap bubbles on the surface of water. He had the sense of being caught in a riptide, drawn backward, his dreams for the future moving ever further away. Now, he was on his own. His life an accumulation of failed relationships, each one greater in its loss than the previous.

He thought back to when Luna and he went to the Spanish church in L.A. and lit a candle. She tried to make him a better person. She gave him hope. Was it possible, he thought, to begin again, to turn back time? Maybe, he thought, this continuing story of humiliation and anguish was his life's purpose—an atonement. Like the Mariner, the penance of retelling his *Rime*, always the same, wore him down and reconciled him to his defeat.

A somber feeling of reminiscence came over him. The yoga studio was filled with soft chanting like wind rustling through leaves. The sweet perfume of incense made his head swim. He saw himself in front of the room soaking up the admiration of beautiful women in tight yoga pants. They were his for the taking. Their gaze predatory, just as hungry for him as he was barren and in need of them. He hadn't really understood it at the time. The passion, the longing, the ambition burned from the inside, consuming him. All of it was a mockery, a mistake.

What he envisioned wasn't his life. He created his own way of seeing the world so that he could make sense of it. He went to Los Angeles determined and with the dream of becoming an unrivaled yoga teacher. Far from mastering his desires, he'd been devoured by the consequences of his appetite. He'd seen the divine face to face, wrestled him to the ground in his own blood. Bad luck? Or a vengeful god?

The swishing of colorful skirts as the women danced by him returned him to the given moment. He looked around the dining hall at the joyful faces. He wanted to fit into this. This was the life he now stood in front of.

As they were leaving the dining hall, he saw Rumi across the room. She smiled at him and waved. Something inside him stirred. She reminded him of the young, long-limbed girls from the university who grabbed his attention all those years ago. Like him, they had been full of dreams and unbound possibilities. He'd tasted their sweetness and been nourished by their innocence. Making love to them, he'd tried to fill the empty space in himself. Their reverence absolved his shame and negated his fears, at least for a time. Like a myth sustaining him on an epic journey, he wanted those unchecked feelings to define him. I was a king, he said to himself. In the end, it all amounted to nothing.

° ° °

Purple clouds partially eclipsed the full moon creating a halo that lit the edges of the sky, like an incandescent crown of glory. Nico lay in his sleeping bag and opened *Love Poems* by Pablo Neruda that Olivia had bought him. It felt like ages ago they walked the antique stalls in Buenos Aires with his head full of ideas. He read from the book, a page she'd dogeared. "I love you as certain dark things are to be loved, in secret, between the shadow and the soul." She'd made promises, but left him, like everyone else had.

He looked across the room. Don Manuel was propped up in his sleeping bag reading, the lengthy tome resting on his chest. He couldn't see the title and asked, "What are you reading?"

"*The Magic Mountain*, by Thomas Mann."

"What's it about?" He hated to admit it, even to himself, but he thought Don M was interesting. The things he said that were philosophical made sense, without making it seem more than it was. Perhaps they'd get along, he thought.

"It's a book of ideas," he said plainly. "I'll give it to you when I finish. I think you'll find it interesting."

Nico couldn't say what he was thinking, it was too embarrassing. He didn't read books. He didn't have the concentration for them. Luna had given him books with her thoughtful inscriptions inside, but they sat on his dresser as decoration. All these grand ideas that people aspire to know, like the meaning of life, and these big emotions they hunger for, like being in love—you read about them in books. When you're young, you want these things to define your life, to make you complete. But they are too big, too grand, too unattainable. What is the likelihood of getting what you want? The accumulation of loss and betrayal met with resentment has shaped me, he thought. Can shame and regret be made to flow backwards? The day had drained him. His eyelids were heavy from the beer and pisco. He stood outside himself and watched a myriad of images, ingrained for all eternity, replay.

17

During the night, the mountains impregnated his dreams. His mind was as restless as his soul, and he mumbled in his sleep, "But I need to get there...I can't be late..." he pleaded loudly leaning into the round opening in the glass window.

The stationmaster shrugged disinterestedly. "Next bus is at noon. Do you want a ticket, or not?"

He would miss the luncheon, but at least he will have shown up. He counted out the money exactly and pushed it under the glass partition. Taking the ticket, he slung his heavy pack over his shoulder and shuffled to a wooden bench in the waiting room. He didn't like waiting, especially alone, and he stared anxiously at the large clock with roman numerals that hung over the ticket booth. A long beam of sunlight clouded with blue-grey swirls of cigarette smoke slanted down from the crescent shaped window near the top of the dome-vaulted ceiling.

He took the last open seat on the bus. More passengers came on board, standing over him in the aisle. Their clothes were soiled and they reeked of their own body odor. The rickety bus climbed higher, lurching along the narrow, rutted, winding dirt road. His nasal passages stung from the smell of diesel, sweat and cigarettes.

The bus ground to a stop at the remote rocky plateau. He stumbled out of the bus, his legs aching and wobbly from the cramped four-hour journey. Everything seemed strange. He felt apart from the place and was alarmed by the silence. He made his way to the fairground intensely aware of how late he was. He hoped to make a good impression, and he was certain his tardiness would be viewed unfavorably. Several tables draped in white linen had been set out in the meadow, appearing incongruous with the informal gathering. The elders sat smoking and drinking coffee while children ran freely, laughing and playing as they scampered up and over the boulders strewn about the terrain. Gazing out, he spotted a boy with long curling locks of black hair and saw that it was himself, and he smiled inwardly—he wasn't too late. Ita's grandfather stood at a bar made of the same lacquered wood as El Federal where he'd gone with his father as a child. He didn't know how he knew it was Ita's grandfather, but he felt certain it was. He draped his arm across the old man's wide shoulders, leaned in and kissed him lovingly on the cheek. The boozy scent of bergamot overpowered him, and he closed his eyes. When he opened them, there was a perfect martini in front of him. It was filled to the brim. He lowered his head and sipped off the top so he wouldn't spill any. He looked up and saw his elder smiling at him the way one does at a toddler who has done something delightful. There were questions he wanted to ask, but he couldn't form the words. It could be that he was afraid to know the answers. He'd already made a mess of his life, and now that he had returned, he didn't want to disappoint the old man. What if he failed again? The fluttering began in his heart and he sipped more of the martini hoping it would calm his nerves. He mouthed the words, asking no one in particular, am I destined to be a paqo? Ita's voice assured him the old man would be his guide. He wanted to see her, but in this dream, she remained hidden from him.

A mournful hymn rose up from the meadow. It was the "Lacrimosa" from Mozart's *Requiem*. Gathering in mountainous forces, dark billows of thunderclouds advanced rapidly across the sky accompanied by the low rumble of thunder. He watched them take shape, long and curvaceous goddesses, like figureheads on the front of a wooden ship, competing for Neptune's favor. With each stroke of lightning he saw the face of a goddess, her elongated finger stretched out toward him. The next explosive thunderclap brought heavy water droplets which fell like tears from her laden breasts. The guests sought the inadequate shelter of a flimsy white canopy erected on the fairgrounds just as great shards of lightning impaled the water-logged earth around them. Nico trembled and crouched to the ground certain this was the end of his days. He was petrified, yet in the faces lit up by the phosphorescent flash, he saw the absence of fear in those around him. Just then a blinding surge of electricity coursed through his body in what felt like a slam to the back of his head. A loud ringing filled his ears. As the bolt struck there was a split-second flash of intense burning heat that dissipated by the time his brain registered he'd been hit. His vision blurred, and the world around him slowed. I'm still alive, he thought. His ears were still ringing when he squinted up at the old man in wonder, even as his hair stood on end in the ozone-saturated air.

o o o

From a place beyond, he heard his name and brushed aside the web of sleep. The voice belonged to Don Manuel saying it was time to prepare for the despacho. The room was solidly dark but for the oil lamp casting long ominous shadows on the wall. In his half-waking state, the tentacles of the dream still gripped him. His terror of lightning impaling him was eclipsed by the fear Ita was dead. He couldn't shrug off the dread that threatened to suffocate him. His night sweat turned to a shiver of anxiety, not knowing whether she was alive, that by his own fault, something vitally important had been destroyed.

"You were crying out in your sleep." Don Manuel stood over him with a mug of coffee encircled in his hands.

The aroma lured Nico from his tortured thoughts. "A bad dream…" he mumbled. Wriggling his way out of the sleeping bag he still felt the jolt of electricity in his muscles.

"Here." He handed the mug to Nico. "Our dreams are guides. What do you make of it?"

A tarp whipping in the wind slapped against the side of the building, like a messenger at the door. Nico put the mug to his lips but his hand trembled, and he set it down before spilling it.

"We were in a field, high in the mountains. My great-great grandfather was there, but he looked like you. There was a storm, and we took cover, and then, I was struck by lightning. I felt the shock, like an explosion in my head. Everything slowed. Somehow, I survived."

"Quite a prophetic dream you had." Don Manuel said nodding.

"What do you mean? It was terrifying." He filled the basin from the hot kettle and splashed water over his face.

"To become Altomesayok you must be struck by lightning. It's a sign you are chosen by the Apu. It marks the beginning of the journey on the path of light."

"The lightning… wouldn't I have to be struck for real?"

"Dreams are the representations of memories and are often clearer. The idea that a memory is linked to imagining the future goes back as far as the study of philosophy. The connection between our memories and experiences exists like traces on paper of what has been written over or the emergence of an underlying image in a painting. Not only events that actually occurred but also events that might have occurred but did not."

"Are you saying it happened to me?"

Don Manuel smiled at the question. "To the Q'ero time isn't linear. They see the future as behind them and the past ahead of them. Have you noticed when Alma is relaying a story about something that happened in the past she gestures forward and when talking about events that happened long ago her gesture moves up and further forward, toward the horizon? When she talks about the future, and about passing knowledge onto her children, she waves over her shoulder, behind her. The past is what's known, what you've seen and experienced, so it has moved on and is in front of you. The future is unknown, behind your back where you can't see it. The Quechua word for tomorrow literally translates as, someday behind one's back. To the Incas and their descendants, Pachamama is both place and time."

"It makes total sense the way you explain it. So, where does our notion of time come from?"

"Temporal landmarks exist only in our head, in the ego. Andean cosmology isn't too esoteric a concept if you accept that time is like a river. The moving water is always in the present tense. Those who have come before are ahead of us, and your children will follow. Time exists simultaneously, spreading in all directions, like concentric ripples in the still water of a pond. Do you see how the women tie their shawls behind them, around their shoulders?"

"Yeah, they're beautiful..."

"They weave elaborate patterns into their shawls to guide the energy forward with intention. I like to think of these designs as prayers, informing the energy that flows through them. We have an impact on what we manifest. We create our lives ahead of us from the future behind."

"How strange, Camille said this to me on the climb to Machu

Picchu."

"That's right. Now is a term just as vague as here."

"I'm worried about my grandmother. In the dream she said I would be guided by an elder. I wanted to see her, but I couldn't. What if she's sick or in danger?"

"Nico, I understand your fear, but I don't think she'd want you to leave because of her."

"She wouldn't..." He closed his eyes and sighed. The weight of sadness felt crushing. "Is it possible to communicate between the living and the dead?"

"For Pachamama, the spirit world and the material world are intertwined. Nature speaks to us. The wind carries the words of the Apu from the mountains, she enfolds us with mist from the cloud forest, she is in the song of water falling. Listen. Life and death coexist, they are merely different aspects of one continuous experience. Spirit flows through us if we remain receptive. It's where inspiration comes from. Your grandmother is a wisdom keeper. She will continue to guide you."

During the night it snowed though sometime in the early hours it had stopped. The crusted snow crackled under his feet as he stepped into the hushed cover of darkness. He thought how much easier it would have been to stay inside the cocoon of his down sleeping bag. Drawing in the deepest breath he could of the cold diluted air, he lost himself in the stillness of the predawn morning. Walking toward the ridge where the ceremony would take place, outlines of the buildings began to rise out of the blackness as a silver mist appeared against a backdrop of the sacred mountain. They placed their blankets on the ground in front of a low stone wall, and Don Manuel began softly chanting as he unpacked the items in his prayer bundle.

The dampness penetrated Nico's limbs, but he felt strangely

alive in the presence of the unknowable, as well as reminded of his insignificance. The sky shifted from darkest blue to grey. The villagers and volunteers, wrapped in ponchos with chullos covering their heads, gathered around Don Manuel who began singing in Quechua to the Apu, the mountain spirits, thanking them on behalf of the community for bringing ayni, a balanced relationship between the people and the universe, aligning them physically, spiritually and with their hearts. Each item Don Manuel placed into the offering was a gift to Pachamama and symbolized the elements of fire, air, earth, water, and spirit—giving back what had been received. First, he placed a k'intu, an arrangement of three coca leaves, to inform each of the prayers. The light was barely there, softening the landscape like an impressionist painting. Nico saw an opportunity to participate by helping the elders make a bonfire. As Don Manuel sang, he added candies for life's sweetness, beans for protection, alpaca fur to bless their relationship with their animals, corn to thank Pachamama for their sustenance, and pisco to honor the ancestors. Folding the corners neatly, he wrapped the bundle, tying it with string. In the east a crack in the flat charcoal curtain opened just enough to emit a sliver of light across the sky washing it with a copper glow. Everyone turned their backs to the bonfire, releasing their claim to that which was being offered, and Don Manuel placed the gift of gratitude into the flames.

As the sun peeked over the mountain, the Apu allied with the living. Everyone shook hands and hugged, reminding Nico of the uncomfortable meet and greet period after church service when the congregation did the same. But here, they were unified in greeting the day with joy. The impulse to run was gone. He was thousands of miles from L.A., New York, and even from home. The dawn, like the despacho, was a gift to the earth—a kiss upon their faces—an invitation to open their hearts. Nico felt something else, something akin to belonging. For now, the fear of death had lessened.

18

The sun had fallen behind the peaks leaving in its wake a giant bruise spread across the darkening sky. In the failing light Nico sat on a nearby boulder watching Rumi lash a ladder to the frame of the water tower. She had the sharp features of a boy with long limbs and slim hips. Her arms were bare, and he noticed the muscle definition as she worked the rope. Her movements, like Don Manuel's, were deliberate, confident.

"I can't believe we finished," he said. "It took all of us to raise it upright. We never would have been able to get the tank onto the platform without the pulley you made."

Earlier, he helped Rumi and the two guys in the army jackets, which he learned were Danish students, assemble a windmill and install it on top of the water tower. While they worked, he asked her questions about how the system worked. As a rule, he wouldn't show his ignorance. That would have made him vulnerable. But she didn't seem to judge his lack of knowledge. She plainly explained the benefit of capturing the wind energy off the mountains to supplement the solar given the number of days without sun. Letting his guard down, he'd admitted to taking so much for granted, to which she said he wasn't alone.

"It takes a village," she chuckled at her use of the cliché. "Literally."

He was still energized by the camaraderie. He'd had a similar feeling of connection at the despacho ceremony, in the early hours of a purple twilight. The sensation had taken him by surprise. He was cautious and often came across as aloof. It was his way of concealing the shame of not being worthy, and of having lost everything he cared about. In the short time he'd been there, he noticed a fearless joy amongst everyone.

"Temperature's dropping fast," she said and picked her sweatshirt up off the ground where she'd tossed it earlier.

"Why'd you removed the bottom rungs?" he asked when she tugged at the ladder to test its strength.

"To discourage the younger children from climbing." The wind had picked up and she looked at the windmill spinning. "Look at that!" she said. A broad smile spread across her face.

"You did a great job." He didn't know if she'd heard him. For someone so young, he thought she was confident. Working on the water tower he noticed the others looked to her for direction.

He'd brought the guitar with him and picked it up. "I wanted to practice before dinner," he said, plucking absent mindedly at the strings. He began playing the opening refrain of "Stairway to Heaven."

Rumi turned toward him and listened, her eyes wide in amazement. "I love that song," she said when he stopped. "My mom used to play it on the guitar, too. It never gets old, does it?"

"Never…" He played the opening all the way through. Her gaze made him uncomfortable. He rolled his eyes comically and sang with exaggeration, purposely dragging out the last few words the way Robert Plant did.

She laughed and clapped her hands.

He was suddenly unbearably self-conscious and felt the need to escape.

"I better go and get washed up," Nico said looking at the ground.

He walked quickly away, then, as an afterthought he called back over his shoulder, "See you at dinner."

He hadn't meant to flirt with Rumi. Playing the guitar had always been a device, his way of connecting with women. He shook his head. Hitting on someone twenty years younger was a line he might have crossed in L.A., but not now, not here. He didn't want her to think he was a player. She was just a college girl, he thought. He felt ashamed, as if he'd committed a crime. Nothing here was like anywhere else, including himself. He knew this place would change him. But he wasn't sure he was ready for that.

Dusk was fast becoming night. A great absence gnawed at him. He was lonely. Not just for sex, although that was important to him. Sex gave him a sense of power and control that he needed. He missed the passion that ensued at the quickening of a new relationship and the certainty that she, whoever she was, would be the one to make him whole. It was the initial intimacy he craved. But then he found fault. Insecurity set in, followed by fear, and then disgust. He was afraid Camille would forget him. It had been she who suggested they work together when she returned from Iquitos. He hadn't yet decided if he even liked her. She was pushy and overbearing but her independence and confidence appealed to him. With Camille he could recover what he lost.

He recalled the argument he had with Luna just before he'd left L.A. She said love makes people stronger. Years ago, she'd handwritten a bible verse in a card and given it to him—Love is patient, Love is kind. He couldn't recall all of the words. What he knew for certain was every relationship left him with a nagging emptiness. It would be better, he thought, if he would just stop his calamitous pursuit of love. When he was younger, he believed love was the absolute state of belonging, a way to make him whole. Now, it was either his near-death experience or his entry into middle age that he decided love was a false promise of contentment and happiness. Love was changeable, and only by chance might it mature and become a stable condition that was reliable and trustworthy. He was certain he would never be in possession of love. Better to pursue immortality and be remembered for what he did in this life.

He stopped to look at the moon rising on a colorless horizon. His thoughts turned bleak. He asked himself, what had his life been? He saw himself as the sum of his misfortunes, and his world a prison from which there was no escape. The weight of his mother's death and his grandmother's mortality crippled him. He longed for home, his grandmother's voice.

The past is never lost, he thought. It was always there leaking in through the cracks, invading the present while he spent all his breath trying to conquer it. It was so strong an obsession that sometimes he felt dissociated from reality, no more than a shadow climbing the wall. He wished it were possible to escape time. To be borne by the river, each moment erased by the next, forever beginning anew. Retreating into the comfort of the knowable past was to embrace a melancholic happiness mingled with an uncharacteristic sense of goodbye. The future was a condition of becoming and a frightening testament to life slipping away.

In front of him was a road unlike any he'd traveled. There was no final destination, only the beginning of a lifelong inner journey to self-knowledge and acceptance. His entire being had been destroyed and yet a euphoric feeling had replaced his anger and sorrow. It was neither a blessing nor a punishment. Lost in the nebulous in-between, his release from material attachments brought its own abundance. To be open to the possibilities was to receive the harmony of the universe.

He was counting on Q'eros to fix him, steady him. It was a bleak landscape, filled with hardship. He knew there were lessons, and they would be unspoken. He would fail many tests. His was the truest quest, the quest for freedom. Freedom from the fear that kept him hostage. He had to let go of everything he once believed and desired. It was his last opportunity to choose something better.

Whatever I do will never be enough, he said to himself. I struggle against everything when all I want is to belong.

He stood in the enormous night, the darkness and dread deepening. In the year that just passed, before he'd been shot, he'd known somewhere within him that part of his life was over. He feared he would never be happy. Love. It was the trophy that always eluded him. Now he was certain it was too late. Instead, he'd been given another chance to find something to hold onto. There were things he'd tried to forget and put behind him, an inheritance of bitter disappointment and longing he'd known as a boy. Only nature itself was perfection, the Apu and Pachamama. It was here he could bring his life to account. He could stand still before the cosmos and be changed.

Nico walked to the one room dwelling he shared with Don Manuel. A deep cold off the mountains seeped into his bones. A light dusting of snow swirled in the air. In the distance was the faint barking of a dog. The llamas huddled together in the corrals. The window was aglow with the yellow light from an oil lamp. When Nico walked in, he was struck by the warmth from the stove. Manuel was dressed for dinner and reading by the light of the lantern next to his pallet. He didn't look up from the book when Nico entered.

"Sorry to be late. Have you been waiting for me to go to dinner?"

"No, it's fine. Everyone worked till sunset. We can head over as soon as you're ready," he said, turning his attention back to the book.

"*The Magic Mountain*?" Nico said. He remembered the title.

"Yes. It's interesting to read the exchanges between characters who hold such diverse ideologies and have lost all sense of time while cloistered in a sanatorium."

"What's a sanatorium?" Nico asked. He liked when others told him about books. He wished he had the attention needed to read. He was embarrassed that he couldn't set his mind to it. Luna had given him books that she said he would like. He tried.

"It was a medical facility where people went to be treated for tuberculosis around the first World War, before there were antibiotics. It's genius that Thomas Mann set this book in the Swiss Alps in a sanatorium, a clever way to put these people together and where his young protagonist learns about art, love, politics… and humanity."

Don Manuel described the characters in the novel and explained their different perspectives on life. Although the book was written and set long ago, it struck Nico that people's desires were no different. If asked months ago what he wanted, Nico would have said power, wealth, and the skill to influence others. He had been living with his obsessions and fantasies, and with his own set of rules. They were what made him who he was. He coveted acclaim for his achievements.

He had been living in the past, worried about the future, and there was never enough time to make his mark on the world. He'd only just arrived in Q'eros and he'd observed something he hadn't appreciated during his time here twenty years ago. These people and everyone he'd met lived in the present and embraced life. They were happy to share their time and knowledge.

Nico poured hot water from a big kettle into a tin basin. He stripped down and washed his body in the steaming water. Even this haphazard sponge bath helped to relieve the penetrating cold. He realized how much he'd taken for granted the luxury of indoor plumbing. The solar showers they were installing were going to make a huge difference in the lives of the Q'ero. Generations of families have lived in these stone shelters without running water. They hauled water from the stream and heated it on the stove. Smoke from fuel cakes of llama dung burned their nostrils and stung their eyes.

In the amber light he saw the long shadow of his nakedness on the wall. He looked at the pale scar on his torso. The residual pain had faded, but it was only the physical wound that had healed. He wouldn't be here if he hadn't been shot. He returned more and more frequently to that night. It was a state of unreality where he left his body and observed himself. Oddly, he wasn't very troubled by the dissociative experience. He thought it might be a mental healing process he was experiencing and that he should mention it to Don Manuel.

He didn't shave, deciding it was easier to let his beard grow. Taking the neatly folded black pants and dark woven dress shirt he'd worn the night before from his duffle bag, he dressed quickly.

"Will there be music again tonight?" Nico asked.

"I'm sure." Don Manuel said, setting the book down. "Music is integral to their lives here in Q'eros."

"Is it okay if I bring my guitar to dinner," Nico asked. "I can try to pick up some of the songs."

"They would like that." He took a well-worn military green parka off the hook in the wall, the kind an explorer would own.

Nico zipped his new down jacket up to his chin and wrapped the scarf he'd bought in Pisac around his neck. He slung the guitar case over his shoulder, and they walked over to the dining hall. Nico hoped there would be more of the local beer and brandy at dinner, it would give him the confidence he needed to play the guitar in front of so many people.

The room was a cacophony of accents. Everyone speaking at once. He looked around the room and spotted Rumi with her friends. She looked up and nodded at him; a small smile lifted the corners of her mouth. Saskia waved them over and they took the last remaining seats next to her. She was deep in conversation with a volunteer from an NGO that provided water filtration systems to remote villages around the world.

Don Rafael stood, and the room quieted. He held up a potato like it was a national treasure. It is believed the Inca were the first to cultivate potatoes as early as 8000 BC. Speaking in Quechua he thanked Pachamama for keeping his people alive.

Alma served and passed the plates down the table. She stood no taller than five feet. Her face was heart-shaped, its countenance serene with skin the color of gingerbread and black hair down to her waist. She was ageless. Her dark eyes possessed the knowledge of generations. She wore a white blouse embroidered with flowers and a tiered skirt that rustled when she walked. Her scarf was knotted at her collar bone in the traditional fashion. Nico remembered that the intricate pattern woven into the scarf brought the future forward. He was still shy around her, afraid to speak in her presence. She never demanded respect or admiration; it was just given to her.

"I'll grab us some beers," Nico said.

He brought three beers from the cooler and set them down next to their plates. Saskia had turned her attention back to Don Manuel. They discussed the day's work.

"Isn't that right, Nico?" Saskia asked.

"Yes, of course," Nico answered without knowing the question. He was somehow drawn back to the past, unable to find his way forward. It was as though he sat facing backwards as the train pulled away.

When bowls of whole boiled potatoes were passed around the table, Nico thought how much he craved french fries. They were his favorite comfort food that reminded him of diners and fast-food chains in the United States. He imagined sitting in a booth across from his father in the diner near their apartment in New York City. He ordered a plate of fries and a Coke. First, he shook just the right amount of salt on them. He didn't like drizzling the ketchup haphazardly over the perfect golden sticks of potato. He squeezed a little puddle of ketchup on the side, dunking each fry only once. He missed New York. People walked everywhere, nothing ever closed. The diner was open twenty-four hours. If it were late, after midnight, a man might be mopping the floor, a yellow bucket on wheels next to him. He looked up from his daydream when he heard Don Manuel's voice.

"When was the last time you thanked Mother Earth for the bounty she supplies?" Don Manuel said. "Indigenous culture is based on respect for the land. Many people today think food comes from the supermarket, from factories. Food is sacred. For the Q'ero, the potato is holy. We live because of the plants and the animals. Ayni, the principle of reciprocity, teaches us to honor life. Honor death."

"We said grace at Sunday dinner. Until my father left. Then, I don't remember much after that. Most of my memories are of cooking and eating with Ita. I spent a lot of time in the kitchen with her. She taught me to make empanadas and locro. Her chimichurri is the best." He smiled at the thought. "I remember Thanksgiving in the States. There was a huge parade with humongous balloons of cartoon characters and superheroes. One of my father's friends from the restaurant always invited us to their home for dinner. There was so much food. Afterward we sprawled on the sofa and watched American football. My friend Luna told me they didn't teach the truth about Thanksgiving in school, how the Europeans stole the land from the American Indians and brought disease to the tribes killing most of them, just like the conquistadors did here."

"Luna. That's a pretty name. Was she your girlfriend?"

Nico fell silent. He heard Luna in his head saying that he'd pushed everyone away. Nico wanted Don Manuel to approve of him. He experienced a twinge of shame. Luna said if you love someone, you don't control them. Was she right? Does love really make people stronger? Luna had been a true friend to him, and he'd treated her terribly.

"No, she was never my girlfriend, not like that. I sometimes forget that she's a lot older than me. Luna was one of my students and we became friends. She was always there for me…" Nico said with certainty.

A platter of empanadas landed in front of him, and Nico served himself then passed it down. He wanted Don Manuel to know he had a worthy friend.

"She's American Indian," he added, "she taught me about their beliefs and ceremonies." He was relieved Don Manuel didn't press him for more information since he'd forgotten if she were only part Native American and to which tribe she belonged.

"Is that so?" Don Manuel thought for a minute. "Apart from having different creation stories, their spiritual teachings stem from a single source. Honoring all life, all elements in nature—the animals, the trees, rivers, mountains, and even the wind share the same spiritual essence. It is up to us to live responsibly and have respect for the energies that gave us life. We are how we live, and our experiences bring self-awareness."

Nico felt insecure. He worried that he would be seen as ignorant.

He wished he could be like Don Manuel. Everyone adored him, they were drawn to him, they trusted him. He made them feel accepted. What Don Manuel possessed was magic. He was completely unselfconscious, and as smart as he was, there was nothing about him that was flamboyant or pretentious. If you tried to capture his essence, to define it too clearly, it vanished. Nico had spent long periods of time with him in the car. He'd listened to him explain philosophy and the ancient teachings. It struck Nico that he knew little about Don Manuel's personal life. Yet, he had willingly entrusted him with his own.

"I'll work hard. I won't fail you, Don Manuel."

"Fail me? You can't fail me or Don Castillo."

"I guess… I failed myself."

"You are your own teacher, Nico. The lessons come when you listen to your voice, observe it. Free yourself of fear and anger. They have paralyzed you. You know this. You're a wounded healer. You have everything you need within you."

"You aren't the first person to call me that—a wounded healer." He thought of Luna, then remembered Camille had called him that, too. "Why me?" he asked.

"You're descended from the ancestors, the blood of the paqo and the Spanish. You can move between both worlds. But it's up to you to confront yourself. Let go of your fears and your desires. They are your downfall. Stop believing you are nothing without them. When we have no love for the self, then what else matters?"

Nico pursed his lips, as though considering. The words tripped so easily off Don Manuel's tongue, like fat raindrops from a leaf after a downpour. Until now, Nico rarely considered changing his beliefs. His entire life he'd been driven by his desire for wealth, for celebrity. He believed that without the recognition, without everything he valued he was worthless; it was all that mattered. He believed that all men wanted to be famous. To be famous was to be loved. But once he had them, it was never enough. For all his pursuits, life had shown him the more he craved glory, the further it receded from him. He'd manipulated and controlled everyone, demanded their loyalty. The drugs and the lies had twisted him into something he no longer recognized. It wasn't that he couldn't be a healer, but the obsession, his desires, had destroyed him. The fear of loss and the loneliness he felt, had been his downfall. It was true, he had driven everyone away. Everything he'd believed in was a monument to a false religion from which he ought to turn away.

"Let go, you say?" He felt himself wither.

To let go. To accept blame. It was inconceivable. Impossible. It had to be someone else's fault. He prayed to be free of the anguish and the longing, so immeasurable it could barely be contained. Whether it was some unhappiness in childhood solidified by time or carried into this life from another, he didn't know. It was a pervasive sadness so vast he couldn't name it. All he knew was he could no longer bear it. The only way to dismiss the truth would be to leave Q'eros, to abandon his dream of being a healer. He wasn't willing to do that. It seemed to him now that this was the road that would lead him elsewhere. It wasn't the first time he'd been given this message. In passing years there had been a chorus of voices—pleading, anxious, angry, wise. But it now seemed clearer coming from Don Manuel, a medicine man, who had accepted him into this remote society. He wanted to know more.

Everyone had received their plated meal. After the gratitude blessing, Alma signaled it was time to eat. Saskia leaned in to talk about projects she hoped to complete in the days ahead. There were only a few weeks left before the students and volunteers would have to return to their schools and jobs. It was imperative that as outsiders they didn't do more than what had been requested by the village elders. They'd been invited to help improve living conditions that did not threaten the cultural integrity of the Q'ero who, it is said, are the indigenous spirit keepers that hold the world together.

Don Manuel said he would have to head down to the Sacred Valley soon and give despacho to the tourists while it was still the height of the season. This came as a surprise to Nico. The fellow next to him tapped his arm and Nico turned to the fair-skinned freckled face of the British student sitting in the seat beside him. Nico couldn't recall his name and was relieved the boy started the conversation by announcing himself.

"Finch," he said and put out his hand.

"Nico." They shook hands.

"Tomorrow we're putting up solar panels on the bathrooms and greenhouse. Will you be able to give us a hand with that?" Finch asked.

"Sure…" Nico hesitated not knowing if it was his decision to make. "I don't see why not. I think we finished the water tower today."

Nico couldn't help worrying that Don Manuel was going without him. He would have to wait until later to find out. He wanted more time with him. He needed to learn more about what it meant to be a wounded healer. Was it a good thing? Could he be a high paqo? He felt he was running out of time. He didn't want to be left behind.

Finch continued the conversation by asking Nico where he was from and what had brought him to Q'eros. He hated answering questions. He was tired of making up stories, tired of telling lies.

19

After the long day working outside, Nico was hungry as a ravenous wolf. Even the boiled potatoes exploded with flavor. He'd come to appreciate the colorful tubers. Grown in their country of origin at such a high altitude, they had a deep rich flavor which tasted nothing like those from a supermarket in California.

Everyone at the table was talking, it was very loud. He told Finch a little about himself. He said he'd been to Q'eros years ago, when he was around Finch's age, and decided to come back. He left out the details. Finch was a student in London studying sustainable agriculture. He and a few of his classmates had come on a work study program. Nico noted the difference in their backgrounds, but they had ended up in the same place. It was as if Nico were given a second chance. He saw in this intelligent boy a different version of himself. He muddled through the questions Finch asked, giving answers that didn't reveal much. Nico hated feeling like he was being interviewed. His confidence only came when he was conscious of being charming and seductive with women. He couldn't summon that bravado here. It would be foolish to try. He pushed back the terrible loneliness that threatened to claim him. The emptiness of those who are ruined.

The plates were cleared and jugs of pisco were set out. There was the scrape of chairs being pushed back from the table. Guitars and flutes materialized as though they'd been conjured. The discordant sound of them all being tuned at once was exhilarating. Nico hesitated, then reached behind him for his guitar. He poured himself a brandy, filling the glass to the brim and left the jug close at hand. Two of the fellows across the room began a traditional folk song with an upbeat tempo that was easy for him to follow. He'd moved stacks of lumber with them earlier in the day. He remembered their names were Alphonse and Juan, although he wasn't sure which one was which. They nodded to him, and he followed along, getting the feel of the music with chords then adding fingerpicking. The women began to dance and Rafael's daughter, Illa, was among them. It was hard to tell, but Nico guessed she was around Rumi's age. Her shawl moved with her body, first one side then the other, light as a bird's wing. Rumi finally joined in, and Nico watched her mirroring Illa, their smiles growing wider until they giggled girlishly like children at recess.

Several songs into the evening, Alphonse, or maybe it was Juan, began to play "Habla Me" by Gipsy Kings. Their modern flamenco music was world famous and Nico had learned to play many of their songs. This song stirred memories that caused feelings of heartache, and he was glad for the brandy to help him overcome his inhibition. When it was his turn Nico picked a popular tune by Jesse Cook, an acclaimed classical jazz guitarist. Nico played the catchy melody in the fast, frenetic style he'd mastered. The other players kept up the percussive rhythm and by midway through the song everyone was dancing, including the children. He watched Saskia and Manuel, they appeared comfortable with each other and enjoying themselves. Later into the evening he noticed they'd gone. He wondered if they were together romantically. For a while he felt angry believing they had abandoned him. Then he realized he'd been included in the evening's festivities and that he enjoyed himself singing and playing guitar. He'd been a part of something.

When everyone left the hall, Nico helped Alma and Ch'aska turn the chairs up on the table. He knew once the volunteers had decamped from the village there would no longer be feasts held in the community center which for now acted as a dining hall. It was typical to eat a meal consisting of only boiled potatoes, peeling them with your fingers while sitting on the ground. He offered to sweep the floor, but they wouldn't hear of it. The exhaustion showed in his eyes. He thanked them and bundled up before stepping outside where the cold air took his breath away.

Snow sweatered the rocky ground with a white softness. There wasn't a footprint to be seen in any direction. The coming months would become increasingly colder and wetter. In his mind he would leave, open a studio somewhere, make money again. He was anxious about Camille's offer and if she would contact him. There was no future he could see for himself; life had stopped like a broken watch. His past, everything he'd known and cared to remember, was in front of him moving further down the river. A Christmas dinner at home in San Telmo held laughter and the aroma of cumin and sauteed onions. His hands wrapped around his father's waist as they sped through Pinamar on a motorcycle, the smell of salt and the wind in his hair. He could resurrect the images with such potency and brilliance, the sounds and smells were indelible. He may be uncertain about the future, but his memories were deeply drawn. They were sun bleached photographs he'd overwritten.

Stars, like the eyes of the universe, appeared the brightest this time of year. Close enough to touch, they blanketed the sky. Walking to the hut, the gravel sounding under his feet broke the silence. He felt himself removed from reality, as if he were floating. He was able to observe himself with a sort of numbness brought on by too much brandy. Things could not be more transparent than they were in this light. Q'eros was unfolding to him. This was a place of healing where he didn't need to hide. This village with its damp, unforgiving climate. Its pale sky and mist covered mountains. Its barren shelters with earthen floors and walls stained with the smoke from burnt cakes of llama dung. He began to see another side of himself. He'd been caught between the currents. Here, they came together to reveal the future that was coming from behind.

Don Manuel was reading his book when Nico entered the room. Some warmth remained from the hearth and the sting of smoke lingered in the air. He was wearing his chullo pulled down over his ears and mittens with the finger flaps pulled back so he could turn the pages. He looked up when Nico walked in.

"Good music tonight, my friend. You play well. Everyone had a fun time and stayed late."

"Thanks, it was pretty great." He was thrilled to receive the compliment and that Don Manuel called him his friend.

Nico glanced at his watch and saw it was only ten o'clock. It felt much later but that was because they'd gone to dinner just after sunset. He'd fallen out of the custom of wearing a wristwatch and felt a touch of sentimentality each time he looked at his father's old Rolex. Nico desperately wanted to get the question off his chest. He was glad for the boldness given to him by the brandy.

"When are you leaving?" Nico asked casually. What was it, he wondered, that he'd done wrong? Was Don Manuel abandoning him? He was distraught, overcome with defeat. There was no place for him to go. In the spillover light from Manuel's lantern he changed out of his dinner clothes and tugged on a long sleeve thermal and sweatpants to sleep in.

"Not for a few days," Don Manuel answered. He lay the open

book against his chest and looked over his reading glasses at Nico. "First, there is a blessing to thank the llamas."

"What's that?"

"Now is when the villagers harvest the corn. They journey down with the llamas to bring up the harvest, as well as squash, peppers, and wood. The corn is stored up here, in shelters at roughly 16,000 feet, with potatoes and alpaca meat. The women sort the best ears and set aside the seeds to plant in December. Some of the corn is coaxed into sprouting, then fermented to make chicha, the corn beer. It's quite an endeavor, but then there's a big celebration. The llamas are decorated with colorful yarn and bells. The villagers sing and play flutes and bang drums to thank the llamas for carrying the heavy loads back up here. Offerings are made to ask the spirits for protection, good health, and fertility of the animals." He laughed, and even in the dim light Nico saw the glint in his eyes. "And of course, there's lots of chicha to drink!"

"I wouldn't want to miss it!"

"Afterward we'll go to the Sacred Valley to give despacho to the tourists."

"I didn't know if you wanted me to go with you." He needed to be sure.

There was an awkward silence, as if he were considering. When Don Manuel continued his voice had become more serious.

"Many people are judgmental about spiritual tourism, but giving despacho at the retreats does more than provide a much-needed income to the entire village. The ceremonies and cleansing rituals strengthen the connection between people and the natural world. Offerings to Pachamama and the Apu are tributes signifying that everything is connected; humans, the animals, and plants all contain kawsay, the living energy. The Q'eros worldview is integral to their daily life. They are in a constant dialog with Pachamama and the cosmos to keep everything in balance. To restore harmony, to be in right relationship with nature and with Mother Earth, the Q'ero willingly share their wisdom with others. They believe it is crucial for the preservation of life on this planet. They are the keepers of an ancient spiritual knowledge. We need to keep the teachings alive by making them accessible."

"You're a great teacher…" Nico said. Everything Don Manuel said was true. He wished he found the right words, but there was nothing he could say. He hoped he wouldn't be judged too harshly for giving despacho to his students. He'd done the best he could.

"As a paqo I give despacho. As a philosopher and religion professor, I teach indigenous knowledge systems to my students. But it is essential that they follow the teachings and not the teacher. The work of a paqo is integral to reciprocity. The Lakota say *Mitakuye Oyasin*, we are all related. It reflects the ideology of interconnectedness; it's a concept that crosses all the universal teachings. When we gave despacho to the volunteers who are donating their time and efforts to Q'eros, it was to unite us, to bring harmony and right relationship to the work we are doing."

"Do paqos go often to the retreats?" It was time consuming to get there and most didn't own vehicles. They would have to arrange with drivers in Paucartambo.

"July and August are the height of the tourist season. The paqos have been traveling to Cuzco and the Sacred Valley since the end of June, after Qoyllur Rit'i."

"Did you go to Qoyllur Rit'i this year?" Ita had made a big deal over his childhood trip to the Snow Star Festival.

"Yeah, I went with Tica and her family. I try and go every year, but it's becoming harder because I have arthritis. Even with the bus to Mahuayani, the walk to the Sanctuary is still four hours from midnight to dawn. Although, a moonlit trek to the sanctuary is magical."

"I was too young to remember. What's it like?"

"There is nothing more spectacular. Imagine thousands of pilgrims, mostly indigenous Quechua and Aymara wearing colorful costumes, carrying flags and crosses, and playing musical instruments, walk to the sanctuary at the foot of the Qollqepunku glacier in the Sinakara Valley where they pay homage to Señor de Qoyllur Rit'i and the sacred Apu." Manuel yawned and set the book down on the ledge next to him.

"How did this festival come to be? I never knew…"

Manuel heard the genuine interest in Nico's voice, and the professor in him had no objection to telling the story.

"Qoyllur Rit'i loosely translates as Snow Star, which symbolizes purity. Its mystical significance is essentially about retrieving your highest vision. The festival is a blend of Andean and Christian religious cultures. It celebrates the reappearance of the Pleiades—a constellation seen at the winter solstice in the southern hemisphere the week before the Christian feast of Corpus Christi—which is the beginning of harvest. The festival's origin story was that Christ appeared to a Native shepherd boy in the form of a mestizo boy. The mysterious boy helped the shepherd and then disappeared leaving the image of Christ embedded in a rock which became the symbolic focus of the pilgrimage. Much like what you saw at the Virgen del Carmen in Paucartambo, there are troupes of dancers. Ukukus, men dressed in bear costumes are the guardians of the Qoyllur Rit'i festival and the only ones allowed on the sacred glacier whose melting water was believed to have healing powers. It used to be we brought back ice from the glacier, but since global warming that's not done anymore."

Manuel glanced at the small travel alarm clock he'd set on the windowsill. "Good God, look what time it is? We ought to get some sleep." He waited for Nico to zip himself into his sleeping bag and then turned off the lantern.

Nico lay sleepless in the dark. His memories billowed in, like curtains during a storm, terrifying and unforgettable. He contemplated the death of his mother and the fear of losing Ita. He cried when his dog Stella died, and one time he saw the spirit leave the body of a deer he'd shot. He wondered if animals were aware of their mortality. After a time, he too would pass into eternity. The beauty of life is its transience, he thought. If in death he were remembered, then he will have lived.

He couldn't remember when it began. Like a fever that had broken, the longing and unfulfilled desire had been cleared by the storm. Perhaps he was here to be closer to obscurity. He listened to Manuel breathing in a slow and steady rhythm. The comforting sound reminded him of his dog sleeping next to him on his bed.

° ° °

He awoke in darkness. Out the small window, he watched as the sky gradually whitened and the mountains appeared from under the mist. Manuel was brushing his teeth.

"I didn't hear the alarm,' Nico said.

"I woke up before it went off. I let you sleep a while longer."

"I'll hurry." He was embarrassed to keep Manuel waiting.

"Are you going to work on the greenhouse today?" Don Manuel asked while lacing his work boots.

"I can, unless there's something I can help you with." He preferred to be in his company.

"Go ahead and help Finch until the llama blessing begins."

After breakfast they headed in opposite directions. It was bitter cold. The frost, like gossamer filaments, lay over everything and crunched underfoot. Nico hadn't asked but guessed Manuel would be engaged somehow in making chicha. Finch drove the truck loaded with solar panels over to the greenhouse. Two other guys from a university in Lima joined them. The mounting apparatus for the solar panels had to be attached to the outside frame of the greenhouse. By noon they'd made considerable progress installing the clamps and racking on the bathrooms. They were tired and hungry when the lunch bell rang. As they approached the community center, they saw the llamas on the distant hillside.

The sound of flutes and drums echoed off the mountains. Children gathered the youngest llamas and decorated them with garlands of plastic flowers. An offering of burnt coca leaves was made to the Apu and chicha was tossed over the herd as a blessing to insure their health and fertility. Then, everyone celebrated by drinking chicha and chewing coca leaves all afternoon and into the night.

Don Manuel held a glass bottle of corn beer that at one time may have contained Burgundy. He threw his arm over Nico's shoulder in joyful inebriated camaraderie.

"This is a rowdy event," Don Manuel said slurring his words. "But by dancing, and singing, and drinking chicha, the ritual becomes a reintegration with the forces of nature. Jung called it the collective unconscious, a reservoir of shared knowledge and experience. I like to think of it as a psychic inheritance of memories passed down by our ancestors."

The flutes played to the mountain spirits, long drawn-out whistles like an eagle's call. The singers' voices crescendoed in a high falsetto that seeped under the skin. The bells on the necks of the llamas clanged wildly as they circled, chased by children and dogs alike. The hypnotic effect might be compared to the trancelike state one experiences during a gospel sermon.

Nico allowed himself to become one with the wildness, to

experience what might best be described as a burning atonement.

I can survive my life, he thought. This is a place to quench the rage and lust in my heart and be reborn.

It had never been in his nature to accept this condition of belonging, a feeling akin to happiness, to be a part of this eclectic band of revelers. These Quechua families who live as one. It was nothing like he imagined.

I'm making a new memory, he said to himself under the beer's influence. It was impossible for him to express how he felt and know how the experience would change him.

He stretched his mind backward and forward through time, weaving them together. Whether by blood or circumstance he connected the past with the future. He was sent to Q'eros to be healed by the apus; to learn to accept love where it was offered. Anything was possible in this rugged mountain landscape and under this sky full of stars.

20

Nico squeezed his eyes shut and pressed his hands to his temples. The blaring alarm resounded in his head long after Manuel turned it off. A sour taste from the corn beer lingered in his mouth, and the thought of several hours in the car on the winding, bumpy road made his stomach turn over.

"You'll feel better after some breakfast," said Don Manuel encouragingly.

"Oh, God." Nico said, rubbing his head with both hands. He went over to the wash basin and splashed cold water on his face.

"If you finished hooking up the shower yesterday, we can check it out."

"It's working. But there might not be any warm water yet," Nico said.

"Well, then we can leave right after breakfast."

They took only what they needed. Nico loaded their bags and his guitar into the back of the Jeep. Somehow, the rickety sounding vehicle managed to get them everywhere they went. Manuel characterized their impending trip through the Sacred Valley as an odyssey. Then he began to tell Nico about Homer's epic poem. Nico wondered why Manuel didn't seem to have a hangover from the chicha.

Once they were on the road, Nico put on his headphones and listened to meditative music. Manuel played a recorded lecture by one of his colleagues at the university. It was comforting that they didn't need to converse. He thought about Camille and wondered if anyone would know where she was. If he was honest with himself, he didn't expect her to contact him.

They followed the winding road down the mountain range. Alma had sent them off with thermoses of hot coffee and a paper sack of corn empanadas. The view, like from a travel postcard, was breathtaking in its beauty. Islands of clouds dotted the pale blue sky, like wreathes they encircled the peaks. The wind blew hard sometimes shaking the vehicle which caused Nico to gasp. Manuel slowed and then came to a full stop at the sight of an Andean condor soaring on the thermal updrafts. The sight of it was extraordinary.

"They can fly for hours without once flapping their wings." Manuel said.

"I've only seen a photograph. Until you see one in person you can't imagine the wingspan. It must be at least ten feet."

Don Manuel pulled slowly ahead, his eyes back on the treacherous road. Nico tried not to look at the sheer drop off the cliff's edge, which terrified him.

"Are you sure no one will come up the mountain today?" he asked doubtfully.

"Hope not."

Nico thought he saw him wink. By now, he had learned Don Manuel didn't worry about things he couldn't control. Nico put his headphones back on and fell asleep to quell his fear.

The whine of the Jeep's engine subsided. Looming mountains stood guard over the valley of rolling green hills. The staggered terraces planted with corn ascended, like a grand staircase. Sheep huddled together in the pastures. In the distance a dog barked. Long stretches of road meandered through lazy villages. Smoke spiraled from the chimney of a stone house with a dried grass roof.

Nico was awakened by the sun on his face.

"I'm sorry I fell asleep," he said.

"My kids always fell asleep in the car. When they were small, the only way I could get them down for a nap was to drive them around."

This was the first time Don Manuel mentioned he had children. Nico wondered how old they were and where they lived. He didn't venture to ask. He thought if Manuel wanted to tell him, he would.

Nico opened the car window letting in the cool fresh air. They drove as if through a bucolic landscape painting, a Constable perhaps. The light was pure, and the air fragrant with the scent of oranges. In the distance, two girls ran up a hillside in the direction of the flock. For a moment he was riddled with doubt. He questioned if this was where he was supposed to be.

Don Manuel sighed and glanced over at Nico to see if he was still awake. "I think you'll like Adele," he said.

Manuel had mentioned their first stop was the guest house of an old friend. The memory of her was written on his face. Nico didn't say anything. It wasn't a question. Don Manuel was filled with stories of mythology and philosophy. Nico learned they were stories within stories, the legends held ancient wisdom. That's what Don Manuel had taught him. He said, "stories teach people about themselves." Nico waited for a story.

"I met Adele in Paris a long time ago when I was a young lad, years before I met my wife. I was attending a lecture given by her father, a French diplomat. I remember it was springtime. I was completing my doctorate at Harvard and I'd taken time off to meet up with friends in Paris. Adele was still in boarding school but she had come to see her father." Manuel paused, as if imaging the day all those years ago. "She had a quick mind. I remember we had a somewhat provocative discussion about Philip Roth's controversial new novel, *Portnoy's Complaint*." He chuckled softly, taking his eyes off the road only long enough to see if Nico might have understood the reference. "As young as she was, she wasn't naïve. I couldn't help being attracted to her, everyone was."

Don Manuel stopped talking. He sighed again and Nico thought he might continue, but he stayed focused on the road ahead. After a few minutes he picked up where he'd left off.

"Years later, I heard she was in London studying at the Royal College of Art. She'd married a writer only to divorce him a year later. She never remarried, just moved around the world like an itinerant poet. Somehow I always seemed to know her whereabouts. You know, she was possibly the most interesting woman I ever met, but I never pursued her."

"Why not? It seemed like you had a strong connection."

Manuel paused for a moment. When he spoke there was no doubt in his voice.

"She would have been bored with me," he said, shaking his head. "My lifestyle would never be glamorous enough for her. Three years ago, she inherited some money and purchased the property here. The house resembles a European literary salon from an earlier century. So, the first stop on our odyssey around the Sacred Valley is Adele's." He looked over at Nico and smiled. The depth of time and memory reflected in his eyes.

They drove along the Urubamba River in silence until they arrived at a turn that led to a group of blush-pink stucco cottages nestled beneath towering eucalyptus trees. Leaving their bags in the car, they walked on a stone path through the garden to the front porch. When they rang the bell, Adele came to the door.

"Mon chéri!" she exclaimed, greeting Manuel with a kiss on both his cheeks. "Bienvenu!" she chimed, extending her arms to Nico. "Entrez, entrez! Je suis ravi que tu sois là! I am delighted you're here!" Adele ushered them into a large foyer. She spoke quickly to a young man about getting their bags from the car and to put them in their rooms.

She was tall and slender, with flyaway blonde hair and large, pale eyes. The diaphanous vintage Thea Porter caftan she was wearing could have been in the collection of Elizabeth Taylor. She had the air of both a Hollywood movie star and a Haight Ashbury hippy. When she spoke, she fiddled with the strands of beads around her neck. Her French accent caught Nico off guard. To be reminded of Élodie gave him a tingling sensation at the nape of his neck.

It was late morning. Her guests milled about in the sun-drenched parlor. The room filled with the honeyed accents of French, Spanish, and British English. Manuel knew the gentleman with a grey beard from his time teaching at Oxford. A friend of Adele's walked over to say hello. She reminded Manuel they had met last year in Cusco at a fundraiser.

Nico said nothing. His silence was reserved, observant.

Adele pulled them away. "Come, I want you to meet an old friend of mine." She introduced them to a distinguished man about her age. He was from the British Museum and in Peru on a research project. Manuel showed interest and they began to converse.

A woman entered the room, her eyes searched for someone.

"Madelaine!" Adele called out and went over to greet her with double cheek kisses.

Nico looked up and saw she was an attractive young woman with caramel skin and black hair. For a moment, his mind played tricks on him and he thought it was Maya.

Lunch was served in the adjacent sitting room. The decoration was an inviting mix of French antiques that had come down from the family alongside Pre-Columbian pottery and hand-woven textiles by local women in Pisac. The colors were rich and deep. A table was set with Limoges plates and they were served a luncheon of salads and quiches with white wine in cut crystal stemware. Adele must have spoken to her guests about Don Manuel. During lunch he was the focus of their questions about the Q'ero. After lunch, the guests dispersed and Don Manuel suggested a siesta would be restorative. When Nico awoke, the sun had fallen on the horizon and Don M wasn't in his room. He went in search of bottled water and saw Manuel in the parlor in deep conversation with Adele and left them undisturbed.

Before cocktails, Don Manuel made an elaborate despacho ceremony. He handed each guest a k'intu of three coca leaves in which to place their intentions. Adele supplied fresh flowers, gemstones, feathers, tobacco, candies, and other traditional elements. Nico stood next to him during the ritual as he washed the sage smoke over each guest chanting a prayer in Quechua. The ceremony was given to cleanse the negative energies from the body. Nico had practiced this back in Los Angeles, but now he was learning from a master and had written down the words in his notebook.

Later in the evening they gathered in the living room. A wood fire burned in the fireplace. Many of the women wore long filmy dresses. Several men wore sport coats and a tie. Others dressed more casually in linen trousers and button front shirt with the sleeves rolled. Nico was mesmerized by the soft voices of various languages. It wasn't at all what he expected. Guests leaned, as if posing, against the mantel or perched on the back of a chair, wine glass in hand. The room had become perfumed with Gauloises smoke. Don Manuel spoke about Q'eros and Andean cosmology. His gift for storytelling kept them engaged. They were all highly educated and well-read.

A cellist with the Berlin Philharmonic had read Don Manuel's paper on the teachings of the philosopher Krishnamurti. She had studied theosophy and began a conversation that brought everyone to attention. Nico observed how she talked with her hands, her fingers moving as though she were fingering the neck of the instrument. Her eyes rested on Nico when she explained how Krishnamurti had been groomed to be the new world teacher but rejected the idea of being a guru. She went on to say that he'd become interested in psychology and spoke about leading a spiritual life based on awareness and freedom.

An elegant man from Barcelona, his long dark hair pulled into a tight knot on his head, segued to the question of whether one can achieve happiness. His dress showed refined taste and wealth. His mouth was tight and his eyes serious. If he were happy, it didn't show on his face.

"Happiness is completely within our control," Don Manuel said.

This piqued Nico's interest. He'd given up on happiness. It had always eluded him. Nico tried to remember when or if he'd ever been happy. The thrill of joy, shrieking laughter he'd experienced as a child, had vanished long ago. He knew sorrow and anger. They were familiar and at times comforting. He hoped he would be able to find his way to happiness.

The Spaniard said he had spent time at a Buddhist monastery. "You have to train your mind to let go of any attachment to outcomes, basically you mustn't have any expectation of happiness, then happiness will be the result."

"That's an excellent, and simple way to put it." Don Manuel said.

Nico didn't feel they were arrogant or condescending, but he knew he didn't fit in. He didn't possess their education, their sophistication. But he was intrigued. He didn't always know the questions to ask his new teacher, it was much easier to listen to the others converse with him. He didn't want to feel intimidated, but he did. The hours passed. Thankfully, the brandy had been abundant, but was now finished. He felt his head nod and his eyelids were heavy.

"Good God!" Adele said, "What time is it?"

Nico looked at his watch. "Three o'clock."

Seeing the Rolex was a reminder he needed to call his father. Ita might be there if Lucia had sent for her. When they finally retired to their rooms, he looked out the window. The moon had set, and he could barely make out the outline of the mountains.

It was early, around nine. There was no one in the dining room. The cook made them a breakfast of poached eggs and croissants with fresh elderberry jam. Adele hadn't come down and there were only a few guests reading in the sitting room. They loaded their bags in the car and departed quietly.

They had not been driving long when they arrived at a rustic modern chalet cradled in a corn field with a spectacular view of the mountains. Walking into the lobby, a neutral palette of glass and stone with a cathedral ceiling, Nico remarked how it could not be more different than Adele's cozy cottage. Here they found a young, active, mostly American crowd dressed in hiking gear for a climb or suited up for kayaking on the river. The concierge assigned them to adequate rooms in the back near the staff quarters. The despacho ceremony was to follow afternoon tea, and Nico's yoga class would be the next day at ten in the morning. They'd been given permission to use the spa and heated pool. They dropped their bags in the room and ordered lunch on the pool deck. Manuel set an alarm in case they fell asleep in the comfortable lounge chairs. He'd heard the chef was a young, talented Peruvian whose farm to table cuisine had been inspired by the region.

"I could get used to this." Nico said, then regretted how it might have sounded.

"People come from all over the world to the Sacred Valley in search of truth. We're honored to be of service and keep the teachings alive. There's nothing that says we can't enjoy a few of the perks at these resorts." Manuel winked.

Nico laughed. "I also meant to say, I'm grateful to be learning from you. Your ideas about life. You know so much." He could see a future in front him that had been obscured.

There was a pause. The only sound was the soft rustling of queñua trees as the wind slid off the mountain.

"It takes time, Nico. I chose an academic life where I learned about philosophy and religions. The formal education I received wasn't required to become a paqo. I'm a bridge between both worlds. You can be, too. It requires a willingness to step back from the Self and be receptive to new experiences. Just be open, aware, and without an agenda. As a practitioner of Kundalini Yoga, you have experience sitting in deep meditation for a long time. Moving the breath. In Buddhist practice this may bring wisdom. Are you able to achieve this...clarity, walking in the world? Mindfulness is being present while wide awake."

Nico understood. He didn't say anything for fear of sounding foolish.

Before the despacho ceremony they both changed into the traditional clothing of poncho and chullo. They arrived at the pavilion to see a greater than expected number of guests waiting. Nico recognized three paqos from Q'eros who were there to perform coca leaf readings. The guests were eager and asked many questions about the traditional Quechua ceremonies.

Nico performed a sage cleansing before the despacho. It was the first time Don Manuel let him do the ritual. At the closing of the ceremony, he asked Nico to put the despacho into the firepit. The bundle went up in flames against the backdrop of the cliffs. When they were alone Nico thanked him for allowing him to contribute.

"The ability to conduct a ceremony is more than reciting the blessing. Ceremonies commemorate change. They are an opportunity to heal. Everything we give to the apu, to Pachamama is an offering, no matter how small or seemingly insignificant. It is part of leaving the old behind and preparing to be reborn."

"When I had the studio I performed ceremonies, I taught kundalini. Everything I was, everything I had— I lost it all the night I was shot. I have nothing left to give."

"I know you have suffered, but you cling to the memory of all the things and people you have lost. They are your albatross, the weight around your neck. They have tremendous power over you—the power of grief, guilt, and shame. Shame will make you its prisoner if you let it. It keeps you from those you love and who love you. You will not be free until you have let go of all that pain. Forgive yourself, Nico. Leave the past behind and be reborn."

That night he spoke to his father and was relieved to hear both Lucia and Ita were living in the guest house at Claudia's ranch. His house in Temecula had sold. It took him by surprise how sad it made him feel, as if it were another failure. But then he remembered what Don Manuel said about letting go of things.

At dinner they talked about books and movies. Nico said he liked action thrillers like the Bourne movies, apologizing that they were not highbrow. He thought his answer weak and lacking in intellect. He added *Lord of the Rings* and *Star Wars* and talked about the dark side and Yoda.

Don Manuel nodded. "These movie franchises, and I'd add *Harry Potter*, are monomyths. The hero sets out on a journey and undergoes a test of character. The stories are steeped in the ancient teachings making them accessible to everyone. What could be better than the conflict between the light and dark side of the force? It goes back to biblical times, where Jesus made up stories that taught his followers right from wrong. Storytelling is the best way to teach. Have you read *The Lord of the Rings*, too?"

"No, I didn't." Nico shook his head. Now, he was embarrassed about his lack of literacy.

"Actually," Manuel replied quickly, "I love the movies more than the books because Peter Jackson did such a good job with bringing the story to life."

"I'd like to read more," Nico said. He sounded discouraged.

"The spoken word is a viable way to learn. Lectures, theatre, movies, television, podcasts, and even YouTube. Lots of people don't read much anymore. And, in ancient times, most people couldn't read, so they passed down stories generation to generation."

"I read *The Call of the Wild*. Do you know it?"

"Oh, yes. It's a classic. Did you like it?"

"I did… it was sad. It was about how much Buck and John Thornton loved each other and trusted each other. Luna gave it to me, and she wrote something inside. I wish I had it here… She wrote, 'It was never about the gold, it was about the journey."

"That's a fitting summary." Manuel said.

They had been on the road for weeks. Nico stayed back in the shadows. He hesitated to speak, to put himself forward, for fear of being judged or sounding ignorant. Don Manuel was beloved. They all looked to him for a spiritual experience. Like great works of art, he conveyed the truth of existence. Nico thought it was like being on tour, greeted at each stop like a rock star. All were captivated by Don Manuel and listened to him attentively. He became the center of attention without trying to be, belonging naturally wherever the moment found him. The stories he told shed light on the universal teachings, traversing effortlessly between Andean cosmology, Buddhism, and Gnosticism. In his notebook, Nico wrote himself a reminder that gnostic meant knowledge when Don Manuel quoted from the Gnostic gospels, *Bring forth what is within you to save you*, the same quotation Luna had written on the front page of his journal. Nico saw his life as divided into eras and he had entered a new one. What had belonged to the old had been buried. He stopped feeling guilty that he'd survived. He began to let go.

In Pisac they purchased coca leaves and other supplies for making the despacho ceremony. Nico bought a jug of pisco brandy, and they filled the cooler with beer. Nico stood near the ancient oven, a central feature of the plaza, and took a bite from a warm, golden empanada.

"I was here with Camille on our way to the Inca Trail. It's so strange..." he said, "It feels like it was ages ago." The man operating the oven handed him a paper sack with several more pastries to take away.

"They might be better than my wife's. Don't you think?" Manuel said. The baker pulled the wood peel from the oven and handed him another wrapped in paper.

"It's only a trick because the oven is old," Nico joked. "Besides, your wife puts roasted corn which makes them sweeter." He took another from the sack. "Still, these are delicious."

Late in the afternoon they arrived at a secluded modern glass and wood multi-level building at the foot of green hills. An American couple in their thirties greeted Don Manuel with the warmth and enthusiasm given to a favorite uncle. Apparently, they were expected although Nico wasn't aware of a schedule. Their hosts, Neil, and Cheryl had moved to the Sacred Valley five years ago after becoming immensely successful at a technology startup in

Silicon Valley.

Sunlight filled the large room through a floor-length window overlooking the valley. Functional seating of mid-century modern design, good lighting, and vintage advertising posters from the early 20th century complemented the aroma of freshly brewed coffee. An antique cabinet stocked with top-shelf whiskey added a warm and inviting touch to what felt like a conference room. A group of guests wearing designer T-shirts and overpriced sneakers sat around a communal table working on their laptops. Two young Asian women sharing a screen leaned their heads together to confer. A coffee mug on the table read, *Go with the Flow*.

They were served tea in the garden. The air was filled with the fragrance of flowers and the earthy scent of watered soil from the vegetable patch. Birds splashed in a water fountain and hummingbirds were at the feeders. Don Manuel told Nico he'd met Neil and Cheryl when he taught at UC Berkeley. It was rare to have computer science majors in his class, but they'd signed up for his philosophy course on the nature of the human mind. To successfully design and build a product that has traction and will scale, they needed to understand free will and the processes of behavior that make up our social institutions, the way we work, make decisions, and form relationships.

The retreat offered a compelling program designed to increase joy and maximize productivity in work and life. Within months of opening the center they had received favorable press from the technology forums. Guests who had graduated from elite schools and now ran big tech companies arrived in groups. Workshops were held in San Francisco, Austin, and New York but they preferred the Sacred Valley as a natural spiritual center. The method centered on the concept of creating flow, a mental state referred to as being in the zone. It wasn't a new idea, and Don Manuel argued that it was thousands of years old. Its popularity in recent decades had been inspired by the work of psychologist Mihály Csíkszentmihályi whose research and writing about happiness and creativity in the 1970s described the flow state as being immersive and energetically focused, to the point of transforming one's sense of time.

They stayed a week which was days longer than their visits to the other lodges. It was a small number of guests and no other paqos had come to the lodge. Nico gave the blessing to Pachamama offering the k'intu of three coca leaves. Don Manuel asked him to perform the sage smudging, and he washed the smoke over each guest to cleanse away the negative energies.

Still, Nico struggled to control the anxiety and feelings of inadequacy that plagued him. He felt he would always be an outsider. The guests were all young, and even if they came from different parts of the world they understood each other. He knew it was his negative feelings that prompted his arrogance.

"They think they're better than everyone." Nico finally grumbled to Manuel. He'd become starkly aware of the gulf that separated him from them and he was ready to admit he despised these self-absorbed, elitist Millennials.

"I think they have loosened up since we arrived. The tech industry is super competitive and they're under a lot of pressure. The lessons they learn here can help them prevent burnout," Manuel said.

Of course, Nico thought, Manuel was like them, over-educated and privileged.

During the coca leaf reading Nico listened to Don Manuel ask the guests questions about their life, health, and relationships in a way that was sensitive and thoughtful. After a prayer to the apus Don Manuel opened the pouch and read the placement of the coca leaves. Nico watched closely, noting that his readings were keenly insightful.

Nico hadn't used his intuitive skills with clients since leaving L.A. He knew what people were seeking. In his past he'd used that skill to manipulate them. He wanted a chance to show Manuel he was capable and sincere.

At dinner, Nico noticed the various cliques talking amongst themselves. Some drank beer and others wine. Afterwards they read books, played chess, or Catan. Electronic devices weren't allowed in the common room. Two men sat with them, attentive, as Manuel spoke about Krishna's teachings in the *Bhagavad Gita*. He knew how to use his voice to make people listen, its warmth was mesmerizing. Nico was quiet. He felt invisible. These moments left him questioning his faith. He had always found solace in Catholicism. The ritual of a mass with the heavy fragrance of incense, and the solemn voices of a boys' choir. Lighting a candle for his mother contained an element of magic.

Nico walked up to the whiskey bar. There were some top-shelf bourbons that he'd drunk at bars in California. Two slender women with thick framed eyeglasses and a tall willowy fellow with curly hair were considering the choices in front of them. They were lining up a row of small glasses for a tasting flight. Nico poured himself a glass of Woodford Reserve. They asked him where he was from and how he came to be there. When they discovered he taught Kundalini Yoga they requested he lead a session and arranged to meet in the gazebo the next day after the scheduled program classes. Nico thought it possible Manuel had been right, maybe they were opening up to them.

When Nico walked back to the sitting area, Neil and Manuel were deep in conversation. Nico stood beside them, listening, a drink in his hand. They were talking about motivation.

"Extrinsic motivation will never produce extraordinary

developments in science or in any field for that matter," Don Manuel said.

"Studies have proven you right. Of course, workers are initially driven by rewards and recognition. Financial and other extrinsic rewards are based on external validation that ultimately reduces productivity. Boredom and disillusionment set in. The most measurable increase in productivity has come from prosocial motivation. A greater and lasting effect occurs when one can see the positive effect of their work on others. That's what increases motivation and quality of work significantly, and with no additional training, and no extrinsic motivation like bonuses either." Neil was passionate about this topic. It had become the focal point and culmination of his career.

"Intrinsic motivation is powerful because it's rooted in joy. Joy is water. It's the sun. It's an unlimited source of motivation, integral to one's identity and raison d'etre—reason for existence. Your program teaches how striving for meaning and purpose with joy makes a life worth living," Don Manuel said. He was in his element. A bridge between the worlds.

Nico was fascinated. He wanted them to know he understood. He wanted to say something but couldn't decide what it would be. He hadn't fully understood, but he recalled Camille saying that joy brought about fulfillment. They had been on the Inca Trail when she told him to enjoy what he did for the sake of experience, without expecting a reward. He finished his drink; the ice had melted. He would have liked to speak out, to participate. But he lacked the confidence. He thought he would appear unintellectual by their standards. In small ways, that he barely realized, his arrogance and impertinence were eroding.

They moved toward the bar and Neil poured Bushmills, an Irish whiskey. He handed it to Manuel, then poured himself one. Nico hesitated before adding ice to his glass and pouring himself another drink.

"That's what I love about flow," Neil said. "It's about being in the moment. You and the work, whatever it is, become one. It's completely Zen. Focusing on a task and the world dissolves. It disappears, and you are immersed. Calm. In Flow. They say the great composers were able to create flow on demand. I believe that. I used to think you could only get there if you were micro-dosing. Then, I realized that anything produced pharmacologically could be produced naturally. I was blown away. I found once you train yourself to enter the zone, flow becomes natural. You no longer need to rely on psychotropics."

Nico must have looked surprised. He thought psychotropics would be a natural gateway to the flow state. They'd met curanderos offering plant medicine ceremonies at several resorts. He hadn't asked Manuel why he didn't perform them.

"What are your thoughts on the plant teachers, Nico?" Neil asked.

Nico glanced over at Manuel. He didn't want to say the wrong thing.

"Speak your mind, Nico," Manuel said. "None of us here are strangers to San Pedro or ayahuasca."

"Both teachers induce mindfulness and insight. You become focused—hyperaware. I found the mystical experience arouses feelings of acceptance and oneness with the universe. You become nonjudgmental. It's like love is everywhere, in everyone. So, in that case it can most definitely lead to peak-performance. To be able to get to this place, to create a state of flow naturally is extraordinary. I think it's brilliant."

"There is still a role for psychotropics particularly in treating PTSD and addiction which is making major breakthroughs around the world. There are several studies that have shown real progress in the treatment of depression, anxiety, OCD, and personality disorders." Manuel said.

"Absolutely. The plant medicines are valuable teachers." Neil nodded in agreement.

"I agree, there are benefits to psychotropics. With or without them, the practice of Kundalini Yoga channels the body's subtle energy... you know, prana, chi, or the force within us, and moves this energy through the chakras to bring about spiritual awakening. The kriyas are a combination of breathing exercises, the meditation mantra, the asanas which are the postures, and the mudras which are the hand gestures. It is a very ancient practice said to have been practiced by Jesus Christ and his disciples." Nico said.

"I have heard that said and you've done a good job explaining. I'd like to come to your class tomorrow if that's okay?" Neil asked.

"That would be great." Nico glanced over at Manuel. He hadn't thought it possible, but he might be accepted after all.

21

The yoga session was attended by what he thought must have been everyone. Neil brought his laptop and a speaker and played meditation music. He placed his mat in the front near Nico. He saw Cheryl in the back in case she had to jump out if someone needed her. There was a drizzle of rain and mist that swirled in the open gazebo. Nico felt surprisingly relaxed and the session ended with soft clapping to show their appreciation.

° ° °

Manuel lived in the moment. Nico lost track of time. They performed ceremonies and gave blessings. Nico taught yoga. There was nothing to show for it. No money exchanged hands. Others may have been worn down by the repetition, but Manuel regarded each visit as a new fresh experience. Nico learned the money for their services was electronically transferred to a private account that served the needs of the Q'eros provinces.

After the rain, a blue sky wiped clean. The sunlight falling into the valley glinted off droplets of dew on long blades of grass. They drove long stretches in a comfortable silence. The hills rising on either side. The terraces mounting in semicircles stacked on top of each other, like a pyramid to the gods. Nico thought the dog chasing a flock of sheep was familiar. They must have passed by once before from the other direction, he thought.

A rusty gate blocked their entrance to the cobblestone driveway.

Manuel leaned out the Jeep's window and rang the bell. What appeared to be a monastery or cloister had been converted to a wellness center. Guests were seated in the Spanish colonial courtyard. A woman in a long black peasant dress conversed with a younger woman wearing a white robe. The lobby was filled with the warmth of Latin America. Carved, dark wood furniture, plush sofas, and earthenware pottery. On the walls were paintings of reclining nudes, a portrait of Frida Kahlo, and flowers that could have been painted by Georgia O'Keeffe.

At the front desk was an envelope neatly addressed to Nicolás Romero. The letter inside was written in slanted feminine script. His hand trembled as he squinted his eyes into focus.

Nico, I knew you would end up here eventually. You were right. I am back home with Ben and Jackson. I put my acting career aside and started a small production company to develop projects with female driven stories. Everything is coming together with the Sisterhood more quickly than I anticipated. My team found this beautiful property in the Sacred Valley for sale and so I went ahead and bought it. It had been a monastery that was already operating as a retreat, so it needed very little time and investment. Make yourself at home. You are welcome any time to stay and teach yoga and perform ceremonies. I hope you are on the path of healing and finding your place in the world. Rosa has my email and phone number if you want to get in touch. Your friend, Camille

He never doubted she would open a place in the Valley. It was just like her, he thought, to envision something into being. It had all the warmth, elegance, and charm he expected. Rosa assigned them a casita near the caretaker's house. They ordered lunch and beer. The menu was vegetarian, which didn't surprise him.

To serve the large number of guests, they would remain for more than a week. Private appointments for cleansing rituals and coca leaf readings waited for them in the casitas. All were painted yellow with a Spanish red clay tile roof. Flowers overflowed the window boxes. Each had a private cook and housekeeper. The gardens were lush with orchids and large tropical plants. Women lay by the pool reading. It took Nico a few minutes before he realized all the guests were women.

After tea they performed a despacho in the garden with a view of the mountains. They had gemstones, coins, tobacco, and feathers from the Pisac market. Rosa brought them corn from the kitchen and flowers from the garden. She handed Nico a small bottle that he recognized as Camille's lavender oil. He thought about writing to her but didn't know what to say.

The next morning Nico gave a Kundalini Yoga class in the courtyard. The women resembled his former clientele in L.A. Actors and writers, producers, and agents. After the class one of the women, mid-thirties, approached him. Even in her designer yoga pants with matching top she looked aristocratic.

"So, I heard about you from Camille." Her smile was seductive, almost sinister.

"Oh, really? I can't imagine what she said."

"You were all the rage in L.A. Quite the following." Her eyes roamed over his body.

"You're embarrassing me," he said coolly. A chill, probably it was fear, ran through him. He thought of his commitment to becoming a shaman, a teacher as respected as Don Manuel. He was ashamed of his past. Not just his failures.

She shrugged. A quiet humph escaped her lips. She turned her back to him and walked away. He was certain the swivel of her hips was exaggerated for his benefit.

Later in the week, a shaman from the Shipibo tribe arrived to lead an ayahuasca ceremony. After breakfast, they would fast and begin after sunset. He assumed it would be the shaman Camille knew from the valley, but he couldn't be sure. He'd only had one experience with ayahuasca, in L.A. The curandero had been a guy from Brooklyn and the experience wasn't authentic.

He hadn't been honest with Camille. He was afraid of ayahuasca. He didn't trust anyone to lead him in what could be a frightening experience. Facing his truth, his demons, terrified him. He'd been a curandero in the San Pedro ceremony many times. He took care to build a proper mesa and guide participants on a safe journey. His experience with San Pedro was of being carried on the wings of an angel. He'd been faced time and again with his spiritual illness, his fears, and his deep sorrow. It was time to let go of what no longer served him. Would he allow himself to accept happiness?

Ayahuasca, the mother, had something more to teach him. He knew this deep inside. A Shipibo shaman channels icaros, sacred healing songs received from the plant. It's the frequency and resonation of the sounds, chanted into the body of the participant, which release blocked energy and rebalance the chakras. Visions created by the songs are the messages riding the waves, guiding you to the god within. The experience could help bring him closer to the self-actualization Manuel had spoken to him about. He would participate if Manuel would give his blessing. He was ready for a transformation and the integration with his shadow self.

° ° °

The day after the ayahuasca ceremony they left for Cusco. Manuel hadn't participated in the ceremony but remained nearby if Nico needed him. The glittering, neon green of the hills seemed electrified and the clouds appeared to come alive in shapes of circus animals that galloped alongside them on the road. In his head he kept repeating to himself, The mind is everything. What you think, you become. Manuel rephrased it by saying, open your heart, and your destiny will be revealed.

"Is it possible to feel as though I were turned inside out? And yet, at the same time, I have this inexplicable feeling of joy." Nico said, as though speaking to himself. He hadn't slept and wondered if he was making sense.

"Happiness comes from the harmonious concert of mind, body and spirit," Don Manuel said softly, knowing the sound of his voice would be amplified.

"I'm still subtly aware of the healing designs, the icaros embedded in my body, like a tattoo on my heart."

"Those are the patterns of the Arkana. They will remain to guard your spirit."

"I'm seeing everything more clearly. I feel as though the plant teacher has shaken loose memories and relics of the past to clear a space. During the ceremony, I saw my life since birth. It was as fragile as an eggshell with only raw feelings of loss and disappointment. How can I explain this? It's like I've been stuck in childhood tripping over broken toys strewn about the room."

"Now, you can rebuild your relationship with yourself from your heart chakra."

"I suppose everyone undertakes the journey from childhood to adulthood, somehow choosing what to remember. I thought I knew everything… It's only since talking with Ita that I discovered I knew nothing. The memories and heartbreak that have haunted me are the imagination and guilt of a lonely boy. I carry them around like suitcases filled with nightmares that are so heavy, so powerful. They torment me."

"It will take days to absorb everything you learned. It was a good experience."

"The medicine spoke to me. I opened my eyes and it showed me the universe beyond myself, and the universe inside of me. It was like when I was on the Inca Trail, and I saw the Milky Way for the first time. It's like looking into infinite mirrors that go on for eternity."

"Time and memory are entwined. Remember? Our lives are created ahead of us from the future that has informed us from behind."

° ° °

The ancient city. Iron gates guard the doorways. Under majestic churches built with Inca labor sacred sites are buried. Driving through the narrow cobblestone streets it begins to rain. Manuel turns on the windshield wipers. The white stucco buildings lean into the street. Through the windshield they are streaks melting into puddles. The merchants in open stalls pull the racks of woven tapestries inside. Nico worries Don Castillo won't like him. He hasn't shared his fear with Don Manuel.

They parked in the residential neighborhood that is just a short walk to the Plaza de Armas. There's a little green park nearby. The house is modest. Nico is taken by surprise when Sabrina opens the door. He'd forgotten she was related to Don Castillo, too. They remove their shoes in the entranceway. In the bedroom, the bed is neatly made and covered with a colorful blanket. An impressionistic painting of the Andes hangs on the wall above the bed. Don Castillo is sitting in a chair in front of the open window. He's in shadow, backlit by the light. It took Nico a few minutes for his eyes to adjust, but then he recognized him. It was strange that he didn't appear any older than twenty years ago.

Don Manuel kissed him on the forehead. Sabrina greeted them warmly and went into the kitchen to make tea. Manuel said a few words to Don Castillo in Quechua. Nico knew it was about Q'eros. He heard his name and walked over to shake his hand, bowing slightly from the waist.

"Bring the chairs and the folding table over here." His voice was commanding, as if he were a much younger man. "Do you play cards, Nico? Sabrina is tired of losing, she won't play with me anymore." Don Castillo said in excellent English.

"Sure, I love cards. What game do you play?" Nico was relieved that the awkward introductions were over.

"Rummy," he said. They pulled up chairs around the table and Don Castillo shuffled the deck.

Sabrina returned carrying a tray. A pot of tea and biscuits with cheese and sliced apple. It looked heavy and Nico rushed over to give her a hand.

"Will you stay for dinner?" She asked looking over at Manuel.

"Thank you but we are due at Tica's tonight." He poured the tea into cups. "This is perfect," he added,

"Then if you'll excuse me, I'll go to the market while you are here."

She picked up her shawl and Nico walked with her to the door.

"You seem better, Nico. Calmer."

"Don Manuel's a good teacher. If you hadn't…."

She raised her hand as a stop sign. "It was meant to be…"

"Sometimes you just can't make the right decisions alone. It takes someone else to show you the way." He looked down at his feet.

A small smile appeared at the corner of her mouth. "And Camille? Have you spoken to her?"

"No, but we were just at her new center. It was an interesting visit. She left me a note. I suppose I'll call her…"

"When you're ready." She nodded.

He sensed she understood his hesitation.

In all likelihood he was being tested, maybe not. It didn't

matter. Don Castillo won almost every hand. Nico's mind was elsewhere. Besides, he was glad the old man won. They laughed at Don Manuel's stories and told him about the solar panels, the greenhouse, and the party for the llamas. The light from the window faded more each hour until it was time to say goodbye. Sabrina had come back and was in the kitchen preparing dinner. The fragrance of cumin perfumed the room. It seemed to Nico the whole world had opened to him.

° ° °

The river came into view outside the car window. The moon was low in the purple near-darkness. They turned into the carport and parked behind Emilio's truck. The lights were on in the house, the smell of cedar burning in the fireplace. Before they got out of the car Tica was there to greet them, followed by Emilio. Nico stood back at a distance, but they brought him into their fold. They removed their work boots in the mudroom and put on sandals over their wool socks. The room was as he remembered it, homey with colorful rugs and tapestries.

"Hot tea or cold beer?" Emilio called out from the kitchen where he was roasting pork, the same traditional meal he'd made a few months earlier, though it felt longer. Nico remembered it had been tender and delicious.

"I can use a beer." Manuel answered. Nico nodded and went onto the porch to get them from the cooler. Manuel sat with Tica in the living room which was within earshot.

"I'm glad you got here before dark. I'm guessing you had no trouble on the road." Tica said.

"Thankfully, the weather was clear."

"How is Don Castillo?" she asked gently.

"He was in very good spirits. Nico here kept him entertained playing cards. I think he let him win!"

"Actually, I did not! The man is a trickster!" Nico laughed.

"Well, I'm glad to hear he is doing better." Tica said.

Nico looked over at Manuel, then went into the kitchen. He didn't ask what was on everyone's mind."

"He's rallied before," Manuel said. "But I'm not sure. The cancer may have spread and he won't go back for more tests. He welcomes whatever comes. He's right, I suppose. Death is just another realm."

They sat for a few moments in silence and then Manuel said with enthusiasm, "I forgot to tell you, when we left Q'eros we stopped to watch a condor ride the air currents."

"That must have been spectacular," she said.

"I hadn't seen one in a long time. It was beautiful." Manuel sighed. "It feels like that was ages ago." He stood and stretched his arms over his head. "We were a long time in the Sacred Valley."

He poked his head into the kitchen and spotted Nico at the counter with Emilio. "It smells good," he called to them.

"We can serve in just a few minutes," Emilio called out. "

"The kids should be home from school soon. Let's sit down at the table," Tica said.

Nico had made himself useful slicing onions. He felt as if he belonged, as though the past had been altered and bled into the future. Emilio taking charge of the cooking reminded him of his father. It was the grace with which he entertained and made you feel welcome. Fragments of memories merged with newfound familiarity paged through like scenes out the window of a moving train car.

This is how family should be, he thought. If he looked at it straight on, or too closely, he feared it would fall apart, like wet newsprint. At the counter, he cut up the tomatoes into wedges, and tossed them into the red onion and jalapeños. Emilio was pulling the pork. The tortillas were warm, and Nico wrapped them in a tea towel and placed them in a breadbasket.

The twins walked in bickering with each other, just as Nico remembered them. They threw their backpacks on the floor of the mudroom and leapt at Manuel, fawning over their uncle. Nico stood to shake hands and was surprised when they hugged him. He'd forgotten their names if he ever knew them. When Ramon swiped a tortilla, Tica barked his name and ordered them to wash their hands. Later, during dinner, Ray, as he was called, kicked his sister Q'ori under the table when she asked Nico his age. Nico kiddingly leveled his gaze on her, whereby she blushed and looked down at her plate. He was reminded of himself and his sister, the combativeness and the love so deeply intertwined. Ita used to say, it wasn't God who made us. It's in the small things, like cooking and sharing a meal, that we make God. It's what demonstrates our faith in each other, a faith that will be rewarded.

I'm different now, he told himself. My thoughts and the way I perceive everything around me has changed. I'm not the same person. I can't go back again. But where this new course is leading me, I don't know.

22

Nico carried a thermos of pisco onto the porch and looked out at the river. He appreciated the soothing effect of the local brandy. In the distance he saw the yellow halo of light coming from the church. The stillness of the air, the night falling silently, the sound of the water lapping the stone. His thoughts, like bits of his life, floated down like leaves. They caught in an eddy and spun counter-clockwise then continued until they passed out of sight. The silence was so pure he felt it was possible to know forgiveness. Perhaps it was a confirmation of his life, the sense of an ending.

"You have all the answers, don't you?" he asked the river. "So, tell me—What do I need to know?"

The last time he stood there, the chilly bleakness of the water reflected the emptiness of his soul. For as long as he could remember he felt a feverish need to escape his discontent. Like a miner intoxicated by the lust for gold, his eyes had seen only the things he desired—money, power, women, fame. For all his trying he'd found nothing. His obsessions never allowed him to accept the many possibilities that had come to him.

"You know my secrets. The origin of my blindness. I never asked to be born. I just want to know my life's purpose, that there is something beyond misery. I refuse to turn away." It didn't matter who heard him. He looked around but he was alone on the porch.

During meditation, in his practice of kundalini, he'd experienced being outside the limitations of time. He'd voiced the teaching of this experience to his students, but he never mastered releasing himself from its bondage. He'd carried the past with him which had only led him back to the past. Now, it seemed covered by a veil, distant, and less important.

"I'll find my truth," he said so only the river could hear. "My past has fallen into shadow. I fear the future."

We are our memories, he said to himself. They live in us. They shape us. Even the memories we don't remember are the blood in our veins that make us feel the way we do. As a young man he'd been content to travel the globe without thought of how long he would remain in any one place. But now he felt the weight of middle age, a reminder he was in his forty-second year. He wished for the contentment and stability he enjoyed here with Tica's family. There was an effortless joy to their lives. He felt an ease in his soul, as if the torment lodged just below the surface, like a splinter, had been washed away. He stilled his heart and listened to the river. He heard many voices. This time the river wasn't shaming him, it wasn't laughing at him. He couldn't say why, but he sensed the significance would be revealed. His thoughts moved freely. Across the river he thought he saw the church light flicker. A steady beacon in the darkness. There is something I'm remembering—a sermon. To the thirsty I will freely give from the water of life. Camille said you find meaning when you rise to a challenge and give outside of yourself.

He thought again about Sisyphus, pushing that godforsaken boulder uphill only to have it roll back down. His defeat repeating throughout eternity. It had been the story of his life.

Hearing the screen door creak open, Nico turned to see Manuel.

"The river is good company," Don Manuel said. He was drinking a beer.

"Hmmm. It's strange how I hear voices... Is that crazy?"

"Not crazy at all."

"I was just thinking about something Camille said. Do you know the story of Sisyphus?

"Well..." he laughed. "There's the Greek myth of Sisyphus condemned to an eternity of futile labor. Then, there's the essay by Camus postulating that when Sisyphus is heading back down the hill, briefly free from his labor, he is aware of the absurdity of his fate. In this moment of awareness, Sisyphus is happy—possibly considering his task with joy. I theorize *The Myth of Sisyphus* is about relinquishing the goal, liberating oneself from desire. When you accept this state then sorrow vanishes."

"I feel like I'm always starting over, never getting anywhere."

"Mmm well, only when you abandon desire can you attain freedom," Don Manuel replied.

Nico took a few minutes to consider the practicality of what Manuel just said.

"I don't know if it's the brandy, but I think I get it," Nico said. He was quiet, thinking of something. "That night in Q'eros you called me a wounded healer. You never got to finish explaining it to me. The thing is, Luna told me the same thing and then Camille said it, too. Is it because I was shot?"

"Not exactly, but things happen for a reason; they are messages. To become a healer, which you believe is your calling, you must heal yourself by accepting the wound and integrating the brokenness into your higher self."

"Is that even possible?" He shook his head and took a sip of brandy from the thermos.

"We survive by learning from our pain. Embrace the suffering that has held you back."

"You make it sound so easy."

He thought of his mother, and that he was still seeking her approval. But feeling unworthy of the love, might he just turn away from it in disgust? The emotional and physical scars were a burden, and in his effort to cure others, he'd been destroying himself.

"Some healers think they can heal themselves by healing others," Manuel said. "They're mistaken. That's called co-dependency. Others deny the wound and develop a false sense of self, attempting to cover up the pain with the attainment of the glittering goals of wealth and fame."

Nico looked down sensing that statement was directed toward him. "So then, what does it mean to be a wounded healer?"

"Good question. Myths, like Sisyphus and Chiron, teach us about life and about ourselves. Chiron, the wounded healer, is a mythological character who is half-man and half-horse. He represents the challenge of balancing our animal and divine nature. The dichotomy between the material body and the soul or spirit. Chiron was rejected and abandoned at birth and so his story symbolizes the conflict that arises in the process of healing the original identity wound of rejection that comes with independence from the mother. The integration of the wounds and weaknesses into the self is natural to identity development—the process of becoming whole."

Nico thought how fortunate Manuel's students were. They attended university and could listen to his lectures. "You're saying everyone has this wound, and we all have to heal ourselves?" He unconsciously touched his side where the scar was.

"Let's sit down. But first, grab me a beer from the cooler."

Nico twisted off the cap on the bottle and handed it to Manuel.

He sat on the top of the cooler offering him the bench.

"We all have a story we tell ourselves that relates to our wounding. You see, spiritually the wound is a blessing. It will help you know yourself. Viewed through a personal lens it is an expression of the undeveloped, self-centered consciousness that is bound to the past and rooted in time. But the wounding is beyond our individual ego. Individual suffering, like a mirror, reflects the greater suffering of the world. It's an encounter with something greater than ourselves. The struggle of human with the divine weds the two together. The wound and the blessing are inseparable."

"This is pretty deep stuff. I don't know if I understand it…"

"From the beginning there have been stories about wrestling with the divine. They exist in Greek and Egyptian mythology. The Crucifixion. Christ's wounding and union with God is the foundation of Christianity. But let's look at the Christian story of Jacob's encounter with God in the book of Genesis. Jacob was a con artist and a liar. His brother was out to kill him, and he fled. During the night God visited Jacob in the form of an angel and wrestled with him until dawn. The struggle left him crippled. But by facing God and confronting his failures and sins, God blessed him. In the story of Jacob we witness the struggle with his fears, failures, and weaknesses. A cornerstone of the ancient teachings and all great religions holds that through suffering we transform ourselves and evolve our consciousness."

"Ita used to say something like that. Through suffering we are closer to God."

"Ita is very wise." Manuel nodded. "Let's keep going. The avatar of the wounded healer relates to our ability to accept the wound and even be grateful for what it teaches us. Going through the wound is a death of the old self. Born from our wounds and the struggle, we are united with the divine within us. This transformation is the enlightenment that Christians call becoming born again."

"Ah, I had no idea what that really meant…"

"Our willingness, like Jacob, to consciously experience suffering through the wound is how we receive its blessing. The wound is what helps us discover who we are. Essentially, the wound contains its own medicine. Naturally, our instinct is to move away, to avoid suffering, and to project the pain elsewhere. But spiritually, the way to healing is to face and resolve the pain. The source of our pain is our duality: human and divine, mind and feeling, male and female. We are one with the creator. We and all of creation are one. You've seen and felt this every day at Q'eros with their reverence for Pachamama and the Apus."

"They have a sense of connection that feels natural to me."

"I feel the same way. It's the most tangible to me, too. But a lot of people live in the illusion we are separate from the divine. If we stay with Christian teachings for the time being, you will recall what Jesus said, *as the Father in me, and I in thee, that they may be in us*. It's a beautiful expression that says we are all a part of the cosmos, and that everyone and everything is imbued with spirit. It's a struggle. But becoming wedded to the higher power within us is the path to a spiritually evolved consciousness."

"I want to… I've tried. But—"

"Nico, you've been holding on to your pain for too long, and now you're at a crossroads. It's up to you to choose differently. There are times when unaware and blinded by goals we may drive right though that intersection and miss the chance to alter course. Too often, we see our mistakes and missed opportunities in the rear-view mirror, but those past decisions can give insight for the next time. Only by acknowledging the wound and walking the path of recovery, can you become an exceptional healer and truly serve in that capacity."

"How do you go on? There are some things that time cannot heal, some wounds that are too deep." He had no answer to the sorrow that had always been there. It had darkened even the bluest sky.

"The spark of the divine is in here," Don Manuel said touching his upper abdomen. "When you call upon your higher self, the spirit will guide you. To be touched by the divine is to be wounded and healed, and you will feel connected to a force greater than yourself. The god is within you. He is never not here." He placed his hand gently on Nico's solar plexus. "The belonging you are searching for is not behind you, it is ahead."

Nico listened to the soothing murmur of the river. It knew the past and the shadow of the future. In the vast emptiness there was beauty. The water gently lapping the retaining wall sounded like the breathing in of life and the sigh of death. The water was blacker and deeper than before. With an open heart and without desire, he sought the mystery in its depths.

"Moving water is everywhere at the same time, always the same, yet always new," Manuel said as he followed Nico's gaze down river. "It's impossible to step into the same river twice. The river has changed and you have changed."

"I'm always dwelling in the past, picking at the threads of an old life, even though in my heart I know there is no going back."

"Nothing stays the same. Like the river, everything is always changing."

Nico stood looking out across the river. The yellow light blinked on and off in the distance. For years he allowed desire to rule him until his heart was corrupted. All the secrets he harbored had been uncovered.

All his life he'd carried with him hurt and sorrow, struggling like a traveler with too much luggage. He'd told himself it was what he needed and believed was his identity. It was the armor that would shield him and keep him alive.

"Will my wound ever be healed?" Nico asked.

"When you become the river. Water finds its way forward just as the darkest tunnel bends toward the light…" Manuel said.

The only sound was the river kissing the stone. He felt the bruises that time had inflicted, but he was no longer bitter. He recalled the dream he'd had in the hospital. The jaguar had told him it was time to leave.

"I'm ready," Nico said.

He'd come to the end of something and the beginning of something else. He didn't know what it would be, no one did. There was only uncertainty. Whatever came he would still be himself, his true self, full of possibilities of what can be.

Published by Compelled Books
www.compelledbooks.com

Thank you for purchasing and reading my book. I am extremely grateful and hope you found value in reading it. Please consider sharing it with friends or family and leaving a review online. Your feedback and support are always appreciated and allow me to continue doing what I love.

Please go to *The Serpent Awakens* book page on Amazon if you'd like to leave a review.

The Serpent Awakens is less a sequel than a companion novel to *The Sleeping Serpent*. Reading both novels is a fuller experience, but both books can stand alone.

Made in the USA
Middletown, DE
24 September 2022